Readers love *Andre in Flight*
by LAURA LASCARSO

"With a happy ending, interesting and multi-layered characters and a whole bunch of twisty plot, this is a good story that I feel should appeal to many readers."

—Long and Short Reviews

"*Andre in Flight* by Laura Lascarso is a beautifully written story about soul mates and eternal love. The author has done an excellent job in capturing the emotions, longing, grief and creativity which will leave you wanting for more."

—Gay Book Reviews

"…the writing is elegant and the characters well drawn and realistic, which is exactly what I expected."

—Prism Book Alliance

By LAURA LASCARSO

Andre in Flight
The Bravest Thing
One Pulse (Dreamspinner Anthology)

Published by DREAMSPINNER PRESS
www.dreamspinnerpress.com

THE
BRAVEST
THING

LAURA LASCARSO

Published by

DREAMSPINNER PRESS

5032 Capital Circle SW, Suite 2, PMB# 279, Tallahassee, FL 32305-7886 USA
www.dreamspinnerpress.com

The Bravest Thing
© 2017 Laura Lascarso.

Cover Art
© 2017 AngstyG.
www.angstyg.com
Cover content is for illustrative purposes only and any person depicted on the cover is a model.

ISBN: 978-1-63533-635-1
Digital ISBN: 978-1-63533-636-8
Library of Congress Control Number: 2016963404
Published April 2017
v. 1.0

Printed in the United States of America
∞
This paper meets the requirements of
ANSI/NISO Z39.48-1992 (Permanence of Paper).

BERLIN

ONE HUNDRED and eighty days until the end of junior year and I'm already counting down. Not the best thought to be having on the first day of school.

"Berlin, check out the tits on that one."

Trent knocks my shoulder and points to a girl walking by where we sit on the tailgate of my pickup truck in the high school parking lot. He eyes up the freshmen, or *fresh meat* as he calls them, while I pretend to do the same.

I grunt in appreciation, even though breasts don't do it for me. Neither do girls, for that matter. But my reputation at Lowry High depends on me being a normal red-blooded American male. I don't know for sure if I'm gay or not, but judging from my browser history this summer, it's seeming more and more likely.

"I'd hit that in a minute," Trent says, and I grunt again like a bullfrog. Ribbit, ribbit. Trent and I have been friends since fifth grade when we started playing peewee football together. He knows pretty much everything about me. Except this. I've been hiding it from everyone—my team, my friends, my dad, my girlfriend Kayla.

Kayla's breasts, according to Trent, are prime.

I scan the parking lot for Kayla's blonde head, and the whine of a motorcycle catches my attention. I point in that direction, noticing the bike first, a new Kawasaki Ninja, black with neon green fairings, then the driver. He's in all black—jeans, T-shirt, high-tops, even his full-face black helmet. Like a dark, sexy comic book villain.

"Check out the crotch rocket," Trent sneers. He sounds jealous.

The guy docks his bike and takes off his helmet. I've never seen him before—that much I know. I've never seen anyone *like* him before.

His hair's long on one side, black and shiny. The other side's buzzed close to his scalp, punk rock. The way his hair falls over his face reminds me of our horses and how their forelocks will sometimes hide one eye.

The new kid hitches up his tightfitting jeans and slings his backpack, also black, over one shoulder, then struts across the parking lot like he already knows where he's going. He's slim-hipped but on the tall side, an inch or two shorter than me. I'm full-on checking him out when I catch myself doing it and force my eyes away.

I have to be more careful.

Trent sizes him up like he's surveying the field, about to throw a pass, or more likely, preparing to pounce. "The fuck...." he mutters.

I glance back at the new kid and see what caught Trent's attention. It isn't just the haircut, which I've never seen on anyone in real life, or the piercings climbing up his ear like rungs on a ladder. It isn't even the fact that he's Asian, which is pretty rare around these parts. It's his eyes. He's wearing eyeliner, thick and black, like one of those Egyptian pharaohs. And he's smoking hot. Big, dark eyes, smooth skin, and a naturally pouty mouth. There's a pucker just above his upper lip that draws me in. My lower half starts to ache in an awful way. I should stop staring, but I can't tear my eyes away.

The new kid glances over at us: Trent first and then me. He looks bored, but then his eyes lock with mine, and there's something there. At least, I feel it, under my skin and racing through my veins like an itchy, full-body fever.

"Aw hell no," Trent growls. He must be reading my mind. I'm about to soil myself, but it's not me he's talking about. His eyes are still on the new kid's back.

To Trent, a boy wearing eyeliner is an unlit firecracker on the Fourth of July.

A surge of fear races through me. What is this kid thinking, cruising into the Lowry Lions' den wearing eyeliner like it's New York City? Lowry might only be a stone's throw from Austin, but it's full-on Texas when it comes to its small-town prejudices. He must know that.

Trent jumps up like he's going to follow him and whoop his ass right then. I grab his muscled arm to steady him, same as I've been doing on the football field since peewee league.

"Coach wouldn't want us starting trouble on the first day of school," I warn him. I say *us*, but it's Trent who starts the trouble. I mostly try to stay out of it.

"Fuck if I'm going to let that faggot wear makeup in my house."

I shake my head at that. Everyone's a faggot to Trent—the geeks, the band nerds, the arts department... basically any guy who doesn't play sports, and even some of the ones who do. Not me, though. I've somehow managed to dodge his faggot detector all these years, which is a relief. And also terrifying. I live with a constant dread that Trent will one day find out my secret and turn on me.

"You have the whole school year to sort it out." I keep my voice even-keeled. If he knew how I really felt, he'd get suspicious. "He'll figure out soon enough what's what."

Trent massages his fist like it has a mind of its own. Maybe it does. As our quarterback, his hands are magic on the field. He has so much talent and potential. If only his dad were a little nicer to him, maybe Trent would lighten up and not be such an asshole all the time.

As for me, my college plans depend on a football scholarship, which means I have to keep my sexuality to myself if I want to stay on the team and in the good graces of Trent and his dad, Coach Cross, the head of our high school's football program.

It's a tricky situation.

I lose sight of the new kid as Kayla and Madison, Trent's girlfriend, come along. Kayla throws her bare arms around my neck and pulls me in for a kiss. She's a little heavy-handed with the perfume. I always smell like a candy store after hugging her. Despite her love of PDAs, we've only ever made it to second base. Her parents are pretty conservative, and she's saving herself for marriage. I respect her for that. It's also part of the reason we work as a couple. She praises me for my willingness to wait, which takes some of the pressure off me. And we have a lot in common—same friends, same Christian upbringing, same small-town values and love of football....

"I missed you so much, Teddy Bear," Kayla says in between wet, smeary kisses. Her lip gloss tastes like fruit punch, and instead of enjoying our reunion, I'm trying to figure out which kind of fruit that is.

"I missed you too." I hug her tightly. It isn't a lie. We're friends, after all.

Next to us, Trent and Madison grope each other like nobody's watching. They're on and off again, but from the looks of it, it's back on. At least Madison keeps Trent occupied and off my back.

"We're heading in," I tell them, picking up my backpack and slinging it over my shoulder. I guide Kayla's back with my free hand.

"See you in third," Trent calls. His stare follows me across the parking lot. Sometimes when he looks at me like that, it makes me nervous, like he suspects something. But it's probably just my guilty conscience. I hate the lying and sneaking around, but I don't see any other option.

Kayla does most of the talking on our way in to school. I say just enough to let her know I'm listening. It's safer that way. I don't want to accidentally let the wrong thing slip out. I scan the hallways for the new kid, but I don't see him anywhere.

Kayla meets up with her girlfriends at her locker, and I make my way over to the administration building, where I'm an office aide during first period. It's one of the perks of being a football player. Our fall semesters are pretty light, and we're allowed to miss the first three periods if we have a late practice the night before. I try not to take advantage of it too much. I know it's unfair, but I didn't write the rules.

The head secretary gives me the job of sorting and stapling welcome packets for the freshmen. They'll be handed out in homeroom, which is at the end of the day.

As I sort I keep thinking about the new kid. It's only a matter of time before Trent catches up with him, and I can't go around protecting every so-called faggot at Lowry High School. Maybe the new kid will fall in with the drama department. Not that they can offer him much protection, but Trent tends to leave the herds alone. It's only when one gets left behind like a wounded wildebeest that he pounces.

The new kid doesn't seem wounded, though, just out of place. Like his tour van up and left town without him. Even without the makeup, I doubt he'd ever fit in.

"Ahem."

I glance up and there he is. My neck burns like I've been out in the sun all day, and my face is probably cherry red too. My blood's always rushing to the places it shouldn't. It's probably racist of me to think it, but up close he looks like an anime character, especially with the makeup and crazy hairdo. The boys in anime and manga are pretty hot, one of the reasons I'm a fan.

"May I have a student code of conduct?" he asks, all proper-like. His voice is smooth as river rocks. He sounds bored.

The rulebooks are part of the freshmen packets, so I hand him one. I finally get up the nerve to look him in the eye, but he seems distracted. He sits in one of the hard plastic chairs, elbows on his knees, thumbing through the book. His dark eyebrows draw together in the center, forming a wingspan across his forehead. The muscles in his arms are well-defined, even though he's a little on the skinny side. When he finds what he's looking for, he marks the page with a pink referral slip and snaps it shut. He catches me staring at him. My neck gets hot again, and I try to think up something to say.

"Awful early in the school year to be getting a referral," I tell him. He must have gotten it in the hallway before class even started.

"Are you a hall monitor?" he asks.

The hall monitors at Lowry are teachers, not students. Then I realize he's probably making fun of me. His lip curls up on one side, drawing my attention to his mouth, and I forget what we were even talking about.

"Mr. Hayashi?" Mrs. Potts calls from her office. She's the juniors' guidance counselor, which means we're the same year. He strolls over to her office, casual and cool. He wears those skinny jeans well, kind of low on his hips. Broad shoulders, cute round butt. He must play sports—soccer or maybe track. Black suits him, I think, but he'd probably look good in whatever he wore.

He doesn't close the door behind him, so I move in a little closer. I'm not a gossip, but I do pick up some helpful tidbits from working in the front office. It's not really eavesdropping. I just want to know more about this kid. Where'd he come from? What's he doing here? Is he going to stay? I hope so. But maybe he's not even gay. Maybe he just wears eyeliner as part of his getup. Like a rock star or a pirate. Maybe I'm not even gay.

The ache from down below disagrees.

His voice is too low for me to hear. Mrs. Potts is easier to make out. I mess with the copier just outside her office to hear them better. Whatever he did to get a referral must have been small potatoes. Mrs. Potts is using her nice voice.

"I don't understand... I suppose you didn't...."

I edge in closer.

"Lowry can be a fresh start for you, Mr. Hayashi. Your parents and I both want you to succeed here. You wouldn't want to give other students the wrong impression."

"What impression is that?" he asks in a deadened tone.

Mrs. Potts is quiet for a moment. "All I'm saying is you might want to try a little harder to blend in, for your own sake."

Yes, Mrs. Potts, I want to say. *Good advice.*

"With all due respect," he says, "I don't want to blend in. I checked the dress code and there's no rule against eyeliner. If there's nothing else, I'd like to go to class."

He got a referral for breaking the dress code? What teacher would make a big deal about eyeliner? Then I know who it was: Trent's dad, Coach Cross.

I hear the squeak of Mrs. Potts rising from her chair and know she's making her way to the front of the desk to sit on the edge and get real with him. This is my third semester as an office aide. I know Mrs. Potts's go-to play.

"Hiroku," she says, a little softer this time. "I know you've had a difficult summer. Your mother told me a bit about all you've been through. Your family moved to Lowry so you could start over. I think you owe it to them to give it a try, don't you?"

Hiroku Hayashi. I try saying his name under my breath; it makes my mouth feel clumsy. It's strange, just like everything else about him. And kind of hot too. Mrs. Potts made it seem like he got into trouble at his old school. Maybe he started a fire or brought a weapon to school. He seems like a deviant in that way. Maybe he got expelled and had to move to a new county.

I hear shuffling in the room and jump back to my post at the counter just as Hiroku comes strolling out of the office. He glances over like he knows I've been listening. But if he wants to survive Lowry High, he needs to try fitting in. I should know. I'm a pro at it.

"Mrs. Potts is right," I tell him. "Your look won't work here."

He stops and turns a little, slides up to the counter so we're facing each other. He tilts his head and looks at me from under his hair, smirks like I made a joke. Maybe he knifed someone at his old school. He looks kind of insane.

"How about you, cowboy?" he says in a deep, husky voice that goes straight to my balls. "Is that look working for you?" My own throat goes dry as the desert as his eyes rake over me, from my waist to my chest and shoulders, finally my eyes. No guy has ever looked at me like that before. My junk starts throbbing again and I'm glad the counter's between us, giving me some cover. Something about this kid puts me in a tailspin.

He purses his lips and raises one eyebrow. "Well, maybe it is working. For me, at least." The smirk is still on his face when he leaves the office. He has a light step, like a cat. I didn't hear him come in, and I don't hear him leave. I take a deep breath and tell my body to calm the hell down.

He's a dude. I shouldn't want him like that.

But I do.

HIROKU

THREE CHINKS and a faggot. That's my first day at Lowry High. Already I've been labeled and harassed, like some bad joke where I'm the punch line, again and again. Maybe I should have tried harder to blend in like that guidance counselor said, but honestly, these country bumpkins need a break from the monotony of the Aryan nation that is Lowry, Texas. And I'll wear my eyeliner if I feel like it, thank you very much.

Even if I lost the eyeliner, it wouldn't change the fact that I'm gay and Asian. Though maybe I'll correct the ignorant assholes next time and tell them I'm a Jap, not a Chink.

As far as separating the homophobes from the more tolerant of the student body, my look is working just fine. And I'd rather be my authentic self than some cookie-cutter version of the all-American boy. Like that kid Berlin. Who does he think he's fooling? The way he looked at me in the office… he's as queer as they come. But maybe I'm just imagining it. That's how hard up I am for some male companionship.

After school I ride my bike around the outskirts of town, stopping here and there to snap pictures of anything I find interesting. The one good thing about moving out of Austin is the long, empty country roads. I wind up and down highways, then stop at a gas station to get a drink. As I'm walking back out to my bike, my phone rings. I know it can't be Seth. He doesn't have my new number. Still, my spirit lifts at the possibility.

I check my phone and it's my sister, Mai. She's premed at Columbia University. She knew today was my first day. She's probably calling to check on me, make sure I'm not planning to go off myself or something, which isn't a huge vote of confidence on her part.

"Hiroku Hayashi," she says when I answer, as if I'm somebody important. "Tell me about your first day."

I give her the highlights: the football coach who harassed me for wearing eyeliner and then, when I refused to remove it, sent me to the front office. The slurs from Lowry's finest. Team Sports, which should have been the absolute worst but actually wasn't too bad, mainly because that hot farmer boy Berlin was in my class and we were playing basketball, which

I'm pretty decent at. Except that asshole, Troy or something, called me a faggot in the locker room while he might or might not have been checking out my junk. I leave that last part out, though. TMI.

"This town is so small, Mai. There's nothing to do. Nowhere to go. I'm trapped in hillbilly hell."

"Any hot cowboys?" she asks, ignoring everything I just said. She's always had a thing for cowboys. Her boyfriend Terrance couldn't be further from it. He's kind of an egghead. A nice one, though.

"None," I say, though that's not entirely true. That kid Berlin is cute, and I bet he'd look good in a cowboy hat. I made him blush in the front office, but maybe I misread it. He's probably a homophobe like his friend Troy. Just my luck.

"Don't be so negative, Hiroku. It's only your first day. How can you know for sure?"

I've done the math already. There are six hundred kids at Lowry High. If we go by the national average, that means about thirty of them are gay or lesbian, which means *maybe* fifteen gay or bisexual guys. Judging by my first day at Lowry, most of them are probably still in the closet, which means exactly zero of them are available. I share the breakdown with my sister.

"There will be no black-tie ceremonies for me," I tell her with a dramatic sigh. My sister, my mom, and I watched *The Bachelor* and *The Bachelorette* religiously before Mai left for college. Now it's *Finding Prince Charming*, the all-gay version. How progressive are we.

Mai sighs sympathetically. "Well, don't give up just yet. I know leaving Austin sucks, but this is a good change for you. He was toxic, Hiroku. You know that, right?"

"Yes," I say, which is obligatory.

"You haven't tried seeing him, have you?"

"They're on tour." Unless I show up at one of Seth's shows, which I've thought about doing, it's impossible for me to see him.

"Have you talked to him?"

"No." Though I do check Seth's Instagram about ten times a day. Ever since we broke up, he's been posting pictures of himself with other guys. It's uncanny how much they all look like me, as if he's trying to tell me how replaceable I am. But he doth protest too much.

"Stay away from him, Hiroku," she warns me, yet again.

"I got this, Mai," I tell her, yet again.

We talk a little more, then say our good-byes. As I mount my bike, an old, battered truck rumbles up. I recognize the driver as Berlin from Team Sports. His arm rests on the driver's-side door. The rust-colored hairs catch the sunlight. The hair on his head is blond and longish with a curl at the ends, perfect for getting your fingers tangled in. I consider saying hello, if only to make him blush again. He glances my way and looks startled, like I've offended him by coming to this gas station. Like there are more than three gas stations in this tinyass town. Forget it. I make my face blank, don my helmet, and ride off.

When I get home to our empty, ticky-tacky house, I pull up Seth's Instagram, scroll through the pictures, and imagine it's me there with him. But I know the price of being his beloved—body, mind, and soul. I didn't break my mother's heart and spend my summer in rehab just to fall down that rabbit hole again.

I hoped living in Lowry would be an improvement over life with Seth. Judging by day one, the two aren't so different.

That's the problem with me—I like pain.

BERLIN

ANDERSON THROWS another kegger Saturday night. Everyone's there. The football team. Cheerleaders. Some of the more popular band kids and color guard. I never understand how popularity works. It's like some algorithm that chews you up and spits you out. Maybe because I play football, I've always come out on top. I keep thinking about the new kid, Hiroku, wondering if he'll be at the party. Kind of hope he will. He isn't, though. I guess it takes longer than a week to establish the new standard of cool.

The party is full of the usual mischief—keg stands, wrestling matches, chicken fights in the huge inground pool. I drink, but not too much. I can't risk getting drunk and doing something stupid, like make out with a dude or admit I'm crushing on the new kid. I can't lose control, ever.

Toward the end of the night, Kayla and I wind up in one of the bedrooms. Her idea. Cuddles are usually enough to satisfy her, but she's had too much to drink and keeps reaching for my pants.

"Come on, Bear, let's do it." She tugs at my belt like we're playing flag football.

"You're drunk, baby. I don't want to take advantage of you."

She groans. "I want you to."

"You say that now, but you might regret it tomorrow." Usually this works, but she isn't listening to me tonight. She undoes my belt buckle, then fiddles with the button of my jeans.

"Kayla." I try to guide her hands away, but she's like a heat-seeking missile for my crotch.

"Come on, Bear, we've waited so long. Don't you want to?"

Kayla reaches into my pants and starts working me over with her hand, but I can't get hard. I fumble around with her boobs. She glances up like something is wrong. That something is me.

I think about the new kid. *Hiroku Hayashi.* His name sounds like a sexy sports car or an expensive liquor. Something smooth that goes down easy. I imagine unbuttoning his tight black jeans, slipping my hand into his underwear—what kind does he wear? Something expensive. Something you can't buy at Walmart. Silky and black, like his hair.

"Bear," Kayla purrs, pleased at my erection. What kind of jackass makes out with his girlfriend while imagining someone else? I pull Kayla's hands out of my pants and hug them to my chest. They're small compared to mine, like tiny birds. I sit her down on the bed, stuff my junk back in my pants, button up, and belt in.

"We need to talk."

Last year, I thought all I needed was a girlfriend to turn me straight. But no matter how hard I try, I can't stop thinking about guys. Something is wrong with me, and I'd rather be alone than fake it with Kayla. And besides, Kayla deserves someone who really loves her.

She crosses her arms and legs and pouts while she waits for me to say something. But what can I say? She believes gays are misguided and in need of rehabilitation. Our church believes that too. I don't know what I believe, but I'm pretty sure no amount of Bible school or counseling from Pastor Craig is going to straighten me out.

Kayla would tell the whole school. I'd be done for. No football, no friends, no life. It's a lot to lose and not much to be gained.

"Something happened while you were in Dallas," I say.

Her body shifts, her eyes narrow, and she seems to sober up instantly.

"I was with someone else." I hate lying to her, but I don't know what else to do. At least this way she can hate me and move on.

"Who?"

I shake my head. "It doesn't matter."

"Who the fuck was she, Berlin?" For a Christian girl, she sure can curse like a sailor when she gets riled up.

"It was nobody, Kayla. I'm really sorry. You were away, and it just happened."

Kayla's lower lip trembles and she starts crying, big fat tears dripping down her cheeks, smearing her makeup. She kind of sniffles and honks at the same time. I want to hug her, but that seems wrong, so I sit there on the edge of the bed and wait for her to break up with me.

"I cheated on you too," she says in between wiping her face. I almost don't catch it.

"You what?" With all the lying I've been doing, her confession shouldn't hurt so much. But it does. It downright stings. "When?"

"Last year." She pauses. "And again this summer."

"Twice? Really?" If I hadn't lied about cheating, she'd have never told me. She lied to me this whole time too.

"Like you said, it just happened. Can't we start over? I promise I'll never hurt you again."

I pace in front of the bed while she continues to apologize and make promises, but I can't think straight or recover fast enough. I can't believe she cheated on me. Sweet, innocent Kayla. *Who was it?* I want to know, then think, *No, I don't.* I also can't believe she still wants to be with me. Someone has to be reasonable here.

"It's over, Kayla. I cheated. You cheated. We're not right for each other."

Kayla springs at me, yelling and beating her fists against my chest. It doesn't hurt, so I let her have a go at me. I'm not going to change my mind, though. It's the right thing to do.

"You can't do this to me, Berlin. You cheated too. You have to forgive me. I love you. We were meant to be together. Don't you care about me at all?"

I hug her while she cries into my shoulder. I do care about her, but I can't give her what she wants. Maybe some part of her knows that already and that's why she strayed. "I'm sorry, Kayla. Want me to drive you home?"

She pushes me away. "Just go."

I leave the party soon after. I'm tempted to call her over the weekend, just to check in on her, but I don't want to confuse things.

At school on Monday, Trent can't wait to tell me Kayla hooked up with one of the guys on our football team as soon as I left the party.

"What the fuck is that all about?" he asks me.

"We broke up," I say. I really don't want to hear about who she's hooking up with. Makes me kind of angry she couldn't even wait a day.

"She broke up with you?"

I shrug. "More or less." I don't like discussing my love life with Trent, and not just because of the whole maybe-being-gay thing. I'm a pretty private person.

"Why?"

"I don't know. It just happened. You and Madison break up all the time."

"Yeah, because she's fucking insane. Kayla, though, she's a sweetheart. Is it because she wasn't putting out?"

"I don't know, Trent. I just wasn't feeling it." I stop there and worry I've already said too much.

I glance across the parking lot to where Kayla's getting out of her car. She and Madison link up. Kayla looks at me with a long face. Madison glares at me like I ran over her dog. I still feel bad about it. We've been together so long it feels weird to think that I won't be walking her to class or hanging out with her on the weekends. She came to all our home games last year. It was nice looking up into the stands and seeing her there with a big smile on her face. I hope she still wants to be friends. Still, it's better this way. Even if it is a little scary to be alone. Even if it means people might get suspicious.

Trent punches my shoulder lightly. "Don't stress about it, Bear. They'll be lining up around the corner for you. Maybe next time you'll get one that puts out."

Hiroku's motorcycle careens into the parking lot then, sending a surge of adrenaline through me. *There's nothing stopping me now*, I think. A panicked feeling rises up inside me, or maybe it's my breakfast, and I resist the urge to glance over at him. Trent doesn't try to hide his fascination.

"Fucking faggot." Trent spits on the asphalt, a big brown loogie. Dipping on school grounds is illegal, but Trent gets away with it. Teachers look the other way where Trent's concerned.

"I'm going to nail that kid's ass to the wall," Trent says, shifting the wad of tobacco from one side of his mouth to the other. I wonder if he knows how homosexual that sounds.

I hate it when Trent messes with people, but the thought of him messing with Hiroku makes me kind of crazy. My back tenses up and my pits start to sweat. I have to play it cool, though. I can't let Trent know I care either way.

"Whatever, man. He's just a freak. Not worth getting suspended over. Think of the team."

Trent grunts. "He was checking out my package the other day in the locker room."

That's a lie. I was there in the locker room with them. Hiroku keeps to himself, and we have stalls for showering, so it isn't like some peep show either.

"I heard he got expelled from his last school," I say. Maybe if Trent thinks he's dangerous, he'll leave him alone.

"Probably for being queer."

"You can't expel someone for that." Though they've probably tried, maybe even here in Lowry.

"Too bad." He leans over my tailgate and spits again.

I glance over at him. I thought making fun of guys he thinks are gay was just an outlet for Trent, like a group of people who are easy to prey on, but sometimes it seems he truly hates gay people. Like now. I never understood hating people just because. It isn't like gays are going around making trouble or picking fights. They're not hurting anyone, and they don't deserve to be punished for something they can't even control.

I don't deserve to be punished, do I?

The warning bell sounds, and I grab my stuff to head to the office, relieved to get away from Trent. It feels strange not having Kayla to walk to class, but it's one less act to put on. As I'm passing through the school gate, Hiroku cuts in front of me. My eyes focus straight ahead, but I can't help noticing the bend of his neck where his hair is short on one side, and the tawny color of his skin. Like a palomino. Wondering what it might be like to follow that smooth curve with my fingers, or maybe even my lips.

HIROKU

IT'S ONLY a matter of time. I know this Trent kid is hot about something when I keep scoring on him in basketball. He says it's because I'm such a fucking fairy I'm able to fly in my layups. I tell him I hope he's better at football, because he fucking sucks at basketball. Coach Gebhardt tells us to play nice. Despite Lowry's No Bullying policy, the faculty sure does let a lot of shitty behavior go by.

"Nice shot," Berlin says to me after a sweet little hook shot.

"Thanks." His eyes linger on mine, and I think maybe he's feeling me in a gaytastic way, when Trent comes up and knocks my shoulder, hard.

"Watch it," Trent says, like it's my fault he ran into me, and throws the ball to Berlin harder than necessary. Berlin doesn't talk or look at me for the rest of the game.

After class, I'm getting ready to shower when someone comes up from behind and slams me into the lockers. I catch myself just in time. My palms smack against the cold metal and save my nose from being smashed. My mother loves my face. She'd be beside herself if anyone messed it up.

I spin around to find Trent and his groupies staring me down. A whole mountain range of assholes. Berlin isn't with them.

"Let's see what moves you got now, you fucking faggot," Trent says. His henchmen close in on either side, trying to look intimidating. It's working. My heart rate spikes and I can hear it throbbing in my ears. I imagine I'm trapped in some low-budget PSA about school bullying. It helps me get on top of the fear.

I drop my shirt on the bench between us and square my shoulders, thinking maybe I can reason with him. "Why don't we try transcending stereotypes, Trent? You can do better than the small-minded, homophobic jock, can't you?"

"You like to suck dick, faggot?" he asks.

I'm guessing that's a no.

"Not as much as your mom," I answer back because I clearly know how to take the high road.

Trent shoves me again, hard enough that the back of my head bangs against the metal locker, rattling my brains and causing me to bite down on my tongue. I taste the coppery tang of my blood. *Hello, old friend.*

The masochist in me wants Trent to hit me. Ever since I overdosed and then painfully and some days regrettably got off painkillers, I've felt so little that even a good punch in the face seems like a welcome change. And maybe too I want Trent to confirm exactly who he is.

I recognize the primal desire in Trent's eyes. To wound, maybe even kill. Seth has it too. They get off on the thrill of beating someone else into submission. Domination.

"You know what we do to faggots around here?" Trent says.

"No, but I'm pretty sure I know what you do to the goats."

Trent swings, and I turn to take it on the side of my face. My bottom jaw feels like it popped out of place and my lower lip is on fire. I taste more blood. A surge of adrenaline rolls through me, heightening my senses. Turning me on. Like a maniac, I grin.

"You like that?" Trent seems bewildered and maybe a little disturbed I'm not trembling in the corner. I didn't even try to block his blow, though I probably could have.

"You hit like a girl," I say, spitting blood on his T-shirt. Like a girl boxer on steroids, I should add.

At that same moment, Berlin enters the locker room, still wet from the shower, bare chested, with a towel around his waist. A new kind of arousal takes hold of me. He's built like a gladiator, all muscle and athletic grace, but not too beefy like some of the other guys on the team. Curly blond hair and blue-gray eyes. Ben-Hur. That's how I imagine him during my me time.

His eyes lock on mine, and he looks like he's going to shit his pants, if he was wearing any.

"Trent, man, what the fuck?" he says.

Trent turns, and I know Berlin is going to blow his cover. I heard he broke up with his girlfriend over the weekend, though I try not to read into it. I'm a little ashamed I let an asshat like Trent hit me just to feel something. How messed up is that?

I rush Trent and grab his right hand, his throwing arm, and give him a jiujitsu handshake. He cries out and goes up on his toes to alleviate the pressure I'm putting on his arm. With one blow I could break it and ruin his football career forever.

Lucky for him I'm not that kind of person.

"Listen to me, fucktard," I say quietly, because this message is for his ears only. "I'm a faggot and you're a homophobic prick, and while you may feel it's your God-given duty to beat the gay out of me, I can assure you, it won't work. Touch me again and I'll break this arm before you can say the word *touchdown*. You feel me?"

The look in his eyes is lethal, but I know he's in extreme pain. I apply a bit more pressure and he gasps, the muscles in his neck straining, the vein in his neck popping out. He swallows tightly, then nods. I release him, giving him a little extra shove at the end so he'll stumble backward. Him falling on his ass is accidental, but it's definitely the best part of my day.

Trent groans, still holding his arm, and I turn away. If he comes at me again, he'll have to kill me. I grab my clothes and head for the showers, glancing at Berlin as I pass as if to tell him his secret is safe with me.

With a friend like Trent, it seems Berlin is the one in need of protection.

BERLIN

WHERE DID that kung fu trick even come from? When Hiroku passes by me in the locker room, I'm so stunned I forget I'm staring, openmouthed and catching flies. Makes me wonder if he only did it to keep me from getting involved, like he knew I have something to hide. But if he's got some kind of martial arts training, why is he letting Trent smack him around at all?

Meanwhile, Trent's flopping on the ground, gripping his arm like it's broken, and the guys are all looking to me for a sign.

"I wouldn't mess with that kid if I were you," I tell them, then offer my hand to Trent. He climbs up and skulks off to his locker, grumbling under his breath. Serves him right. After I dress, I see Hiroku breeze out of the locker room without looking back. He might be my new personal hero.

I've got to talk to Hiroku, but how? School's out of the question—that's a death wish for both of us. I tried friending him on Facebook but got no response. I want to meet up with him somewhere outside of school. Then it occurs to me—maybe I should just grow a pair and ask him out.

It doesn't have to be a date or anything, just two guys hanging out. That's normal enough, right?

Later that night, I ask my best friend Google for advice. *How do you ask a guy out?* How people got by before the Internet, I have no idea. My dad hardly talks about anything other than the farm or football. Sex, even the straight kind, never comes up. My youth group preaches abstinence, and my mother… she passed on too early for all of this. I like to think she might have been able to help.

I've never asked out a total stranger. Kayla and I were friends already. It was easy because I knew there was a pretty good chance she'd say yes. I'm not so sure about Hiroku.

Luckily, wikiHow has some pretty good advice, even if it does assume I'm a girl. Pick a place that's private at a time when he's not stressed. Don't make a big deal about it or give off creepy vibes. Okay. Have a date in mind. That might be a little harder. I review what I know about Hiroku so far.

He likes music and wears band shirts nearly every day to school. (I haven't heard of any of them.)

He rides a motorcycle.

He's good at basketball.

He's had some kind of martial arts training.

He may or may not have been expelled from his last school.

He's pretty decent at applying eyeliner.

He turns me on without even trying.

I've already figured out his schedule. He has Digital Arts during first period, which is in B-wing. The kids in that class are always going out on assignment around campus. I pass through B-wing while I'm delivering hall passes during first period. Maybe I can hang around there and intercept him.

I also look up the bands on his T-shirts. One of them, Petty Crime, is coming to Austin this weekend. It's last-minute, but maybe Hiroku would go with me. The music on their website is decent. The lead singer, Seth Barrett, is openly gay and posts a lot of pictures of himself with guys on Instagram. I check out one of their music videos, shot in black and white, set in some kind of opium den or something. Lots of flimsy curtains and smoke curling around Seth and another shirtless guy. The other guy's face is turned away from the camera, but his body is on full display as Seth kisses and touches him everywhere—shoulders, bare back, chest. His fingers scale down his abs to the waistband of his jeans, undo the button, reach inside his pants....

"Dinner's ready."

I slam my laptop shut, but I don't turn around since I probably look guilty as sin. I hope my dad's far enough away that he can't see what I'm watching. He probably knows I've been looking at porn pretty regularly, but I don't think he knows it's gay porn. Not that the video is porn or anything.

"Be right there," I say. It takes me a few minutes to cool down. Images from the video are burned in my head. I rub my hands against the outside of my jeans, then go into the bathroom, wash them, and splash some cold water on my face. I meet my dad out back on the deck. We usually eat outside, whatever my dad grills that night. He's a boss at grilling—vegetables and potatoes along with every kind of meat. He even uses the grill to heat up things like beans still in the can. It makes for fewer dishes, and the food's always good.

Dad says a prayer, then catches me up on what's been going on around the farm. With school and football practice every afternoon, we haven't seen much of each other lately.

"We need to fix the fence in the back quarter so we can put the bulls on the cows before too long," he says.

"Yes, sir."

"You got practice Saturday?"

"Yeah, but I'll get home early enough to put in a few hours. We can pick it back up Sunday morning."

"After church," he reminds me. I wouldn't mind missing church, but my dad's devout.

"Yes, sir."

He glances up at me, wrinkles lining his tanned forehead. "Saw Mrs. Carmichael at the Pac N Sac. She told me you and Kayla broke up."

"Yes, sir. Last weekend." I was hoping he wouldn't ask me about it.

"Everything all right there?"

I sit back and try to appear casual. "We had a good run. It was time."

He nods, and I sense that's the end of it. I lean in to take another bite of my steak.

"How's your steak?" he asks.

"Perfect. As always."

Later that night I shut my door, turn the TV up loud, and watch the music video again with my headphones on. Petty Crime is coming to Austin. I'll ask Hiroku to go with me to their show. It doesn't have to be a date, just two guys who appreciate the same music.

What if he says no?

What if he says yes?

I DON'T have to wait too long. At school the next day, I see Hiroku leave the multimedia room during first period while I'm out on one of my errands. My eyes center on his back like a target, and my heart speeds up so fast I feel it pounding in my throat. I take a deep breath and give myself a pep talk like I'm amping up for a football game. I jog a little to catch up with him.

"Hey," I say. "Hiroku, right?"

He glances over and scowls at me. Still hot.

"Just Hiro," he says, like it would kill him to say anything more.

Maybe I'm wrong about him, or about trying to talk to him.

"I'm Berlin," I say, which is stupid because we already know each other's names, even if we've never talked to each other before.

"Yeah, I know. I've been playing basketball with you for the last two weeks."

I glance around to make sure the hallway's still empty. I don't know what I'll do if someone sees us. Maybe run like hell in the other direction. For now we're alone and he's talking to me. We're having a conversation, even if it's a lame one.

I try again. "So, where you headed?"

"Why do you care?"

Damn, wikiHow didn't prepare me for this. What if he thinks I was in on that stunt Trent pulled? "Just making conversation, I guess."

"When your bros aren't around."

I don't have an answer to that. He's right. I've never talked to him before now. I know when I'm losing. I'm about to bail when he lifts the camera in his hand.

"I'm going to the football field to film the cheerleaders' practice. I've never heard of cheerleading being an actual class. That's crazy."

"That's Lowry," I say. He snorts in agreement. It isn't much, but I'll take it. "I guess your old school was pretty different."

He nods. "Yeah. Just a little."

We're nearing the football field, which means I'm running out of time. I wish he was wearing his Petty Crime shirt. Then I could bring it up without it being weird and creepy.

"Where are you going?" he asks, glancing over at me. He looks a little uncomfortable.

I point ahead of us. "Oh, um, this way." I run my hand through my hair. I'm sweating all over and I feel like I just sprinted the length of the football field. This must be what it feels like to have a heart attack. "So, you like that band Petty Crime?"

His eyes go wide, and he looks at me like I'm from outer space. "How do you know about them?" He looks pissed.

"You wear that shirt a lot. I looked them up online. They seem... interesting."

He stops in the hallway and sizes me up. The intensity of his gaze makes me tongue-tied. I wipe my sweaty hands on my jeans.

"Well, what about them?" He sounds so hostile. I'm pretty sure he hates me. I should give up, but I've come too far to back out now, so I barrel through it.

"They're playing a show in Austin this weekend. I was thinking about going. Maybe you want to, uh, go… with me?"

His eyebrows draw together in confusion, his face softens, and he starts walking again, slower this time. I match his pace as his frown deepens.

"I'm not that into them anymore," he says at last. "I just wear the shirt because I like it. I'm not going to their show."

"Oh, okay." I lag behind a little. I guess that's a no. Is it because he doesn't want to go with me? He probably has a boyfriend already. Or he's just not interested.

We reach the end of the hallway and the glass door that opens up onto the football field. If I go through that door, the entire cheerleading squad will see us together. I stop as he's reaching for the door handle. He turns around.

"Maybe some other time," he says.

I stare after him in a stupor as he crosses the track with his camera slung across his back, butt twitching, black T-shirt hugging his shoulder blades. Maybe I read him wrong. Maybe he's not even gay and I just ruined my life by asking him out. But he did say *some other time*, and that must mean something.

But what?

HIROKU

I'M A little distracted while filming the cheerleaders, going over the conversation with Berlin in my head. I'm pretty sure he just asked me out, unless he happens to have an interest in obscure emo rock bands. But he said he looked up Petty Crime because of me. Was he doing, like, research?

Panic is what hits me first. And guilt, when I think about having to tell Seth about it. *But I don't have to*, I remind myself. We're not together and we haven't been for months. Still, their show is about the worst possible place to bring another guy. The last thing I want is to confront Seth after months of no contact while on a date with Berlin. Talk about baggage. I wouldn't want to subject Berlin to that shit show.

Berlin could be setting me up. Maybe it was a prank he and his friend Trent came up with. But I don't think so. The way Berlin looks at me…. Which means the reason he asked me out is because he's interested in me. Enough to risk being outed for it. He's either brave or crazy.

But I've already decided I'm not going to Seth's show. My parents won't allow it, obviously. All forms of contact are forbidden, which is why I never go on Facebook. I might not be able to resist friending Seth again. Besides, my parents have all my passwords and probably check my accounts regularly. The NSA has nothing on my mother.

"Are you getting this, Hiroku?" calls one of the cheerleaders, Tamara, as she high-kicks her long leg in the air. They're dressed out in their navy-and-gold uniforms for today's filming. Tamara's the one who recruited me to make this video. I showed some of my past work to the kids in Digital Arts and word got around. She cornered me in the hallway and asked me to film the squad. She even batted her eyelashes a little. It wasn't hard to convince me. I need to be working.

"I think I'm going to need you to do that again," I call to her with a flirty grin.

She struts up to the camera and makes a kissy face, then whispers in my ear, "I've got other tricks I could show you."

I stop filming for a moment and tell her honestly, "I'm gay, Tamara." I don't want her to get the wrong idea.

She tilts her head and looks me up and down. "How gay are you?"

I laugh at her persistence. "Pretty fucking gay."

She sighs and winds one finger through her long, curly ponytail. "Too bad. We'd make beautiful babies."

"I have no doubt."

She sashays back to the other girls, and we take it again from the top. As I'm leaving she knocks her hip into mine and says, "See you around, Hiroku. If you ever get bi-curious, I've got dibs." She licks one finger and dabs the air to make her point.

"You'll be first in line," I assure her with a smile.

When I get home that afternoon, I put together the footage of the cheerleaders. The school's editing equipment is subpar, and their computers are maddeningly slow. At home with my software, it takes me about two hours to create a bitching video that makes the cheerleaders look hot and cool and independent all at once. I add in some comic book transitions like *Bam! Ka-Pow! Bang!* and set it to a superhero-sounding fight song. It's a far cry from creating music videos, but it's something, at least.

After I upload the cheerleading video to the YouTube page for Lowry's Digital Arts class, I go onto my Facebook page for the first time in weeks. I miss my old school, my old friends. It wasn't like I had a ton of them, but I did have some good ones. I can't hang out with them anymore, though. A lot of them are still using.

I notice a friend request, and my heart jumps. Is it Seth again? Earlier in the summer he tried friending me, sometimes using other people's accounts. I didn't see the requests until I got out of rehab, and I ignored them all. Avoiding past triggers is part of my treatment plan.

I click the icon, but it isn't Seth. It's Berlin.

Berlin, whose friends would all know if I accepted his request. Wouldn't that look suspicious? I don't know how he's managed to stay in the closet this long.

As I sit there staring at Berlin's profile picture, a chat box pops up from Sabrina, Petty Crime's drummer and my best friend.

How are you?

Sabrina is the one who called my parents from the hospital after I overdosed and told them about the drugs and Seth. She's part of the reason I'm on extended vacation in Lowry. I haven't talked to her in months. At first it was because I was mad at her. Then it seemed easier to cut her off, since she's still part of Seth's life and I don't want to be tempted. Still, I miss her.

Pretty shitty.

:(

How about you? How's the tour going?

Not the same without you.

Wish I was there.

Everyone misses you.

Ditto.

Seth misses you too. He wants you to know he's sorry.

My breath hitches. There's no way in hell Sabrina would ever mention Seth to me, and especially not like that. He's a dirty word as far as she's concerned. She stays in the band because she loves the music, but she's warned me again and again I need to get away from him.

Seth?

I wait, drumming my knuckles, my heart beating faster, my knees bouncing up and down underneath my desk. Is he using Sabrina's account to contact me? Does she know he's doing it?

I miss you, baby.

I stare at the screen until my vision blurs. When I left Seth, I had to cut out internal organs, like you would an arm with gangrene. He's poison, and I know that. But I still miss him. He was my first and my only. He nurtured the artist in me, made me feel things I've never felt before or since. He made me cool and accepted. For three years he was my whole world.

He also got me hooked on pain pills, embarrassed me in front of our friends for fun, and pressured me to do things I didn't want to do. Sometimes he got violent.

I can't..., I start to type.

Can't what?

I can't talk to him, can't see him, can't listen to his music or any other music that reminds me of him, can't look at old pictures or movies. I can't even wear my own clothes without thinking of something we did together when I last wore them, which is why I only wear black now. My room is a mausoleum because his fingerprints are on every goddamned thing I own. I can't think about the past three years of my life, because he's so wrapped up in everything I did and everything I am.

I can't *anything* with him. I delete the words and start over.

Tell Sabrina and the band I say hey.

Don't go. I just want to talk.

I type nothing, just sit there and stare at the screen, waiting for I have no idea what. My next instruction? I've already made up my mind it's over between us, so why am I giving him an opening?

Come to my show. I need to see you. They can't keep you locked away in a tower forever.

He includes a link, and against my better judgment, I click it. It opens a new screen with a single ticket to Petty Crime, their Austin show, the one Berlin invited me to. My name is already on the ticket.

I sign out of Facebook, determined to never open it again. It isn't safe for me. Seth took that away from me. My friends, my school, and Austin too. It isn't my parents who locked me away in this tower.

It's him.

BERLIN

PRACTICE THAT afternoon is brutal. The heat slows us down, especially with all the pads and helmet. I feel like I'm running through quicksand, and every yard is a struggle. An hour into it we're all fading. Coach has us practicing sweeps but Trent is sluggish from the heat and keeps getting tagged by the defensive line before he can make the handoff, which puts Coach in a tizzy.

"Goddammit, Trent," he spits and throws down his clipboard, "What the hell is your problem today? You get hit in the head or something?"

"No, sir."

"You got dirt in your eyes?"

Trent huffs and says nothing.

"You need to run some stadiums to get your head screwed on right?"

"No, sir."

"Get back out there and get it right." He glances over at the defense. "This time, tackle his candyass. We need to make it real for him."

We start again. The first two drills are successful, but Coach isn't satisfied. The third time, Trent takes a shoulder in the gut and falls backward, kind of rolls over and curls into a fetal position. Coach pounces on him right away.

"Get up on your feet and take that hit like a man."

Trent rises slowly to his feet, still hunched over gripping his stomach. He's sweating and wheezing and looks like he might pass out. Coach either doesn't notice or doesn't care, because he barrels on. "You see any women out here, Trent? Look around, you see any women?"

"No, sir."

"You know why? Because we don't allow pussies to play football. This is my field and it's for men only, so unless you're vomiting or shitting blood, I expect you to suck it up and run that goddamned drill again."

There's no way Trent is going to make it through another play. He can barely stand on his own two feet.

"Coach," I cut in. "I think we need a water break."

Coach turns his mean, beady eyes on me. "You telling me how to run my team, Webber?" I glance across the field to the empty bleachers. When he's in a state like this, it's better if you don't look him directly in the eyes.

"No, sir."

"Sounds like you are. You think I don't know it's hotter than hellfire out here right now? You think I'm not sweating my balls off like the rest of you? If you and Trent could get this very simple play right, we could be taking that water break right now, but I got a couple of nancies bitching and moaning at every turn."

Coach goes on about it. I tune him out and eye Trent. His face has gone ghost white and his eyes are at half-mast. He looks wobbly on his feet. I go over and catch him just as he's about to collapse. This interrupts Coach's tirade long enough for him to call over a trainer and a water boy to get him hydrated. "Everyone else get water," he snaps, "except you, Webber. Hang up your helmet. You're done for the day."

What kind of bullshit is he trying to pull now?

"You want me to hit the showers, Coach?" I ask, trying not to let on how pissed I am.

He gets right up in my face and grabs hold of my face mask so I can't look away. His breath is tangy like he's been drinking and his eyes are bloodshot. Rumor is he keeps his sports bottles liquored up. What I know about the man would support it.

"I want you running stadiums until the end of practice. That'll teach you to challenge my authority."

I don't care about his authority. He's being an idiot and putting Trent and the rest of our team in danger. "Coach, heatstroke is serious. You can have a seizure and die from it."

He yanks on my face mask to intimidate me, jerking my head around. Short of laying him out on the field, there's nothing I can do about it. I fucking hate that shit. I rip off my helmet and throw it to the ground. Coach narrows his eyes at me and crosses his arms over his chest.

"You got something to say to me, Webber?"

I take a few heated breaths and wipe the sweat from my brow. "No, sir."

"I thought so. Now, get out of my face before I decide to make you come back here tomorrow and do a few hours of suicides."

I stride away from him, drop my helmet and pads on the bench and head for the bleachers. He calls after me, loud enough for everyone to hear, "And cut your goddamned hair. You look like a faggot."

I tackle the stadiums, pounding the concrete stairs with all my anger and frustration. Boy, what I wouldn't give to tackle Coach, just one good hit to remind him he's not the big badass he thinks he is. After a while the heat and physical strain sap the anger out of me and I feel empty and bitter. Coach is still yelling at Trent down on the field, even though it only makes him play worse. As much as I despise Coach Cross, at least I only have to put up with him for two more seasons.

Trent is stuck, though. He has the man for life.

Later, in the locker room, Trent comes up to me, claps me on the back, and says quietly, "Next time, don't interfere."

"You were dying out there, Trent."

His tone is black when he says, "Don't get between Coach and me again. You know better."

My fingers curl into fists and my back stiffens. Since we were eleven, he's been telling me that. *Don't tell anyone. I'll handle it myself.* It's not just the beatings either; it's the bullying too, calling Trent worthless and stupid, making threats. I want Trent to stand up to the man and expose him for the piece of shit he is.

"You hear?" Trent says when I don't respond.

I nod. "Loud and clear."

HIROKU

I HAVE another failing: I'm weak when it comes to saying no. My rehab therapist Dr. Denovo called that having an addictive personality. I don't know if I was always this way or if it's a product of being with Seth for so long. Did he weaken my resolve, or did he prey on that part of me that was already vulnerable?

I did a lot of reflecting in rehab. I took a long, hard look in the mirror, retraced all the shitty decisions I made, and devised a plan to not make those same shitty decisions again.

Yet here I am on my way to Austin to see Petty Crime, but really, it's to see Seth. Everyone who loves me will be disappointed, except one person. Seth will be thrilled.

I arrive at the Depot after they've already started. The stage is an old feedstore, slightly raised off the ground. The warehouse doors are open. Other businesses have come in and taken over the surrounding buildings to form an industrial-looking outdoor courtyard. The bars are strung with tea lights, as is the stage. This is a big venue for Petty Crime, and the place is already so packed, people have to thread through the crowd to get a place up front. I find a spot toward the back. I don't know yet what I'm going to do, but I do know I want to see Seth before he sees me. A test of my own willpower.

Onstage, Seth is gorgeous, as always. Electric. His dark hair is already damp with sweat. The corded muscles in his arms glisten under the stage lights. He holds his guitar like a lover, like he once held me, alternating between strumming and striking it. He croons and he screams. That's Seth, from tender to vicious in the blink of an eye. Part of it is that he's bipolar. Another part is his desire to control people. I actually wrote a song about it called "Queen of Hearts." I shot the video too and ended up starring in it, my first paying gig. I bought my bike with the money from the video, and also a lot of drugs.

I avoid looking at him so I won't be swayed by his appearance, but his voice has the same effect. When I met him, he was Seth from down the street, three years older, who sometimes dropped in on our basketball games. He sucked at basketball, though. He told me later he only played because he thought I was cute.

He had a band then, but they weren't very good. My friend Sabrina played drums for the high school marching band, and I introduced them. The two of them recruited a lead guitarist and a bassist, and I watched them go from total suck to partial suck to pretty damn good from the beat-up couch in Seth's garage.

I did all their promo stuff and wrote some of their songs. Now they're touring bigger venues and selling out shows. They're on the cusp. Part of me feels like I should still be there with them, since I've given so much over the years. Another part knows better.

On stage Seth whispers promises into the microphone, and I close my eyes to listen.

Use my skin
Burrow deep down in
I will take the dive
I will make you mine

He sings like a siren. He once told me all his songs were for me, that when he looked out at the crowd, the only face he cared about was mine. It was the artist I fell in love with. His mind, the part of him that can be so thoughtful and loving.

I take a deep breath and open my eyes, only to see Seth staring straight at me. He's found me in the crowd. He always had a sixth sense about me.

I shiver as our eyes lock, but he doesn't miss a beat, doesn't trip over the lyrics or even stutter. He motions with his hand for me to come closer.

Like his puppet, I do.

The song ends and the crowd roars. Seth takes a moment to drink it all in. He feeds off the crowd's energy like a vampire. He says something to his bandmates, then takes the microphone again, commanding the room into silence.

"This next song is for a special someone here tonight, a pretty bird who flew away from me but has finally returned. I hurt him…."

Here, the crowd boos as if they can't believe a person as charming and talented as Seth could hurt anyone. He plays along with their reaction while looking me dead in the eyes. "It's true," he continues. "I was a very bad boy, but only because I love the pretty bird so much. And this song is to tell him I'm sorry."

Behind the drum kit, Sabrina strains to look for me. When she finds me, she slices across her throat with her drumstick. She's going to kill me before I give Seth the chance. I can still get away. If I leave before Seth finishes the set....

Then Seth strums the first few chords of "Queen of Hearts," and the crowd loses their shit. It's a fan favorite, even more popular now thanks to the video, the same one that got me in trouble with my parents. The video—and the song—is about Seth and me.

I rise and you fall
I push and you pull
away
I scream and you cry
I beg and you fly
away
I take a little at a time
Give you just enough
to make you mine
you waste
away

I stand there spellbound, imagining Seth's garage where I wrote that song, the smell of sawdust and car oil, how Seth would distract me with kisses when I was trying to compose and laugh at me when I told him I was working. "You take yourself too seriously," he'd say and unravel my resolve with his hands and his mouth. And the drugs, ever present in our last year together. They were the glue holding our relationship together through his cheating and abuse.

Now Seth watches me as he sings, perhaps to see if his magic is having the intended effect. And I watch him, a closed loop of all we've shared. Did he choose that song to acknowledge what he's done to me or to throw it in my face that I can't leave him? The fact I have to ask means I should run like hell, but my body remains, swaying along to the music.

Seth is infecting me all over again, working his way through my bloodstream. The song reaches its crescendo, and I know when it's over I'll go to him, follow him down that rabbit hole all over again.

None of what I've been through matters anymore. Not my mother's face in the hospital when she found out how bad it had gotten. Not the nine weeks I spent in rehab. Not the times I scared even myself at how willing I was to do what he wanted. None of it will matter, because I'll be in Seth's orbit again. The song is in its final throes and my feet are leading me to the stage. Within minutes we'll be reunited. My body will betray me, as it's done time and time again.

"Hiro."

A six-foot wall erupts from the ground and blocks my path.

His name is Berlin Webber.

BERLIN

"WHAT ARE *you* doing here?" Hiro asks as I step in front of him. He looks past me, his eyes still on the stage.

"I like their music," I say, which is part of the reason. I was also hoping he'd be here, but I keep that to myself.

Hiro doesn't answer. It's like he's off in another world, stoned or something. I wonder if he came here alone. He shouldn't be driving if he's high.

"You okay? You want a ride home after?" I put my hand on his shoulder.

Hiro glances down at my hand. "I have my bike."

"I can put it in the back of my truck."

"It's pretty heavy."

"I keep a two-by-four in the back in case I get stuck in the mud."

He looks confused and glances again toward the stage, where the band is winding down. Then he leans in close and says into my ear, "If you want me to go with you, we have to leave now."

I follow his gaze to where the lead singer of Petty Crime is staring at the two of us. "I think they're going to play another set." Hiro licks his lips, which distracts me from the band. Something about his eyes reminds me of an animal on the run. Maybe he's on something more than just weed. "Fine, yeah. Let's go now," I say.

He grabs my arm and leads me out a side door that empties right into the parking lot. He's obviously been here before. "Where'd you park?" he asks, glancing behind him like we're being chased. I point at my truck. "Can you bring it over to my bike? I don't want to start it up."

He's definitely trying to dodge someone, but who? And why? I don't ask, though. I drive over to his bike. Hiro bounces on his toes while I load it up into the back of my truck and strap it in. In the cab his jitters get worse, and he rubs at his knees over and over. Across the parking lot, the lead singer of Petty Crime is jogging toward us, waving his arms kind of crazy-like.

I point toward him. "I think he wants to talk to you."

Hiro grabs my arm. He has my full attention now.

"Just go, Berlin."

The singer must be who he's running from. He isn't very big. I could take him if it came to that, but there must be a reason Hiro's acting so frightened, especially after I saw him stand up to a guy like Trent. Instead of asking questions, I hit the gas, and we haul ass out of the parking lot.

Hiro sticks his face out the open window like he needs one last look. The wind catches his hair. I need to pay attention to the road.

In my rearview I see the singer break into a run. He shouts something, but I can't hear it over the growl of my engine.

"You owe that guy money or something?" I ask once we're a few blocks away and it seems safer to talk.

Hiro collapses into the seat like a punched paper bag. "Something like that."

Maybe that guy's his dealer, or Hiro's selling drugs for him. That would explain some things.

"Is that why you didn't want to come to the show?"

He sticks out his lower lip and chews on it. I wonder what it tastes like. "Yes."

I go over it in my mind. The dedication that singer made, it was for the same song as that video I'd seen. I glance over at Hiro, kind of check out his physique. I've seen him in the locker room without his shirt on. A lightning bolt strikes me.

"You're the guy in the video," I say. I've watched it more times than I care to admit. I practically have his body memorized, which is weird and something I'd never say out loud.

He sighs but says nothing. I've been fantasizing about that guy right alongside Hiro, not realizing they were the same person.

"You guys were together?" They had to be. That video was way too real, more like a documentary than a music video.

Another sigh.

The singer said he'd been bad to someone. Hiro's parents had moved to Lowry to give him a fresh start. "He's the reason you left Austin?"

Hiro fidgets in his seat. "My parents thought I needed a change of scenery."

"Do they know you're here?"

"According to the GPS on my phone, I'm at Lowry High School, working late on a video for school."

This is serious if his parents are tracking him and Hiro's lying to them about it. That guy has to be bad news. I remember the stoned look in Hiro's eyes earlier.

"You came back to see him."

He claps his hands once, hard. "Enough about me, Berlin. Let's talk about you. What position do you play?"

It takes me a second to realize he's changed the subject to football. I guess he doesn't want to answer my questions. "Running back."

"You fast?"

"Pretty fast."

"Your team any good?"

He sounds like he's interested. Football is an easy subject, one I can talk about all day long. "We went to the play-offs last year. Almost made it to state. You follow football?"

He shakes his head. "Not in the least."

He's too cool for school, apparently. I imagine him in the stands, wearing our team colors, cheering for me, of course. But then, I can't really see Hiro jumping around and shouting for any sports team. More like slouched back and scowling with his perfect, pouty mouth.

"You should come to a game sometime," I tell him. "Might improve your school spirit."

He snorts at that. "School spirit is not my top priority right now."

I figured that was the case. "So what is?"

He tucks the long side of his hair behind his ear. I wonder how many piercings he has and if he has any in places I can't see. The singer had them too. Maybe they did that for fun, pierced each other.

"Staying off drugs," he says, then leans forward and scratches at his arms. He looks like he wants to crawl right out of his skin.

Drugs too? He grew up fast in Austin. When I think about that video, the way the singer touched Hiro seemed like he was handling his property more than a person. I wonder if drugs were involved.

"Are you on something now?" I ask him.

"No, unfortunately. Just high on life."

We drive another few miles in silence while I turn it over in my mind. Hiro doesn't offer any more explanation, and I don't know what to say without sounding judgmental. As we approach the outskirts of Lowry, I realize I don't want to take him home just yet, but there's nowhere in town we can go without being seen.

I pull off a side road and then onto a dirt road. Hiro doesn't ask where I'm taking him. He still seems pretty checked out. When we come to the edge of my property, I get out and open the gate, drive through, then close it on the other side. I pull into a grove of trees, park the truck, and shut off the engine.

He turns toward me. "Is this the part where I suck you off in exchange for protection?"

It takes me a second to realize what he's suggesting. "What? No." My neck gets hot and my junk starts throbbing at the mere mention of it. "Is that how it was at your old school?"

Hiro chews on his lower lip and stares down at his hands. "No. I was actually pretty popular at my old school. I didn't need protection."

I believe him. He has that cool air about him, like he doesn't give a shit what other people think. I thought it was confidence, but maybe it's only a cover.

"I just wanted to talk to you since I can't at school."

"Yeah, about that." He drapes one toned arm across the back of the seat and rests his knee on the bench. His shirt is black and tight, with slash marks across the front, like some wild animal swiped at it. I can't stop staring at the skin showing through. My hands get itchy, like when I'm about to get the ball in a game. I kind of want to rip the rest of his shirt away.

"Are you a homo or what, Berlin?" he asks.

My face feels like it's on fire as I run my fingers through my hair, then remember my hair is short. "I don't know." Why do people have to put a label on everything? Why can't I just be?

"You want to find out?" He lifts one eyebrow suggestively, a smirk on his face. Is that an invitation? We hardly even know each other, but still….

"No," I stammer while images from that video flood me. All his body parts swim in my head, so much smooth skin and hard muscle, the smell of him in the cab of my truck. Of course I want to… do stuff… but this seems way too soon. "I mean, maybe, but that's not what this is about. I didn't come here to mess around. I just want to talk to you."

He shrugs and glances out the window. He looks bored. I'm boring him. He's been with a rock star. He probably sees me as just some dumb hick. I don't have any experience with guys. I barely have any experience with girls. I can't even say for sure if I'm gay or not.

I take a deep breath and try to muster up my courage. He came with me over his ex. That has to count for something. "Why'd you guys break up?" It's none of my business, but I'm curious. In the video they looked very… close.

"I liked your hair long," he says, changing the subject yet again. "Why'd you cut it?"

I'm surprised he noticed. I rub my palm across the top of my buzz cut. "Coach told me I looked like a faggot." I clipped it the same day.

Hiro shakes his head slowly. His mouth turns down to a frown. I want to kiss him pretty bad. He turns away from me and gets a faraway look in his eyes.

"Must be hard for you living in a place like this," he says softly.

I follow his gaze to where he looks out at the land, my birthright. Even if I get through high school, I'll still have to hide my sexuality in college if I want to play football. And then eventually I'll come back here to Lowry to manage the farm, and what? Come out then? I don't see any solution in sight, which means I can't think too far ahead.

"I take it one day at a time," I say.

He nods and leans the back of his head against the seat, exposing his neck. Even his throat is sexy. "Yeah, me too," he says.

We're quiet after that. He knows things without me having to tell him. I'm not sure if that's a good thing.

"How'd you know?" I ask him. "About me?"

He tilts his head to look at me sideways. "About you?"

He's playing dumb. He wants me to say it. "About me maybe, possibly, being gay."

He snickers. "You asked me out. Don't you remember?"

"Before that."

He purses his lips and squints like he's trying to remember. "I don't know. I guess I just… felt you. You seemed interested. Was I wrong?"

I swallow, afraid to admit it to him. He's the only one who knows this about me. It feels dangerous but also like a huge relief. I'm so tired of hiding it from everyone, always glancing over my shoulder or covering something up. Feels like I'm bound up in chains.

"You weren't wrong," I tell him. Not in the least. I'm very interested, and it's making me kind of crazy. "Do you think other people can tell?"

"I don't know. Do you check out a lot of other dudes?"

"No," I practically shout.

He chuckles.

I grip the steering wheel because I need something to hold on to. I feel like I'm on a Tilt-A-Whirl with him. "What's so funny?"

"I don't know." He waves one hand. "You're such a contradiction."

I'm not sure what he means by that. Maybe because I try to fit in. Hiro clearly isn't interested in hiding anything, even when that means getting bullied. His parents could have sent him to another school in Austin. It seems extreme to bring him all the way out to the country, like putting a wild bird in a cage. Like a punishment.

"Are your parents mad at you?" I ask. "Is that why they brought you here?"

Hiro sighs and clasps his hands in front of him like a well-behaved child. "My dad is, but that's nothing new. I'm not exactly what he bargained for. Luckily, my older sister makes up for it. I don't really blame him for giving up on me, though. I've made some bad choices."

"What about your mom?"

His eyes soften. "My mom's more hopeful."

"That's good. Are you?"

He tucks in his chin so half his face is hidden behind his hair. "Some days more so than others." He says it so quietly, like he's in pain. I want to hug him or rub his shoulders, do something to make him feel better like I would with Kayla, but I don't want to weird him out.

"You're probably, like, my mom's favorite person right now," he says with a sad smile.

"Why's that?"

He glances up at me with eyes that look empty. "Because you're not Seth."

That doesn't seem like a compliment to me, more like a default. Seth must have really done a number on Hiro for his parents to move out here. And for Hiro to sneak back to see him. Some kind of mind control.

Their relationship interests me. I don't know any gay couples in Lowry. And the people who might be gay are only rumors, usually meant to shame them. I guess things are a lot different in Austin. "How long were you guys together?" I ask.

"Too long." He shakes his head like he's ridding himself of some bad memory. His eyes focus on mine. "How about you? Your parents are ranchers?"

"My dad. My mom died when I was ten. Breast cancer."

His lips pucker. "That really sucks. I'm sorry, Berlin."

He has no idea. My mom was the lighthearted one in the family, the fun one. My dad only smiled for her. And she could get me to crack up laughing with her ribbing, which was always good-natured.

"She had a great sense of humor," I tell Hiro.

"You have any brothers or sisters?"

"No, just my dad and me." But we have our land and our animals. I have my football team and Trent, even if he is an asshole sometimes. I'm not alone, except for in this one thing.

"Does your dad know about you maybe, possibly, being gay?"

Hiro's teasing me again, but I don't think he's trying to hurt my feelings.

"No."

"Would he be mad?"

My dad isn't a hateful person, but he is a man's man, a meat-and-potatoes kind of guy, a God-fearing Christian. If he suspects anything, he keeps it to himself, maybe hoping it's something I'll grow out of. "I don't know," I say at last. "I'm afraid to find out."

"What about your friend Trent?"

I don't have to think twice about that. "He'd flip. So would Coach Cross. I'd get kicked off the team, lose my chance at a scholarship." Lose my friends, become the butt of their every joke, maybe get jumped, be treated just like....

"I won't tell anyone," Hiro says quietly, like he knows how important this secret is to me. I believe him when he says it. He could have told someone before now and he didn't.

"Thank you." The words aren't enough to show how grateful I am.

"I should get going, though." His gaze veers back out the window. "My parents are going to put out a missing persons any minute."

With some reluctance I start up the truck and go back out the way we came. I don't want him to go, but I can't say it without it sounding weird. On the other side of the fence, I unload his bike, then stand there next to it, not sure how to tell him I want to see him again.

"You want to go shooting with me tomorrow?" I ask. The fence shouldn't take too long to finish fixing, and then I'll have the afternoon to do what I want.

He runs his hand along his bike seat. His fingers are long and nicely shaped, with trim, unbitten nails. My own hands are full of scars and calluses from working on the farm.

"I'm not really into hunting," he says. "I'm actually a vegetarian."

I smack my forehead. It would figure. "You're killing me, Smalls. This is cattle country. Beef is what's for dinner." Hiro smiles at that, and it's such a pretty sight that I'd do just about anything to see it again. I wave him away. "It's fine. We don't have to hunt or anything. We can just shoot bottles or whatever." Shit, we don't even have to bring guns. I just want an excuse to be with him.

"Okay. Let me text myself from your phone." I hand him my phone, and he sends himself a text. "We can talk this way," he says, looking at me with purpose. "You really don't want to friend me on Facebook. Besides, I'm never on it."

He hands me my phone, and I shove it in my pocket. I don't know what to do with my hands, which is strange. On the farm and in football, I'm good with my hands.

"Well." He grabs his helmet. "See you tomorrow, then."

As he mounts his bike, the back of his shirt lifts up over his waistband, exposing the small of his back and the triangle of muscles that point downward like an arrow. My throat goes dry as I imagine my hand there, steering him underneath me. My stomach flip-flops. Not butterflies, more like anxiety. My maybe, possibly, being gay is seeming more and more likely.

One day at a time.

HIROKU

I PARK my bike on the side of the road and pull out my phone to text Berlin that I'm here at his property's fence line. Before I can hit Send, his truck rumbles up to the gate from the inside. Berlin hops out, opens the gate wide, and I roll my bike through. Right away he takes the handlebars from me and guides my bike to a cluster of trees.

It strikes me that Berlin is a true gentleman. My standards aren't that high—I mean, I don't expect a guy to hold the door open for me, but it would be nice if he made sure it didn't close on my face. Seth always said he didn't hold doors because we were equals, but I suspect it didn't occur to him to be a gentleman unless there was something in it for him.

"Come on," Berlin says with an easy smile and motions to his truck. His biceps are impressive. Shoulders and chest too; really his musculature in general. He's wearing a T-shirt and blue jeans, work boots, and a ball cap. Muscles, golden hair, and sun-kissed skin. Raised on beef and farm work. *Da-yum.* If we as a species chose one man to preserve as an example of masculine beauty, Berlin would be a top contender.

I climb into his truck, feeling kind of nervous. I assumed, when he asked me to go shooting, we would go somewhere on his land. There really isn't any other place in this town where we can be seen together without dire consequences for him. I have no idea, though, where he's taking me. I'm at his mercy.

Relax, Hiroku.

The weather is nice, not oppressively hot like it had been this summer. The breeze tickles my arms and the back of my neck. I glance over at Berlin, and he smiles shyly. I miss his long hair, though. The stupid football coach who told him he looked like a faggot is the same one who gave me a referral the first day of school and still eyeballs me whenever he sees me in the hallway. Trent's dad. The homophobia doesn't fall far from the tree.

We ride for a while on dirt roads and through fields. Their property stretches out as far as I can see. As we pass by some cows grazing next to a pond, Berlin tells me about their ranch, how many head of cattle they have. Theirs is a cow-calf operation, not a dairy, Berlin explains. They keep a standing herd and raise them for meat. Not veal, though, which is good. That shit is straight-up animal cruelty.

He rambles on—I think he's nervous too—and I listen, forming a picture of his quiet country life in my mind.

"You have horses?" I ask when he mentions them. I've never ridden before, but I've always wanted to.

"Yeah. You ride?"

"No."

"It's not hard," he says. He looks embarrassed. "I could take you sometime."

The way he says it makes it seem like this is going to be a long-term thing between us. That isn't taking it one day at a time. "Yeah, sure. Whatever."

He's quiet after that. I don't know if it's him or me, but there's a tension in the air. It was never this way with Seth, the getting-to-know you weirdness. If anything, I had to peel Seth off me like a leech.

"You have any alcohol on you, Berlin?" Maybe that would help this along.

"No." He looks insulted. "It's Sunday."

"Right. I forgot." He must go to church too. How does that work? Is it a progressive church where gays are welcomed with open arms, or one of those "all gays go to hell" type places? My parents call themselves Christians, but I suspect it's more a way to fit in with the locals than a source of true belief. I can count on one hand how many times we've been to church in the past few years.

Berlin parks the truck, and we get out at a clearing in the woods. There are about a dozen lawn chairs in a circle around what looks like the ashes of a fire. There are also a few two-by-fours nailed together to form a shooting range, with bottles and cans balanced on the ledge. The grass is tall, and the seed stalks beckon in the light breeze like jilted lovers.

I turn around to see Berlin toting a shotgun. Wow. I thought shooting was an excuse to get me alone, but we're really going to do this.

"You ever used one of these?" he asks.

"I've never shot any kind of gun before."

"Not even a BB gun?" His face screws up like he feels sorry for me.

I shake my head, amused by his reaction. "We're a live-and-let-live type of family."

He leans to one side and eyes me from under the brim of his ball cap, blue eyes twinkling. "Let me guess. You're one of those people who doesn't believe in war either?"

There's a flirtatiousness to his teasing, like he doesn't really mind that we're so different. "The word you're searching for is *pacifist*, and while I've never taken the blood oath, I'd guess that yeah, I probably am."

Berlin adjusts his hat as if to see me better. "Didn't seem like a pacifist when Trent came at you in the locker room." I detect a note of admiration.

"That was self-defense."

"Why'd you let him hit you, then?"

I glance away, avoiding his eyes. I don't think he'd understand. I'm not even sure I could explain it. "I didn't see it coming," I lie.

He raises his eyebrows but doesn't comment, which makes me think maybe he understands a lot more than he lets on.

"So are you a black belt in karate, then?" Berlin asks.

"No. It's jiu-jitsu, and I'm not a black belt. My dad wanted me to take a martial arts class after I told him I was gay. To be able to defend myself. I chose my school because they teach Brazilian jiu-jitsu instead of the traditional Japanese form, and I knew that would piss him off."

"You do things just to piss him off?" Berlin asks with sincerity and I realize our relationships with our fathers must be very different.

"Sometimes. He's kind of controlling, so…." I think about how I basically do the opposite of everything my dad tells me as a way to exert my own will, how rebellious I was in Austin. Seth offered me a way to really stick it to him with all the sneaking around and staying out late, partying and drugs. How shitty that must have been for my dad. I've thought about it before, but never quite like that. No wonder my dad is still so angry with me.

"I hate it when my dad's mad at me," Berlin says. "It's, like, the worst feeling in the world."

"It kind of is, isn't it?" Makes me feel like a piece of shit, all in all.

Berlin lifts the gun and spends a few minutes giving me the basics. How to load it, how to hold it, where to position it against my body. For the last one he comes up behind me and circles his arms around my back like a winter coat, overlapping his arms with mine. I feel the heat of his body, and the muscles in his chest tighten against my shoulders. His arms are twice the thickness of mine. His hands are huge. I don't know if this is standard protocol for gun range safety, but I'm definitely digging it.

He positions the butt of the gun against the fleshy part between my shoulder and chest. "Rest the back of it here," he says as his breath tickles my neck. "I'll hold it with you the first time, so you can get a feel for the kickback."

I swallow as he shows me how to put my finger on the trigger and lean my cheek against the stock. This seems an intimate relationship to have with an inanimate object.

"Keep your eyes open," he says. His breath is hot on my ear, his mouth just inches away. "And exhale before you pull the trigger."

I stare down the sight and aim for a green soda can about ten yards away. I take a deep breath, still cocooned in Berlin's arm.

"Ready?" he whispers.

"Yeah." I'm a little breathless.

"Pull."

I squeeze the trigger and the gun kicks back into me, forcing me into Berlin's chest. He doesn't budge. It's like his feet are rooted in the ground. A thrill races through me, and I'm not sure if it's the gun or being so close to Berlin. I miss the mark completely, but I don't really care.

"Well?" he asks when I finally step away from him.

I rub my shoulder and squint at him. "I think I'm going to need you to show me again."

His face turns bright red all the way to the tips of his ears. It's kind of adorable.

"Hiro," he says like some old schoolmarm.

"What? Haven't you ever flirted with a guy before?"

He shakes his head, smiling in spite of himself. "Actually, no."

His innocence is endearing. "It gets easier."

I take a few more shots on my own, no thanks to him. Berlin seems afraid to come near me, like I might use my wiles to try to seduce him. He's so different from Seth, who I always had to push off me, carve out my own territory in order to have any existence of my own. With Seth I always knew what he wanted—everything, immediately. I can't say for sure with Berlin. Is he looking for a friend, one who happens to be gay, like a queer Yoda? Or is he looking for a hookup? His words say one thing, but his eyes say another.

And me, what do I want?

After I finally hit a couple of cans, Berlin takes a few shots. His aim is deadly. I imagine him with a dead buck draped across his shoulders. In my vision he's shirtless, of course. Blue jeans, boots, longish hair, broad chest, and ripped abs. The picture is both grotesque and arousing at once.

"Your turn." He offers me the gun, startling me from my daydream. I take a few more shots. The sun shifts in the sky and it gets hotter. I'm wearing black, as usual, and jeans. Shorts aren't my thing. I consider taking off my shirt, but I don't want to make him uncomfortable.

"You want to go swimming?" he asks, perhaps noticing my discomfort. His arms are shiny with sweat too. "There's a creek about a half mile from here." He jerks his thumb in that direction.

"Yeah." I rest the gun so the barrel points to the ground as he instructed. "I don't have a suit, though."

"I don't either." Berlin gets real quiet then, like a scared rabbit, and looks kind of terrified as he takes the gun from me while keeping his distance. We walk back to his truck in silence. Is he worried I'm going to try something? Does he want me to? I have no clue. Talk about mixed messages.

We drive for a little ways, and then he turns down a narrow dirt path framed on either side with wispy trees swaying in the breeze like hula dancers. The creek is wide and meandering. Berlin checks the current with a stick. "It's deep enough to swim."

There are smooth, flat rocks on the banks for sunbathing. I squat at the edge a few yards away from him and test the temperature with my hand, using some of the water to wet my hair and the back of my neck. Berlin watches my every move like he's afraid I might turn rabid and bite him.

It seems obvious I'm going to take off my clothes, but I'm not trying to make a production out of it.

"I'm going in," I say. "Do you want to watch me or turn around?"

"Uh." His face darkens and he starts waving his hands like he's swimming. He turns abruptly like he's been sent to the corner. I don't think I'd do the same if our roles were reversed.

I take off my shoes and clothes and toss them in a pile, along with my wallet, keys, and phone. I wade into the creek and dive under. The water makes me shiver, but it's cool and refreshing. Cleansing. Everything about this day has a bright, shiny newness to it. I've hardly even thought about getting high, or Seth. A bubble of hope rises in me. Maybe I can beat this whole addiction thing.

I glance over to where Berlin sits on a rock ledge, dangling his feet in the water, still wearing his boxers and ball cap. Maybe the water's too cold for him. "Berlin?" I call. "You coming in?"

"Yeah, in a minute."

I dive down to the bottom and surface again, let the current carry me for a while, then wade over to where he still sits. He hasn't moved in ten minutes, and he looks like he's all twisted up inside, gripping his belly like he has a stomachache.

"What's up with you?" I ask.

He swallows, his Adam's apple bobbing in his throat. "I don't know. I just feel frozen."

He looks like he's in pain. I suspect his body and mind are sending him conflicting messages. It probably doesn't help having a friend like Trent calling people *faggots* and *pussies* all the time. I want to make him feel better, but I don't want to scare him.

"Is it okay if I come closer?"

He nods, tracking me with his eyes. His attention is focused and deliberate, a hunter. I stop when I'm an arm's length away.

"Have you ever kissed a guy before?" I ask, trying to sound casual.

His face gets red again. I don't want to embarrass him, but I think it's too late. His hands are shaking as his eyes dart around, looking everywhere but at me.

"No." He says it so quietly, like he's ashamed. I rest one hand on his knee, and he stares at it.

"Do you want to kiss me?" I ask gently.

He scratches the back of his neck, and I admire the weight of his arms, remembering how they felt wrapped around me. His chest heaves and he nods, still avoiding me.

"You can look at me."

His eyes lift slowly, taking me in, hungrily. The water's about waist-high, and I wait patiently until he's had his fill. I understand desire. I know what it looks, smells, and tastes like. I want to make it easier for him, so I reach for his hands and place them on my hips. His skin is warm. His hands are surprisingly gentle. I take off his ball cap and toss it on one of the rocks, rough up what little hair is left on his head. The water from my arms drips down his shoulders and traces small rivulets on his bronzed skin. A wrinkle appears in the middle of his forehead, and I smooth it down with my thumb.

"Relax."

His shoulders heave and his hands shift on my waist, gripping me tighter. My cock bobs up in the water, never one to be left out of fun times. I drape my arms around his neck and tilt my head a little. I've never been the initiator before, and I worry I'm doing it wrong. He looks at me as if to make sure this is okay, and I lean into him, going up on my toes.

His lips press against mine timidly, a question. I answer by gripping the back of his trembling neck. He comes in again, fiercer this time and with more confidence. His tongue slides along my lower lip, tasting me. My mouth opens wider and his tongue curls, twining with mine. We take turns taking the lead, exploring with our tongues and lips. The kiss blooms with fervor and Berlin groans from somewhere deep down. I feel it in my balls, a twitchy ache, as he draws me in closer so I'm straddled between his thick thighs.

His knees lock around my hips. Chest to chest. Skin on skin. His one hand grips the base of my back and the other tugs at my hair, drawing my mouth open so he can kiss me deeper. He smells like soil and cut grass, and his body feels solid as a boulder. My nerves are raw where our skin makes contact. A surge of desire rolls through me, blood rushes to my cock, and I'm painfully hard.

I lean back to check in on him. I've never been with anyone but Seth before, so in a way this is like my first kiss all over again, exciting and nerve-racking at the same time, not knowing what the other person is thinking or what they want. "How was that?" I ask him.

"It was nice." Berlin's smile is slow to form, like he's waking from a pleasant dream. This gives me confidence. We kiss again, and it's no less thrilling than before. He draws one hand down the center of my back, coming to rest gently on my tailbone. With the other hand he tugs my hair so my head falls at an angle. Berlin's lips drift away from mine, and he kisses my neck and then my shoulder, making my toes curl in the sandy creek bottom and my fingers cinch into the meat of his back. I love how strong and muscular he is—powerful, yet gentle at the same time.

My cock slaps against his thigh, and I tug at it a few times to relieve some of the pressure. Berlin draws back and watches me, pupils dilated, mouth hanging open, a greedy look in his eyes. He wants me to do that for him, I think, so I let go of my own cock and reach inside his boxers. Rock solid. He flinches a little, maybe because my hand is still cold from the water, but he doesn't pull away. I stroke him a few times, massaging the ridge of his head with my thumb. A shudder rolls through him and he straightens his back, letting out a low growl. The muscles in his chest tighten and the rusty hairs catch the sunlight. He's magnificent. I kneel down in the water and mold my lips around his smooth cock, running my tongue along the underside of it and sweeping around his head.

"Hiro." Berlin moans and grabs my hair again, tugging at it like a rein, urging me to take in more of him. I swallow him up until the tip of his cock touches the back of my throat. I want his first time with a guy to be memorable. I grip the base with my hand and slide my mouth up and down, applying just the right amount of pressure. He moans and squirms on the rocks as I work him over. His cock throbs in my mouth, approaching climax, as he fists my hair, squeezing tighter, turning me on. I take him in deep one last time and slide him out, using my hand to take him to the final throes. He comes like a garden hose. I catch some of it as it dribbles down my fist and mixes with the water on the rocks. His cock, like the rest of him, is a marvel, and the thought of him inside me makes me shudder all the way to my toes.

He drapes his arms over my shoulders and pants on my neck. I let go of him and start to back away, but he grabs my shoulders and pulls me into a bear hug, not like he's trying to dominate me, just showing his affection. He reaches for my still-throbbing cock. Something inside me switches, and my body goes rigid. I pull away.

"That one was for you," I tell him, dipping down into the water. I dive under before he can protest, swim a few yards away, and with my back turned, get myself off. Seth was the only one who'd done that for me. I don't know if it's some kind of twisted loyalty or if my subconscious is trying to protect me, but I can't have Berlin go there just yet.

"Did I do something wrong?" Berlin asks when I return.

I make my face blank. I like him even more after what we just shared, but I don't want to spoil his moment with my own drama. This is about him. I meant it when I said it. "You were perfect." I lay my hand on the center of his chest as if staking my claim.

Berlin's face breaks into a wide grin. He's positively glowing.

"I have some news for you, Berlin." I give him a long face.

"What is it?" He looks worried.

I deliver it like I'm a doctor giving him his prognosis. "I think you might be gay."

He chuckles, then grabs my shoulder. "Come here." He pulls me into another hug, kisses my neck and whispers, "Thank you."

I sigh, melting into him. Something in my chest breaks open just a little bit, letting light into the darkened corners where I like to hide. I draw my hand down the center of his smooth, strong back. "Anytime."

Berlin

AT DINNER that night, I can hardly keep the smile off my face. I'm afraid to say more than two words to my dad because I know it must be written all over my face. I just had sex for the first time. With a guy. And it was awesome.

"Ants in your pants?" Dad asks me toward the end of the meal.

"Got homework to do," I say, a white lie. We hardly ever get assigned homework during football season.

"Homework, huh?" He looks at me skeptically.

"Yes, sir. May I be excused?"

He nods and I escape to my bedroom, warm memories of Hiro and the creek swimming in my head. I want to be near him, taste and touch him, but the closest I can get right now is texting. There's probably some stupid rule about how long you're supposed to wait before texting a guy, and I'm sure it's more than two hours, but I can't help myself. I want him to know I'm thinking about him.

I pull out my phone, then get stuck on what to say. I spend about five minutes going over it in my head. It's lame, but it's the best I can come up with.

I had fun today.

I stare at the phone, waiting for him to respond, hoping he will. I don't have to wait too long.

Me too.

My chest expands. Feeling braver, I let my fingers do the talking.

I want to do that again.

I press Send, then wish I hadn't. He might think that means I want him to blow me again. I try to explain.

Hang out. Not the other stuff.

Well, that's not exactly true.

But the other stuff is nice.

Shit. What if he thinks I'm using him for sex?

Only if you want to. We can just hang out. And I can do stuff for you too.

I reread what I've texted. I sound like an idiot. I sit there staring at my phone, stressing for the longest ten seconds of my life, until he finally texts me back.

Are you finished?

If there were an emoji of a hangman, I'd use it.

I hope so.

I'd like to hang out with you again. And I like doing stuff. The stuff we do is hot.

You're hot.

He sends me a picture of himself lying back in his bed with his head on his pillow, headphones covering his ears, making a peace sign over his chest. I take one of my own, but I don't look nearly as hot as him, so I try again and this one's a little better. I send it, then stare at his picture, getting caught up in his dark, brooding eyes and full lips. I imagine lying in his bed next to him, reaching up under his shirt to feel the grooves in his chest. Kissing and undressing him, doing for him what he did for me earlier today. The fantasy plays out until I'm in such a state that I need to jump in the shower to relieve myself.

I wake up Monday morning thinking about when I can see him again, planning my next move. In the parking lot before school, I'm in such a good mood that Trent asks me if I got laid that weekend.

"No, man." I punch his shoulder, embarrassed and also a little scared by his instinct. I tell him it must be the good feeling I'm having about Friday, our first game of the season against the Bruins. Our team is coming together. "It's going to be a win," I say confidently. "I can feel it."

"Just keep eating your Wheaties, big man. This crop of receivers is skittish. I don't know if I can trust them."

I agree with him outwardly, but in my mind I have doubts. I've been playing with Trent for years. When he's feeling confident, he throws beautiful passes that drop right into the receivers' hands like special deliveries. But when the pressure is on, he sometimes cracks and throws bad balls. Then Coach gets all over him, which only makes it worse. I'm the Band-Aid. My running game makes it so that he doesn't have to throw interceptions, gives him a little breathing room so he can recover from a bad play. And for receiving his short passes, I'm his best wingman.

I hear the drone of Hiro's motorcycle, and a thrill races through me. He swerves into the parking lot, and I risk a glance over at him, my throat tight and my pulse racing, as if the sight of him might quench my thirst. Meanwhile Trent eyes him up like a mountain lion would its prey.

"Wonder what Faggy did this weekend," Trent says. I freeze because if he knew, it'd be the end of me. I wish Trent wasn't so obsessed with Hiro. Ever since Hiro stood up to him in the locker room, he's like a conquest to Trent, which is stupid as hell, but that's how his mind works.

"Who cares, man?" The less attention Trent gives Hiro, the better for everyone.

He snorts. "Can you imagine it, though? Doing that nasty shit? Sucking some other guy's dick? Putting your junk in another guy's asshole? That's just, like, disgusting."

"I don't really think about it," I lie. I think about it all the time. I thought about it all last night. Before it was a fantasy man I imagined myself with. Now it's Hiro in high-definition, playing on a loop: Hiro's fleshy lips around my cock, the grip of my fist in his silky hair as he bobbed up and down on it, his smooth skin in my rough hands. My cock swells in my pants, so I think about football plays in order to keep my flag at half-mast.

I bite my tongue as Hiro draws nearer, wondering if he'll glance my way or pass by like we're strangers. I don't know which is worse.

"Hey, faggot," Trent calls, "suck any dick this weekend?"

I almost choke on my own spit. Hiro's eyes lift just enough to meet Trent's. "No, man, your mom got there first."

It's so middle school, but the mom comebacks get Trent every time. "Fuck you, man," Trent yells, flustered.

"Not my type." Hiro keeps walking, not looking at me once, which stings, but I have to admit, he's got bigger balls than me. This gets me thinking about his actual balls and the weight of his cock against my leg. I wish we were at the creek right now. I want another chance with him and soon.

"I fucking hate that kid," Trent says. The vein in his neck is throbbing. "It's not just because he's gay. I hate his whole fucking attitude."

I watch Hiro walk away, my gut sinking. "I think he's kind of funny."

Trent turns his blazing eyes on me. "You messing with me right now, Webber?"

I shrug. "You've been calling him a faggot since the first day of school. You tried to kick his ass. What do you expect?"

"Guys like him shouldn't even exist. They're like genetic mutations."

"Like the Teenaged Mutant Ninja Turtles?" I joke, hoping it'll distract him from wanting to pursue Hiro.

"No, like a lame horse that needs to be put down." The look in Trent's eyes is vicious and mean, like he truly believes gays should be rounded up and executed. An icy fear creeps up my spine. What if yesterday was a mistake? Maybe I shouldn't be taking such risks.

"That's not very Christian of you." I throw my backpack over my shoulder. I don't want to be around him anymore. He's making me sick to my stomach.

"Haven't you heard, Berlin? God hates fags."

His eyes are flat when he says it, and I shudder without meaning to. I used to think Trent's homophobia was more for his dad, but this seems deeper than that. Like it's his own thing. And it's disturbing.

"Leave him alone, Trent." If it sounds like a threat, that's fine by me.

I head off to class, leaving Trent behind, thinking about what he might do if he found out he had a real live faggot hiding right under his nose all these years.

I'm afraid to find out.

FOOTBALL PRACTICE keeps me busy that whole week. Sometimes we don't get out until around nine. My dad always leaves my dinner under Saran Wrap so I can heat it up when I get home. He goes to bed pretty early, so some nights I don't see him at all.

Hiro and I text most nights, but in school he keeps his distance. I guess he always did. I look for him in the hallways, the lunchroom, before and after school. He's making friends. People like him. Of course they do. Part of me wishes I was brave enough to hang out with him instead of putting up with Trent.

No matter how much I look at Hiro, I can never get enough.

The bullshit between Trent and Hiro doesn't let up either. In basketball on Tuesday, Trent checks Hiro's face, giving him a red welt on his cheek. The next day Hiro bumps him in a pass and sends him sprawling across the gym floor. I watch it all, doing nothing, saying nothing, my stomach in knots, knowing that if nothing changes, it will come to a head. I'd hoped they'd reach some kind of mutual respect for each other, but the more Hiro puts him in his place, the more Trent wants to mess with him.

"That kid has a smart fucking mouth," Trent says to me on Wednesday in the locker room after Hiro's team beat ours in basketball. "I'd like to shut him the hell up."

I want to tell Trent he should probably stop with the fag jokes, since Hiro outsmarts him every time. But that would seem like a defeat to Trent, and it'd only rile him up more.

"Just ignore him, Trent." Code for *leave him the hell alone*.

"I wish I could," Trent mutters so low I almost don't hear him.

In the evenings I look forward to the hour or so after my dinner and shower when I can relax and text Hiro. It's easier for me to talk to him this way. I'm not so overwhelmed by looking at him and thinking about all the things I want to do with him. I usually get comfortable in my bed with the lights off. I like to imagine him here with me.

Home now. What are you up to?

Calc homework. How was practice?

He's in all AP Honors classes. I asked him a few days before if he was trying to graduate early. He told me that wasn't the reason. I don't blame him, though, if it is.

Long. I'm beat.

Score any goals?

Touchdowns. A couple. You coming to my game on Friday?

Dunno. I may have to wash my hair.

The thought of Hiro washing his hair gets me going. Naked in the shower with the water running down his smooth, muscled back. Bare ass and thighs slick with soap....

I'll wash it for you after.

Tempting. Don't you make ritualistic animal sacrifices after a game?

Barbeques. After after then.

I'll be sleeping.

No, you won't. You're a night owl.

I even know his sleeping habits. He stays up late working on videos, then catches up on his sleep when he gets home from school. He's probably thinking about all the reasons not to come to the game. The football team is a pack of assholes, especially to him, but I want him to see me play. Part of it is me wanting to show off, but I also want him to see why I sacrifice so much. I fucking love football, always have. Everything about it—running fast enough to fly, receiving a pass, knocking into people, getting knocked down, scoring touchdowns, being part of a team, winning. Even if he isn't into football, I want to share it with him.

I'll be there. On assignment.

That cheerleading video you made was sick.

They asked me to join the squad.

Really?

I told them only if I could wear black.

I laugh. With his eyeliner and punk hair, he'd look like a goth, cross-dressing cheerleader. I can get behind that.

You'd look hot in a black skirt. I can imagine it.

Please don't.

I imagine other things, the way his jeans hang low on his narrow hips, how he struts across the parking lot on his way into school, bumping into him on the basketball court, his mouth opened just a little bit when he's making a shot. I think about his mouth on my cock and I'm hard.

I want to see you again.

I wait for his reply. And wait.

Friday night. After after.

After after.

I cradle my phone in my hand and spread my arms across the bed. Damn, I want him here with me right now. I want to be with him all the time. Hold him, touch him, make him feel good the way he did for me. At the moment I don't even care about Trent and his bullshit. Hiro feels right to me in a way no one else ever has before. Right as rain.

Friday night can't come fast enough.

HIROKU

FOR THE first time in three years, someone else is occupying the frequency I once reserved for Seth. I hate ignoring Berlin at school—it feels like lying—but if I can see his desire, then others probably can too. The last thing he needs is for his friends to notice the googly eyes between us. The activist in me wants him to come out loud and proud, but the realist worries about the fallout if he did.

Having my camera at his football game gives me cover. I have a job to do. I'm a professional. I'm not admiring Berlin's athleticism on the field as much as I'm making sure I have the best angle to capture the run. Those tight pants are just part of the uniform. His ass hardly even crosses my mind. The bulge in his crotch isn't a consideration. Damn, he's big, though. Built like an ox. I keep thinking about shooting that gun, the way he held me in his arms and then later, at the creek.

Focus, Hiroku.

Berlin might not fit in with the football team, but he belongs on the field. His team relies on him. Especially Trent. He and Berlin are in constant communication, to the point that Berlin seems like the shadow quarterback in a way. The coach, too, seems to depend on Berlin's leadership and his ability to rally the team together. Everyone loves a winner, and Berlin is that.

I get some good footage of the rest of the team, a truly beautiful long pass by Trent, caught in the end zone by one of the receivers. Some rough-and-tumble tackles, and Berlin, weaving in and out of the other team's defense like a salsa dancer. Graceful, yet still knocking guys down left and right. He has a good center of gravity and he's tough to bring down, like going up against a mountain.

I'm going to enjoy editing this project.

At halftime I film the cheerleaders and color guard. Tamara blows me a kiss on her way back to the sidelines, strutting so her skirt flaps up and shows off her toned thighs and tight bloomers. "I'm going to change your mind about girls, Hiroku," she promises and reaches down to touch her toes, tempting me.

I grin at her cheekiness. "Don't give up on me, Tamara." I'm confident she's wasting her time, but I do enjoy flirting—guys, girls, whatever.

By the fourth quarter, it's pretty obvious the Lowry Lions are going to win it. I start packing up my equipment. Berlin doesn't need to acknowledge me. He knows I was here and that's enough.

I leave the stadium and grab dinner at a Vietnamese restaurant in a strip mall halfway between Lowry and Austin that makes pho with vegetable broth. Then I ride around town, waiting for Berlin to text. He finally does around eleven o'clock. He asks me to meet him at the fence.

I pull up to where he sits on the tailgate of his truck, still shining from his recent victory. He's freshly showered and shaved, some kind of product in his short hair. I wonder if it's for me.

"Awesome game," I say, feeling bashful all of a sudden. It takes a lot of effort to keep my distance at school, which makes it hard to switch off now. I keep glancing over my shoulder like the bigot brigade is hiding in the bushes waiting to ambush us, but we're alone, so I come a little closer. The smell of him tickles my nose, like pine trees and fresh rain.

"You liked it?" he asks with a shy smile.

"I loved it. Got some great footage too. You were…." *Hot, sexy, strapping. Strapping? What does that even mean?* "You were really good."

He looks relieved. "I'm glad you came," he says, and I'm not sure if he means to the game or right now.

"Me too." I wipe my sweaty hands on my jeans, getting more anxious by the minute. Waiting for the thing, whatever the thing might be, just about kills me. I motion to my bike. "I brought an extra helmet. You want to go for a ride?"

"Is it safe?" He looks nervous, which amuses me. He's just gone up against several two-hundred-plus-pound defensive linemen. That seems like a much bigger risk to me.

"Safe enough."

"Okay." He hops off the tailgate of his truck, and I fit the helmet on his head and adjust the strap for him. I stand with the bike between my legs while he gingerly climbs on. He takes up most of the seat, which means I kind of have to perch on his crotch, but I don't mind. I tell him to lean into the curves, since he has about fifty pounds on me. A little ways into the ride, I feel his bulge pressing up against me. I hear him mumble an apology, and I smile with satisfaction. The feeling is mutual.

On the ride I go slower than I normally would and take the turns with more care. If this is Berlin's first time on a motorcycle, I don't want to freak him out. I take him out to the quarry I discovered when school first started and I was exploring the town. It was daylight when I came before, and I checked the water depth before I jumped. There are other cliffs where jumping would be suicide. I stay away from those.

I park outside the chain-link fence and give him a few minutes to walk it off. I mess with my bike to look busy. I don't want to embarrass him any more than he already is. Secretly, though, I'm flattered. I like that I turn him on.

"Can you climb it?" I ask, motioning to the fence.

"In there?" he asks like it's a cardinal sin. "Isn't that trespassing?"

I shrug. "It's only trespassing if you get caught. Besides, no one's here." He glances around like a cop is going to spring out of the bushes and arrest us. "I came here in the daytime and there wasn't any equipment. I don't think they even use it anymore. Come on."

I scale the fence pretty quickly. It takes Berlin a little longer. For a moment it looks like the fence might win, but he makes it to the other side. I suppose he hasn't jumped fences much in his life. Country boy. I lead him down the path to where there's a large pool of water and a rocky ledge that leads to the top of a cliff about three stories tall.

"Want to jump with me?" I ask. A nervous energy buzzes through me at the prospect, and everything around us feels charged with electricity. I feel alive.

His eyes widen. "I don't think so." He shakes his head. "Looks dangerous."

"Not as dangerous as football."

"Football has rules."

"Rules don't make it safe. Wait here for me. I'll go first." I jog up the rocks in a few bounds, strip down naked at the top, and stand at the edge, letting the cool night air wash over me.

"Hiro," he calls. His voice sounds panicked. "Come back."

"Berlin, it's fine. I've done it before."

"No," he shouts in his deep, manly voice. He sounds like my dad. "Come down here right now."

"Are you serious?" I'm right at the ledge. One more step and I'll be there.

"Yes, I'm serious. Don't jump. Come down."

I groan dramatically, turn and walk back a few steps, and then think *fuck it*. I sprint toward the edge and take a flying leap, my arms wide. Berlin calls my name, but I'm already in the air. Flying. What a fucking rush. Nothing compares to this feeling of being on top of everything, conquering your fears. My whole body is electrified. I'm powerful—invincible—the way drugs used to make me feel, and Seth too, sometimes. I hit the cold water and drop down so deep my toes scrape the rocky bottom.

When I surface, Berlin is standing at the edge of the pool. He looks pissed. I wade over and climb out. "I told you it was safe."

"You see that rock over there?" Berlin points to a slab jutting just above the surface, about ten feet from where I hit the water. It must have been submerged the last time I was here. I kind of wish I'd known it was there. More danger means more thrill.

The worry line is back between his eyebrows. I want to smooth it down. "I'm fine."

"I told you to come down," he says. "What the hell's wrong with you?"

I shiver from the cool night air on my wet skin. I don't know how to answer him; so many things are wrong with me. Where to begin? I climb the rocks again and go over to my pile of clothes. I glance out at the ledge. I must be crazy, because I want to do it again. One more rush. One more hit. One more chance to feel limitless, like a god.

"You take another step toward that ledge…." Berlin's voice booms in the still night.

I glance down at him. He's in full-on Hulk mode, massive, heaving shoulders, arms tense. His head looks like it's about to explode.

"I won't." At least not with him here.

I shrug back into my clothes and join him where he's pacing on a spit of gravel. Even though he's pissed at me, he's still pretty hot. I wonder what it might feel like to channel all that energy to one purpose. What would Berlin do with all that anger and aggression?

"You want to hit me?" I ask. Seth would get angry like that, when I did something he didn't like, especially when he told me not to. Sometimes he'd hit me.

Berlin stops to look at me. "No, I don't want to hit you."

"You want to fuck me, then?" It could go either way with Seth too.

The color drains from his face, and he looks at me like I'm totally mental. "Why do you say things like that?"

Jeez, he's uptight. "Like what?"

"Like you want me to hurt you?"

I turn away, feeling stupid. I have to remind myself that Berlin is a normal, caring person. Maybe I was too once. I don't know how to be with someone without picking a fight or waiting for the bottom to fall out. With Seth I learned to get my kicks when I could, because there was no telling what five minutes from now would look like.

"Is that how it was with Seth?" Berlin asks.

The anger in his voice is gone, replaced with something like pity. If I was on that ledge right now, I'd take my chances with the rock. He waits for an answer, but I don't know what to tell him. It was a lot of ways with Seth, and that was one of them. Toward the end it seemed my body was a debt I owed him for simply existing, for having the nerve to attract him to me. It was my fault he couldn't control himself. Everything I got, I deserved. I know how messed up that kind of thinking is, but I never claimed to be rational.

They say drugs alter your brain chemistry, even after you quit them. Seth did too—he scrambled my emotions.

"It's late," I say to Berlin. I want him to stop looking at me like I'm wounded or damaged. I head back toward the fence and scale it.

"Don't walk away," he says when he catches up to me. "What's going on here?"

"Nothing." My voice catches and my whole body shakes. *It's the cold water*, I tell myself. I hate feeling weak. A heightened sensitivity, Dr. Denovo called it. The rush I felt from jumping is gone and my body still wants more, more, more. Whatever it takes to drown out the noise in my head.

I mount the bike, but Berlin refuses to get on. He looks like one of those marble statues of a Greek god. Like he'd stand there, unmoving, for centuries.

"Take off your helmet, Hiro," he says.

"You don't even say my name right." I know it's mean and childish to pick on him, but he's backing me into a corner.

"Take off your helmet, *Hiroku*."

God, he's butchering it. My mother would be offended. He's so goddamned stubborn.

I stand and rest the bike on its kickstand, take off my helmet, and set it on the seat. He opens his arms.

"No," I say.

He doesn't move. Just stands there like he can do this all night long. He'll wait me out. I don't like seeing his arms open, knowing they're for me. I hate seeing him vulnerable like that.

He motions again with his hands, gently.

God, can't he just put his damn arms down already? I step forward and he takes my head in his massive hand and rests it against his shoulder. His other arm wraps around my back, squeezing lightly. He strokes my hair, tucking it behind my ear, then rubs my back up and down. I feel his chest heave with every breath like a metronome. Finally my body relaxes against his. My slack arms take hold around his lower back.

"I don't want to hurt you," he says softly. "That's it. Okay?"

I nod. My eyes burn and a lump rises up in my throat, but I swallow it down. Jesus, if I cry right now, I'll have to find another cliff to jump off. I take a deep breath and take a step back. I put on my helmet so he won't see my face. I mount the bike again, and this time he slides in behind me. I'm grateful for the ride. I need a few minutes to get my shit together.

We wind through the outskirts of town until we're back in front of the gate to his property, where I park to let him off. I take off my helmet but stay on the bike.

He glances down at his shoes shyly, tugs at his collar. "My dad has to go out of town next weekend. I was thinking maybe you could come over."

I'm silent, already retreating into one of my shadowy corners like a spider. "Maybe," I say noncommittally.

"Well, just let me know. Good night." He leans in and kisses my cheek quickly, then backs away like he's worried he did something wrong. He's making it impossible for me to stay mad at him.

"Good night."

I stay there for a moment, watching him get into his truck and drive off, thinking about Berlin and his deep well of understanding. For as long as I can remember, I've always clung to the shadows. It feels like Berlin is trying to drag me, kicking and screaming, into the light. At any moment he might change his mind and decide I'm not worth the trouble.

But I want to be.

BERLIN

WHEN I get in from herding cattle with my dad the next afternoon, I notice a missed call from Hiro. He doesn't usually call me—we mostly text—and I wonder if it's about last night. I hope he's not trying to end it with me. Still feels like we're just getting started.

I'm in the barn where it's dark and cool, alone except for the horses, when I call him back. His sigh is so long and miserable when he picks up, I think someone has up and died on him. "My mom wants to meet you," he says instead of a hello.

A warm feeling spreads throughout my chest. I worry this thing between us is one-sided, with me only pursuing him, but this seems like a good sign to me. "Your mom knows about me?"

"I may have mentioned you in passing."

I smile at that. "Only in passing?"

He chuckles. "Maybe more than just in passing."

I'm not too scared of parents, though I do wonder if she thinks we're just friends or something more. "When?" I ask him.

"Really?" He sounds like he doesn't believe me. "I thought it'd be a lot harder than that."

"Yeah, I don't mind. I'm good with parents."

"Tonight for dinner? It doesn't have to be tonight, but she basically told me I can't see you again until she meets you. Um, my dad too."

I'm supposed to go to a party tonight with Trent and some of the other guys from the team, but I can meet them there later. I'll have to tell my dad, but I'll figure it out.

"Should I bring something?" I ask.

"Nothing that was once living."

I laugh. "Do your parents know that we, uh...." I don't know how to say it.

"Do they know that we what?" he asks all innocent-like. I can imagine the smirk on his face.

"That I'm, um, into you. Like that."

"She knows I like you, *like that*. My dad would rather not know the details."

Hiro gives me their address and a time and we hang up after that. Later that afternoon, while my dad and I are washing up in the barn, I tell him I made other plans for dinner. "A friend invited me over," I say, hoping to sound casual about it.

"Trent?"

"No, he's new in town."

My dad raises his eyebrows like he's waiting for something more. "Your friend have a name?" he asks.

"Hiroku Hayashi," I say, not meeting his eyes. It's probably written all over my face.

"That's a mouthful. Where's he from?"

"Austin. He's Japanese."

"Oh." He goes back to washing his hands.

"There's something else." Dad glances up at me. "Trent and Hiro don't get along, so if Trent calls or stops by, maybe don't let on where I'm at?"

My dad frowns a little but nods. Maybe it's my imagination, but he seems to be taking an extra long time washing up. My stomach turns because I hate lying to him, and it feels like everything I say anymore is a lie.

"Anything else you want to tell me?" he asks.

I study the dirt under my fingernails. "No, sir."

He shakes out his hands, wipes them on his shirtfront. The way he looks at me makes me think he might know something about what's going on. I hold my breath. "Well, all right, then. Good work today." He pats my shoulder, puts his hat back on his head, and saunters out of the barn.

I SHOW up to Hiro's house ten minutes early with a bouquet of sunflowers I cut from our yard, technically once living, but I think it will pass. A tiny woman who looks a lot like Hiro answers the door when I knock.

"You must be Berlin," she says with a smile and a little clap of her hands. I like her immediately.

"Yes, ma'am." I take off my hat and offer her the bouquet.

"Such pretty flowers. These are for Hiroku?" she asks, gathering them up in her arms.

I blush all the way to my toes. "No, ma'am. They're, um, for you."

"How nice. Please come in." She opens the door wide and introduces herself. I don't catch her first name, but her last name is the same as Hiro's.

"Come in, come in. Sit down." She motions to a small couch on delicately carved wooden legs. All the furniture is small and dainty like dollhouse furniture. If I sit down on it, it might break, so I sit awkwardly on the edge, trying to keep some of my weight off it.

"Be comfortable, please. You like tea?" She flutters around the room like a bird.

"Yes, ma'am. That'd be great." I'm expecting something like sweet tea, but she comes back with a platter of tiny cups with no handles. They're a little bigger than shot glasses, only they look expensive and breakable. She sets the tray on the coffee table and pours me a glass. Her hands are like his, long, graceful fingers.

"It's very hot," she says and hands me the cup. I hold it between my thumb and forefinger, blow on it, then take a sip. She stares at me expectantly.

"It's good," I say, though it's kind of bitter. "Thank you."

"You want sugar?"

"Yes, please."

Mrs. H nods and spoons some sugar into it for me. She says it's jasmine tea. Kind of smells like Hiro's hair. She pats my arm, then lifts her chin and calls for Hiroku like a bird trilling. She says it much more beautifully than I ever could. I really am screwing it up. There's something else in the way she says his name. Affection, I guess. It reminds me of how my mom would call me in for supper when I was little. I get a little teary thinking about it.

Hiro appears a few seconds later. He seems nervous, hanging back in the doorway. I didn't hear him come in. He wears all black, as usual, and his wet hair is slicked back. He could be a model with those full lips and angular jaw, eyes that pull me in like a target.

"He's so big," Mrs. H says to Hiro. I think she's talking about me. Hiro grins and nods. He looks pleased by her observation. My size has utility on the farm and in football, but in a lot ways, it sets me apart from everyone else. People are usually intimidated by me. I have to be careful about how I move and speak so I don't scare people off.

"Sit, Hiroku. Be a good host." She pats the seat next to hers, and Hiro sits with his elbows on his knees, leaned forward like the three of us are in a huddle together. He still hasn't said a word to me, just smiles a little and watches his mother and me with a shy look on his face. Mrs. H. pours herself a cup of tea, then asks me how long I've lived in Lowry and what my parents do for a living. I don't go into it about my mom, just tell her we have a ranch and raise cattle. Hiro already told me they both work at UT Austin, his mom as an accountant and his dad in IT, so I let her ask the questions.

"You play football, Berlin?" she asks. The way she asks questions makes it seem like she'll be delighted with any answer.

"Yes, ma'am."

She points at Hiro and nods. "I've always told Hiroku to play sports. He's very good at basketball, but he never wants to play for school. He's too shy." She swats at him affectionately and clucks. I smile at Hiroku. His head is in his hands, mortified.

She says something to him in Japanese, probably something like *go set the table*, because he rises quickly and goes out to the dining room. A few minutes later Mr. Hayashi appears in the doorway. He also has a silent step, broad-shouldered and slim-hipped like Hiro. I stand to greet him, nearly knocking over the tea tray. I catch it in time and only spill a little of the tea.

When I say hello and offer my hand, he seems reluctant to take it. I don't think he's happy about me being here. I'm not sure why.

He looks me over, seeming unimpressed. "You're Hiroku's new friend," he says sourly, finally shaking my hand. His manner of speaking is formal and refined, like Hiro's. His face is expressionless.

"Yes, sir."

"You two spend a lot of time together?"

I'm not sure how to answer that question. Is he really asking me something else?

"Enough, I suppose."

"Is Hiroku behaving himself?"

What a strange question. I'm completely thrown by it. Luckily, Mrs. H saves us from the awkward silence.

"Dinner is ready," she says and herds us into their dining room, where Hiro is waiting by a table set for four. He pulls out a chair for me.

"Is this your sister's seat?"

"She's studying at Columbia University," Mr. H. says, kind of arrogantly. "She's going to be a doctor."

I nod. "That's great."

"Yes, it is great." He picks up his napkin, flicks it so it opens, then lays it on his lap. Formal dining. Okay, then. I do the same.

Mrs. H. starts passing around the bowls without saying a prayer. I take a little of everything. There's a soup with noodles, a cold, stringy green salad, rice and deep-fried vegetables, and something else that's rubbery and definitely not meat. I try not to inspect it too closely. I don't want to be rude. Mr. H. eats with chopsticks. The rest of us use forks and spoons. Hiro keeps glancing at me from across the table with a nervous smile. I wish I could cancel my plans with Trent and hang out with Hiro without his parents.

Mrs. H. does most of the talking at first. Then Mr. H. starts asking me questions—do I have a job? *No, but I help out on the ranch.* Have I applied to any universities? *No, I aim to be recruited this season and will see what my options are then.*

"And how is my son adjusting at school?"

I glance over at Hiro, and he shakes his head slightly.

"He makes great videos," I say, then remember the video of him and Seth. From the way Mr. H.'s eyes narrow to slits, he must be thinking of that one too. I worry Hiro will be mad, but when I glance over at him, he seems to be trying not to laugh.

"You think that's funny?" his father snaps, followed by a string of Japanese. Hiro drops his smile immediately. Then Mrs. H. breaks in. She seems to be scolding her husband more so than Hiro, and suddenly I'm not hungry anymore. Mr. H. puts down his chopsticks and glares at me.

"You do drugs, Berlin?" he asks with a face like a human lie detector test.

"No, sir."

"Alcohol?"

"Just an occasional beer with my dad." And sometimes one or two at parties, but I don't get drunk. I don't like feeling out of control. That's the truth.

"Did you know Hiroku is a recovering addict?"

The way he says *addict*, like it's a dirty word or an accusation, makes me feel bad for Hiro.

Hiro glares at his plate. "Dad, come on."

"Oh, now you're embarrassed?" Mr. H. says something else in Japanese, and Hiro responds. Another argument. I want to defend Hiro to his dad, but it's not my place, and besides, I have no idea what they're saying.

Mrs. H. lays her hand on mine. "Berlin, come help me with dessert."

She leads me out of the room like it's a combat zone and shuts the door behind us. "They're so much alike," she says. Her brow furrows. "They just *nih, nih, nih.*" She makes her two hands like ducks quacking at each other. Then her eyes light up. "You're so tall. Can you reach the special bowls?" She points to a top cupboard, and I pull down four impossibly delicate bowls, holding them as if they were fresh eggs.

"So careful," she says with a smile. "Hiroku needs someone careful. That other boy…." She shakes her head, her face clouding over. She must be talking about Seth. "He was not careful. Hiroku is very sensitive. He doesn't like to show it, but he gets very sad sometimes." She makes a sad face, then reaches into the freezer and pulls out a tub of ice cream. "You like ice cream?"

"Yes, ma'am." I hope she'll say something more about Seth, give me some clues as to what happened between them, but she starts talking about their move to Lowry and how hard it's been on Hiro.

"I worry about him at his new school. It's not like his old school. He's a very special boy. You know." She nods with importance. I wonder if by *special* she means *gay*, and I would know because I'm gay too. Strange that she knows this about me when my own father doesn't.

"He's very artistic," I say.

She points to her temple. "His head is so smart, but his mouth is so stupid. I worry about him and the other boys."

I worry too. Did his smart mouth get him into trouble at his old school?

"You're a big boy, Berlin. Watch out for my Hiroku. Make sure nobody hurts him."

"Of course, ma'am." I take the oath seriously. I'll keep Trent off his back, or anyone else who tries to mess with him.

Mrs. H. scoops ice cream into the four bowls. I don't know much about Hiro's life before Lowry, only what I've been able to piece together. When he jumped off the cliff at the quarry, it scared the shit out of me, but what worried me more was that he wanted to do it again. Was it only about the thrill, or does he really want to hurt himself?

Back in the dining room, Hiro and his dad are silent and sulking. Mrs. H. presents the ice cream, and Hiro asks if we can take it up to his room.

"Leave the door open," she says. "None of that…." She makes kissing noises with her mouth. My face flames up hotter than the sun as I nod good-bye to Mr. H., but he doesn't even acknowledge me.

Upstairs we sit on the edge of Hiro's bed. His room seems so empty and cold—nothing on the walls, no trinkets or mementos. I know he likes to take pictures, but there aren't even any of those. It's so unlike the rest of the house. There's a single bed with a black comforter, a dresser, and a desk. On the desk are three monitors hooked up to tons of electronics and gadgets, like the hub of some spy agency. Hiro sets his empty bowl on his desk, so I do too.

"I had a lot of band posters before," he says when he notices me looking at the empty walls. "I had to get rid of them."

"Did your parents make you throw them out?"

He glances over at me, seems to be thinking about how to respond. "No, they reminded me too much of Seth. I got rid of everything." He swipes the air with his hands. "A total purge."

I've never been in a relationship like that before. Kayla was more like a glorified friend, and since we broke up, I haven't thought much about her. He must have thrown out everything he owned, because the room looks uninhabited. "Seems extreme," I say.

His eyes focus on the floor. "You ever had your heart broken?"

"No," I admit. "I don't have much experience with that sort of thing."

He nods. "I hope you never do."

I feel bad for judging him. He's coping the best way he knows how. Hiro's like an old cottonwood tree with a whole mess of roots beneath the surface you'll never see.

"So now you've met my parents," he says, straightening a little. "Feel free to run like hell."

"Parents don't scare me."

"Not even mine?"

"Maybe your dad. A little."

He smiles and knocks shoulders with me. "You coming over makes things a lot easier. I'm trying not to sneak around so much." His eyes lift to meet mine. He isn't wearing any eyeliner, and it makes him look exposed, like he's missing his armor. I rest my hand on his leg and give it a squeeze.

"I know it's a big deal, having me over here."

He shrugs and looks away. "I hope you're not still mad about last night." He must be thinking about it too.

"I'm not mad." I wasn't really mad at him then either. I was scared, then worried, and then angry at Seth for being so awful to him.

Hiro takes my hand and turns it over, traces the calluses on my palm. "Good, because I'm not sure what... well, that's not exactly true." He rethinks it and starts again. "I'm not always the most... stable person. But I'm trying to do better."

I curl my fingers to hold on to his hand. "I know you are."

"I was kind of worried I wouldn't see you again after last night," he says. "Not that you owe me anything. I like hanging out with you. And stuff." He grins, and I think back to that blubbering string of text messages I sent him.

I smile, pleased with how open he's being with me. All this time I've been waiting for some clue as to how he feels, and now, here it is.

"I invited you over next weekend," I remind him. I leave out the part where he blew me off.

"You want to take it back?"

I flick his hair, which now hangs loose over one eye. "Not at all."

He tilts his head back, tucking the hair behind his ear, and glances over at me. The urge to kiss him overwhelms me when he looks at me like that. The pressure is building down below, but we promised his mother.

"I should get going," I say. I don't want to leave, but I also don't want to ruin the good impression I've made with his mom. And if I don't meet up with Trent and the guys, there will be questions. I wish Hiro and I could just be together without all the sneaking around. Why can't everyone be as cool as Mrs. H.?

Downstairs, we put our ice cream bowls in the sink, and I say good night to Mrs. H., who's watching something on the television. Mr. H. is somewhere else.

"You're a nice boy, Berlin. Come back anytime."

"Yes, ma'am, I will."

Out front, Hiro walks me to my truck, then leans against the driver's side door with little smirk on his face. I press him up against the door, making sure we're mostly hidden from view. He yields to me like a sapling. Maybe I should ask his permission, but I don't want to mess up the moment with my stupid words, so I just reach for the back of his head and hold him like one of those impossibly delicate bowls. His lips part and I press my mouth against his. He tastes sweet, like ice cream. I could kiss him all night long. My hand creeps up his back, skimming along his bare skin. The muscles in his back tense and he pulls me closer, so I'm digging into him. There's so much of him I haven't explored, and I want to.

"Been thinking about that all night," I say when I finally pull away to catch my breath.

"Me too." He licks his lips, which makes me want to kiss him again, so I do, and I still want more. I'm hard enough to rip a hole in my jeans. I turn away and lean my tailbone against my truck.

He eyes my crotch with a mischievous grin. "I wish I could help you out with that."

"Yeah, me too." I'm getting used to his flirtation. He stands there silently, like he's waiting to be dismissed, and I think about football until my body starts to calm down. "I don't say your name right, do I?" I ask, straightening up.

He shrugs. "I didn't mean what I said last night. I like the way you say my name. It's like you're being careful."

His mother said the same thing about me. Hiro needs someone to take care of him, to protect him, maybe even from himself. I grab his hand and draw him close for a moment, then kiss his cheek. "I'll be careful."

He nods with a dreamy look in his eyes. "I believe you."

HIROKU

FOR THE first time ever, my mom actually likes the guy I'm dating. She's so enthusiastic when I tell her Berlin invited me over Saturday night, she wants to help me pick out something to wear. I politely decline. I love my mom, but I have my limits.

"No more black, Hiroku," she calls as I jog up the stairs to my room. "The funeral is over."

I choose a gray shirt instead. I'm breaking all the rules for him.

I get to his place around six and park my bike on the inside of his truck, just in case anyone comes up the drive while I'm here. He opens the door and notices the shirt immediately.

"Is that for me?" he asks with a wide smile. His teeth are perfect, just like the rest of him. I'm dating cowboy Ken.

I shrug, and because I'm an ass, I say, "Don't get too excited. It's basically light black."

He pulls me into a hug, and I inhale his pine-scented cologne and something else that is decidedly Berlin, a woodsy, earthy smell. I like the feel of his arms around me, his scent in my nose. Thinking about where the night may lead makes me both excited and nervous.

The inside of his house is pretty rustic, with wood floors and paneling. Pretty much everything in the house is wood, some polished, some natural. A buck's head hangs above the brick fireplace. Poor fella. The few quilts hanging on the walls are the only feminine touches.

"My mom made those," Berlin says as I step closer to look at them.

It sucks that Berlin lost his mom. I shouldn't be so hard on mine. She's actually pretty awesome. If it were just my dad and me, we'd have killed each other by now.

"They're beautiful," I tell him.

"Yeah." He looks thoughtful for a moment, then motions to an island between the kitchen and living room. On top of the bar is a wide assortment of vegetables already washed and cut. "I figured we could grill."

"Wow, it looks like you robbed a produce stand," I remark. He looks embarrassed, and I feel bad for teasing him. "No, that was really nice of you, Berlin. I didn't know you could cook artichokes on a grill."

"You can cook anything on a grill."

"No steak for you?"

"I like vegetables. I figured you wouldn't want me to taste like meat."

That makes me pause. Seth never once considered I might not want to kiss his meat breath, nor did he ever pass up the opportunity to eat meat in front of me. Sometimes he even ordered me food with meat, then played dumb or got pissy when I wouldn't eat it, like he was testing me.

"You don't have to abstain on my account. That's why God made toothbrushes."

"God didn't make toothbrushes," he says.

Did I offend him? Take the Lord's name in vain or whatever that rule is? Like everything else, Berlin put a lot of thought into this evening, and I was demeaning it. "Boy, I'm hungry," I say to fill the silence.

I help him bring the platters of food to a deck out back. Berlin fires up the grill and offers me a soda. I'd prefer a beer, or even better, a shot, to loosen up, but I doubt that's on the menu, even though it isn't Sunday.

Berlin grabs the barbecue tongs. "Pick some music."

I make a quick playlist from my phone and connect to his outdoor speakers.

"This isn't what I thought you'd like," he says as my mix of bluegrass and honky-tonk songs play. Not the hokey line dancing shit, but the good stuff, mostly new takes on traditional songs where the banjo and mandolin players go off.

"You were expecting music to slit your wrists to?" He seems to not know whether to laugh. "Joking, Berlin."

He nods. "I was expecting something a little more like... well, you know."

"Like Petty Crime?" He nods. He's seen the video. He knows how my dad feels about it. "What did you think of that video? Before you knew it was me?"

His face turns red as he concentrates extra hard on turning the vegetables. "It was very artistic," he says at last.

I laugh because he's trying so hard to be diplomatic. "I shot that video, you know? I had, like, half a dozen tripods going. I was actually pretty proud of it."

He glances over at me. "You should be. It really tells a story."

Berlin surprises me at every turn. I expected him to think it was shameful or embarrassing to be in a video like that. But maybe he really does see the artistry in it. And the honesty.

"I guess we should throw our expectations about each other out the window," I say.

He nods. "That'd be a good place to start."

We eat outside on paper plates. I suspect he and his dad are used to living the bachelor life. I can only eat about half of what Berlin prepared for me. It's all delicious, including the roasted artichokes, basted in butter, which melt in my mouth.

"You want to see the horses?" he asks as we clean up.

"Yeah. Totally."

He leads me across the lawn to a large two-story barn. Inside are about a dozen stalls, half with horses in them. Berlin greets each animal with a kind word and a handful of hay. I can tell they're happy to see him. I would be too.

"This here's Sheila," he says when he reaches a silver horse with gray freckles. "That's a pretty girl, Sheila. She came to us from a property that got foreclosed on. She was skin and bones, hadn't had a proper meal in months. Hooves were a mess. Look at her now, though, all fattened up and healthy."

I pet Sheila's velvety nose, and she side-eyes me as if to inquire about my intentions with her master. *I don't know, Sheila. I'm still figuring this thing out.*

"This is Merlin. He's a draft horse, a hardworking boy." Merlin has a dark brown coat with a shiny black mane.

"He's big," I remark.

"Seventeen hands. He's the only one big enough for me to ride." He explains to me how horses are measured. It seems kind of arbitrary. Like a cubit.

"Seventeen of your hands is like twenty of mine." I lift my hand and compare it to his. He curls his fingertips around mine. His gaze catches mine in the dusty gloom of the barn, and I see the longing in his eyes. I like the way he looks at me, how he lets me know he wants me without demanding anything. He'll wait for a sign.

I take a step closer. He leans in and I meet him halfway. He sucks on my lower lip, gently, and a thrill races through me as our tongues curl around each other. His hand is in my hair, tugging. I reach for his belt buckle, and he clasps his hands around mine.

"Come with me." He pulls me to a wooden door at the end of the barn. It leads up a darkened stairwell. "Sometimes when we have horses as boarders we keep a stable hand who stays up here, but it's empty now."

Upstairs, he turns on a bedside lamp. The apartment takes up the whole upper floor, one big, open room with a small kitchen area, a table and chairs, and an adjoining bathroom. The walls are the same wood as the barn, with exposed rafters and big windows. There's also a large bed with a wooden headboard and footboard. It's warm and inviting and it smells nice, like hay.

He hooks his thumbs on my waistband, pulls me to him, and kisses me again, then reaches for the button on my jeans. I curl inward and back away.

"What is it?" He looks worried, like he might have done something wrong.

"Nothing," I lie. "Let me take care of you first." I come back to him and press my mouth against his before he can protest. My fingers are fast. I have his shirt and pants off in about ten seconds. He tugs at my shirt, and I let him take it off me. I drop down on my knees in front of him and swallow his cock, loving the taste and smell of him, his enthusiasm at every little thing I do.

One of his hands rests on my shoulder and the other tugs at my hair, pulling at the roots. His hips rock and he grunts softly with every thrust into my mouth. I wrap my lips around his stiff cock and let him set the rhythm. I love the way he takes control without demeaning me, how he tells me with his body language and his noises what he wants.

I can tell from the way he's nodding he's about to finish. He starts to pull back and I take him in deep one more time, then slide him out and catch his cum in my fist, carrying him through the last pulsing thrust.

When I rise, he kisses me full on the mouth, guides me backward onto the bed, and climbs on with me. His elbows support his weight on either side as he kisses my neck, then my shoulder, my chest, working his way down. His hands are gentle, as are his lips as he marks my skin with warm, wet kisses. *Not like Seth*, I remind myself. He unbuttons my jeans and peels them down far enough to kiss my waist. But when he reaches inside my boxer briefs, something switches in my brain, and I start thinking about Seth. Mixed emotions assault me like Seth's fists and words. I can't even remember the last time I was with him sober. *This isn't Seth*, I remind myself, *it's Berlin*. But I can't stop seeing Seth's face in my mind, feeling his hands all over me, like pythons, grabbing and dragging me under, squeezing me so tightly I can't breathe.

"Stop." I roll away from Berlin, sit up on the edge of the bed, and try to catch my breath. My head is spinning and my junk is throbbing. Why can't I get my shit together? I need the release, but my body and mind won't play nice.

I hear Berlin breathing behind me. I don't know what the fuck to say, except that I am certifiably insane. *I should just go*, I think. Get the hell out of there before Berlin ends up hating me for it.

"Are you thinking about him?" he asks.

Shit. He knows. He's probably pissed too. How messed up is it to be thinking about someone else while being with him? I swallow down my rising panic and say nothing.

"I used to do that with my girlfriend when I needed to get, um…."

"It's not that. You're doing everything right." I glance back at him, reclined on the bed, naked. A god. I can't believe I'm ruining this right now. What is *wrong* with me? "I don't want to be thinking about him. It's not a fantasy for me. More like a nightmare."

"Oh," he says quietly.

I stand abruptly and look around for my shirt. "I should go."

He rolls up to a sitting position and grabs my hand. "Sit for a minute." He guides me back down to the bed in front of him, straddling me with his muscular thighs like we're back on my motorcycle. His chest presses against my back, and I feel the rhythm of his even breath. After a moment I relax into him.

"I'm not him," Berlin says, nosing the side of my neck, melting me into a puddle of warm goo.

"I know you're not. I'm sorry."

"It's okay." He strokes my hair, the same way he did the horses' manes. The rise and fall of his chest calms me, like his body is regulating mine.

"You want to talk about it?" he asks gently.

I don't know how to explain it. I also don't want him to think I'm hung up on Seth or pining for him, because that isn't it either. Not exactly.

"He's the only guy I've ever been with, and sometimes it's hard to separate sex from everything else. From the drugs and the music and the way he was… with me."

Berlin's chin rests on my shoulder. "How was he?" he asks, not with jealousy, but with curiosity and compassion.

"Demanding. Relentless." Like the Queen of Hearts, all ways were Seth's way.

"Did he hit you?" His tone is guarded.

Only when I deserved it, I think but don't say it. I know how it sounds. "Sometimes."

"That's wrong."

"Yeah," I agree, but sometimes it seemed like a reasonable response. I could push Seth to the limit. I'm not innocent.

"Was he faithful?"

I chuckle darkly. "Not quite." The first time he cheated on me, I broke up with him, but it didn't last. The second time he lured me back with drugs. After that it was too painful to care anymore. Of course the rules were different for me. Most of our fights were about me flirting with other guys, girls too, even though it was usually to get back at him. I played mind games too.

"The highs were high and the lows were bottomless," I say. "Sometimes he'd tell me to meet him, then watch from somewhere nearby to see how I'd react when he didn't show. It was so fucked up, and that's not even the worst of it. But I couldn't stay away from him."

He rubs my shoulders. "Your whole life was tied up in it. Like football is for me, and Trent."

I'm not sure if he means his life is tied up in football or with Trent. Or both. "Yes," I say. "It's exactly like that." Except Berlin is still involved in his abusive relationship with Trent.

He wraps his arms around me, gives a light squeeze. "Maybe you need more time."

Seth has taken so much from me already. I don't want to give him another second of my life. "I don't want more time. Then it's like Seth's still controlling me."

"A safeword, then?" Berlin asks.

I nudge him with my shoulder. "What do you know about safewords?"

He chuckles. "Wouldn't you like to know?"

It makes me curious about Berlin's experience. I figure it's fair to ask since he now knows about mine. "Have you ever done it? With a girl, I mean?"

"I'm a virgin," he says like it's no big deal. "Unless you count what just happened, and the other day at the creek."

I feel pretty honored I gave him his first and second blowjobs. I know he's religious, so maybe that's why he's still a virgin. "Are you waiting?"

"I'm waiting for the right person."

No pressure there, I think. But maybe one day he might consider me to be the right person. What an honor it would be. My mother is right about him. He's a nice boy.

I lean my head back against his shoulder. His nose grazes my neck while his hands massage the tops of my thighs.

"This okay?" he asks.

"Yeah." I'm getting worked up again by the smell and feel of him. So solid and steady. Like a fucking rock. He tilts my head forward and kisses the nape of my neck. My spine tingles. His one hand grips my chest, hugging me to him. His other hand reaches into my pants and tugs at my cock. I feel the calluses on his hand rubbing over my tender skin, and I shiver from his touch.

"Still okay?" he whispers.

I nod, unable to speak. He spits on his hand and strokes me up and down, but he's too timid. I grab his forearm and urge him on. He tightens his grip and pumps faster. I remember the way he cocked that shotgun. *Pull*, he whispered into my ear right before I squeezed the gun's metal tongue.

And while his hand pilots me, his lips move up and down my neck, his breath chasing his kisses. Every nerve in my body is awake and humming under his steady hand. Waves of pleasure roll through me as my cock throbs in his grip, the sensation of his fingers riding up and down my shaft raising me up, up and away. I moan and twist in his arms while he clutches me tightly, tethering me to him. I dig my heels into the floor and press back into his chest to feel his strength.

"Almost there," I breathe. I know it's going to end, and I don't want it to. I want this mount to the top to stretch on indefinitely, but Berlin's doing his job too well. My thighs tremble as I reach behind to grab the back of his neck, giving him total control. His hips rock against my backside, his cock stiffens against my ass, and I imagine how our bodies might connect as one.

With his mouth anchored to my neck, he whispers, "Go on."

I make some animal noise in the back of my throat as my cock pulses and erupts into his hand. I shudder with pleasure, and my arms go slack around his thick neck as I slump back against him. He kisses my shoulder tenderly, trailing up my neck to the sensitive spot just below my ear. I crumple forward and he holds me a moment longer, until the aftershocks subside, then climbs off the bed and washes his hands in the bathroom. Shell-shocked, I sit there for a few seconds in a daze.

He comes back and jumps on the bed like a little kid, throws a pillow at me, then pulls me down to him. I rest my cheek against his chest, the meaty part where the butt of his shotgun would go. We lie there for a while and I listen to his even breathing, watch his chest rise and fall. It's a comfortable silence.

"That felt goooood," I say, my mind and body finally on the same page. Blissed-out and content. I simply want to be near him.

"Stay the night," he says, playing with my hair. "I want to wake up to this tomorrow."

I glance over at him, feeling soft and gooey inside. I'd say yes to just about anything right now, but my parents would freak and probably never let me see him again. I want to do this thing fully with Berlin, but my past keeps getting in the way of my present.

"Overnights aren't part of my treatment plan," I tell him.

His eyebrows pitch in the middle. He must have forgotten he's dating an addict.

"Come back tomorrow, then," he says. "We'll go horseback riding."

Berlin really wants me back, not just for sex, but to hang out with me too. Like I'm a real person. "Only if you wear a cowboy hat," I say. I'm pretty confident my demands will be met.

He laughs. I feel the rumble of his gut throughout my body. "Done." He lifts my chin. "Hiroku Hayashi, is that a smile on your face?"

I didn't even realize I was smiling. I bury my face in his chest, breathing in his earthy, musky scent. He makes me feel like I'm someone worth caring for. I like the person I am with Berlin Webber. Like the light shining from within him is bright enough to wrap us both in a safe, warm glow.

This must be happiness.

BERLIN

THE NEXT day I pack a lunch and bring the horses out to pasture so they'll have a chance to get their jitters out before Hiro arrives. I want them on their best behavior for today's ride. As I think about last night and the prospect of today, the horses aren't the only ones with nerves.

Near noon I hear the whine of Hiro's motorcycle coming down my drive. That sound, to me, is like a cheering crowd at a football game. Gets me excited and amped up. The anticipation of seeing him is a rush all its own.

I greet him around the front of the house. He smiles at the sight of my cowboy hat. I tip the brim and bow slightly in true cowboy fashion. Then I present him with one of his own. Naturally, it's black. "This is for you," I say and fit it on his head. He looks dead sexy. Might be a present for me too.

His face lights up. "For me? Wow, thank you." He adjusts the hat, then pulls out his phone and snaps a picture of the two of us. "Hold on, I want to send this to my sister. She'll be so jealous. She always had a thing for cowboys."

I'm flattered he wants to share me with her. It's so easy for him to express this part of himself with his family. They might have their difficulties, but at least Hiro doesn't have to hide who he really is the way I do.

"Send it to me too," I say.

I lead him around back to where the horses are tied up to a fence post. "You can brush Sheila and I'll take Merlin."

"Do they have to look good to ride?" he asks sincerely.

"No, but it's a way for you to get to know each other. Builds trust."

I show him how to brush the horses' bodies along with the grain of their hair, how to put his hand on Sheila's coat so she knows where he is. "She likes you to tell her how pretty she is," I say. "She's a flirt, like you."

He takes the brush from me and starts brushing out her coat while speaking softly to her. Some of what he says is in Japanese.

"That's cool," I say after listening for a minute. He glances up at me, black lashes framing his big brown eyes. "How you can speak another language. You have this whole other culture. Makes you special."

"I used to wish I wasn't Japanese," he says. "I don't know if you've noticed, but there aren't a whole lot of Asians in Texas, even fewer Japanese. I wanted to be like all the other kids. Blend in, you know?"

I remember how Mrs. Potts told him to blend in on the first day of school. I said pretty much the same thing. "That was bad advice I gave you."

He shakes his head. "No, it wasn't. But people will either accept me or they won't, and I'm not really interested in wasting time on people who get hung up on appearance or ethnicity or sexuality, you know?"

He's already figured it out—himself, Lowry, the way people judge you based on stupid shit. "You're really brave to put yourself out there like that." Makes me feel kind of gutless, not that he's trying to make me feel bad. Sheila tosses her mane and snorts. "She wants your full attention," I say to him. "She's a jealous girl." I pat her rump and go back to brushing Merlin, glancing over at Hiro from time to time. He's a natural with animals. Horses have a sense for people with kind hearts.

When the grooming is finished, I fit Sheila with a bareback saddle, because Hiro is light enough and that's what she prefers. Merlin gets the full saddle to distribute my weight. I show Hiro how to mount her. Once he's on top of Sheila, I give him some instructions on the reins, along with the commands. "*Whoa* is for stop," I tell him. "If you want her to slow down, pull on the reins a little and say *walk*. They're in tune to your body language and tone of voice. Sheila was abused by her past owner, so she's sensitive to harsh words."

Hiro frowns.

"What?" I ask.

He shakes his head. "Nothing."

I mount Merlin, and we lead Sheila and Hiro to the horse trail that follows along the creek. Sheila will follow Merlin with or without Hiro's instruction, so I don't worry too much about them. The trail is slow and meandering. Sheila isn't built for speed, and I'm too heavy a rider for Merlin to do much more than a trot.

We don't talk much on the ride. I point out stuff about the farm or the name of a tree or a bird, some memories I have, places where the blackberries grow. About an hour into it, I glance back and see that Hiro's crying, silently.

"Whoa," I say and Merlin stops. So does Sheila. "You okay?" I ask Hiro.

His head swivels toward mine. His cheeks are wet. He nods, his face still expressionless. "Yeah, I'm fine."

I want to know what's going on in that head of his, but I figure he needs his privacy. We continue on and reach the clearing by the creek where I brought him before. I dismount and help Hiro down off Sheila. "We'll let them get some water and graze while we eat." I start unpacking the food.

Hiro follows my lead, but he still seems off in his own world. I've been noticing he does that sometimes, just disappears. He's standing two feet from me, but it feels like he's miles away.

"What are you thinking about?" I ask him.

"It's so beautiful here." He glances around. "It's a little overwhelming."

"God's creation," I agree, though I'm not sure he's being completely honest.

We sit down on the rocks to eat. A little while into it, Hiro turns to me. "What's that like for you? Being Christian and gay?"

He called me a contradiction before. Maybe he thinks this is proof of it. I don't see it that way. It's not as if I have to choose. I can be both Christian and gay. "My church thinks gays can be turned straight with prayer. I think they're wrong. But most everything else they preach, treating people kindly, living a righteous life, asking forgiveness for your sins, I agree with all that."

Hiro chews on his lower lip. His eyebrows draw together, his thinking face. "But isn't trying to change someone from being gay not treating them kindly? Isn't being gay, according to your church, not living a righteous life?"

"Maybe to some people, but not to me. Faith isn't like a rule book. Just because one small piece of it isn't working doesn't mean you throw the whole thing out the window."

"Being gay is a pretty big piece of who you are."

He's treating faith and religion like they're the same thing. I tell him, "Faith, to me, is a deeply personal relationship with God and our savior, Jesus Christ. Religion changes according to what's acceptable at the time and who's interpreting the text. I may not agree with what some members of my religion believe, but that doesn't mean my faith in God is any less." He rests his chin on his hand and seems to be thinking it over. "Do you believe in God?" I ask. I think I know already, but I don't want to assume.

He shakes his head slowly. "I think God is a concept humans came up with to deal with the things they don't understand."

"Do you understand everything?"

"No, but I'm okay with the not knowing."

I try to imagine what it must be like to not believe in any higher power. It seems so lonely, like I'd imagine an astronaut must feel floating out in deep space, or calling over a canyon and hearing only your echo in response. One of the things I really love about my church is the community and sense of belonging. "Wouldn't it be nice to think there's something out there bigger than us?" I ask.

"Yes, but it seems like people use God as a cop-out too often, or as a way to justify treating other people like shit."

People treat others badly with or without justification. To me, true followers of Christ live by his example—kindness, compassion, and acceptance. I can't speak for other Christians, though, only myself.

"I don't think that's what God is about," I tell him. "When I come out here, I feel God's hand. This land is a gift, and we've been entrusted to take care of it. When I score a touchdown, I thank God. Maybe He had nothing to do with it, but it feels good to give thanks. Makes me feel connected, like I'm not all alone in this. And when I get to missing my mom, I think about her in heaven, looking down on me, like my life is a football game and she's sitting in the bleachers, cheering me on."

Hiro glances up at me. His eyes still look sad. I remember when I first met him, how I thought he didn't care about anything. But the closer we become, the more I realize just how much he cares, so much that he hides his feelings, like the weight of the world will crush him if he gives into it.

"That's a really beautiful way to put it," he says. "I think putting your faith in God is better than putting it in another person. People will let you down."

Is he thinking about Seth? "Even the best people are still sinners," I say. "We're selfish beings. When you think about it, the things we aim to be—compassionate, kind, selfless—they go against every natural survival instinct."

I sit back against a rock and listen to the sounds of the creek, the horses nickering, and the wind in the trees. Even more so than in church, this is the place where I feel closest to God, out on our land. I'm not much into evangelizing—I think people have to come to God in their own good time—but I hope that whatever Hiro believes, it offers him a sense of peace and connectedness. The world can be a lonesome place, especially when it feels like you're only living for yourself.

Hiro picks at the crust of his sandwich but doesn't eat any more of it. "Why are you friends with Trent?" he asks.

I sit up a little. "Why do you ask?" I say cautiously. I know how Hiro feels about him, rightly so.

"He's an asshole and he's mean. I just don't understand why you'd put up with that."

I don't know how to explain it in a way he'll understand, but I've seen the bruises, the way Trent trembles under his father's hand, his father's taunts and criticism. There's goodness in Trent. He'd defend any member of his tribe, even if it meant getting in trouble. He'd give you his lunch if you forgot your own. After a bad storm, he's the first to come help my dad and me haul trees and fix fences. And we've had so many good times together—sleepovers, birthday parties, practices, and games.

"He's not all bad," I answer. "Maybe you could let up on him a bit, lay off the mom jokes."

Hiro's back stiffens, and I know instantly I've said the wrong thing. "*Me* let up on *him*?" Anger flashes in his eyes, and I watch his face go cold. "I'll lay off the mom jokes as soon as he lays off calling me a faggot and trying to beat the shit out of me."

Yeah, I figure it can't be that easy. "He's had a tough row to hoe," I say gently, digging myself deeper into this hole.

"Well, he's not the only one." Hiro kicks at the ground with his heel. "How many more people has he bullied over the years who haven't stood up to him?"

"A few," I admit. He usually gets tired of them pretty quickly. Trent is more like a rooster establishing the pecking order. He doesn't really target one person for very long, except Hiro.

"You think when he finds out you're gay he's going to treat you any differently?" Hiro asks with a fire in his eyes.

I remember the look in Trent's eyes when he talked about gays being put down like lame horses. I hope that if he did find out, he'd realize I'm the same person I've always been. It seems kind of foolish to think that now. "I'm hoping to not have to tell him."

Hiro shakes his head.

"What?" I know he has something to say about that.

"I just hate having to ignore you at school. And seeing you hanging around with the fucking bigot brigade. They think you're one of them."

The bigot brigade? That's pretty harsh. "I *am* one of them." Those guys are my team.

"You're only one of them so long as you keep up the lie."

He's so fired up about it. It feels like he's attacking me. "Why are you mad at me?" I ask.

"Why? I'm sick of the bullshit. Society. Fucking small-mindedness. Homophobia is everywhere, Berlin. It's not going to go away when you leave high school."

"Don't you think I know that?" I yell without meaning to. Sheila lifts her head and glances over. I take off my hat and run my hands through my hair, then stand up to shake out my limbs. My muscles are tight all over, my adrenaline humming through me like a live wire.

Hiro jumps up and follows me to the creek's edge.

"So, we're just going to keep meeting like this?" He flings his arms in the air. "At the fence post? Hiding my motorcycle so people won't see it? Sneaking around when your dad's out of town? We'll bare our souls by the creek but act like strangers at school? Is that what you want?"

"I don't know what I want. I haven't thought that far ahead." How long has he been thinking about all this? He's throwing so much at me. I can't keep up.

"That's your problem, Berlin. You don't think things through. You tried friending me on Facebook, but you didn't think about your friends seeing it. You look at me at school like you want to fuck me right there in the hallway. If you want to keep this thing a secret, you're going to have to be a lot smarter and fucking commit. Because this halfway shit is going to get your ass in trouble."

"Enough," I say sharply.

He stalks off. My blood's running hot and my mind is spinning. It's like Hiro's sprinting toward the finish line, and I'm still at the starting line with a clueless look on my face. He makes me feel like a total dumbass, which pisses me off because everything he said is true. I'm lying to the people closest to me, like a coward. But I like my life the way it is. I don't want to be treated like an outsider. I've always been on the inside, popular, respected. Coming out to my friends, I might lose everything.

Hiro swings back around. "I'm sorry. This is what I do. I push people to the edge. My dad. Seth. I don't know when to stop."

"Whoa," I say.

"What?"

"Our safeword."

He glances up at me. "You're kidding, right?"

I wish I was. I thought he needed a safeword with me, but I need one just as bad. "The word is *whoa*. It means stop whatever the hell it is that you're doing."

He nods. "Okay."

I pace awhile longer until I've cooled off some, then stop in front of him. "You're right. About everything. The first time I saw you tear into that parking lot, with your haircut and your ear piercings and your eyeliner, I was blown away. You're exactly who you are, even if it means having to take so much shit for it. You've got balls, Hiro."

He grins and grabs his crotch. "Yeah, right here."

I glance at the sky. My dad won't be back for another couple of hours. We have some time yet.

I grab his hand and pull him toward me. "I like you a lot. You know that, right?"

He nods, his eyes shifting away. I'm not sure what that's about.

"You like me too?" I hope I haven't invented this.

"Yeah," he says in a throaty voice. I wait for his eyes to come back to me, and when they do, I see his fear. He's scared of his own feelings.

"That's what matters, then, isn't it?" I ask.

He shrugs. "I just worry about you. What they might do to you if they find out."

If Trent finds out, I'll deal with it. Having Hiro in my life and being able to be myself around him, those are two things I wouldn't trade for anything in the world, even if it means giving up my place in the pecking order. "I'll deal with them. Don't worry."

I toss his hat on the ground and tuck his hair behind his ear. I hook my thumbs on his belt loops and bring him in until his hips knock against mine, sending jolts of electricity through me. I kiss his pouty lips and taste his neck. His skin is salty with sweat but still has that sweet, lemony flavor. I feel his erection growing against mine and go for his jeans, pulling them down around his thighs. I kneel down. He's already hard, and I want him in my mouth. "You want this?" I ask, glancing up at him.

"Fuck yes," he says, his hands already on my shoulders.

I've never given anyone head before, but I've seen it done plenty of times on the web. I may be a little sloppy, but judging from all the moaning and pelvic action, Hiro seems to be enjoying it. His fingers curl around my shoulders, digging into my skin. I grip his ass as he rocks his hips forward and arches his back. I stand and finish him off with my hand, holding him to me like a rag doll. When he bites my shoulder, I have the overwhelming urge to turn him around and bend him over. Climb up inside him and let loose. But I don't have protection, and I don't know if either of us is ready for that.

Whoa.

While I'm still standing at the starting line, Hiro has already sprinted ahead, dropping down to his knees and taking my cock into his pretty mouth, blowing my mind. My hand gets tangled in his silky hair, my body's singing like I just scored the winning touchdown, and I never want this feeling to end.

After, we jump in the creek, the horses watching us with interest. And I watch Hiro. He's the hottest, coolest, most badass kid I've ever met.

And he's mine.

WE GET back to the barn around dinnertime. As we're brushing out the horses, my dad's truck rumbles up the driveway.

Hiro looks like he's ready to bolt. "Should I go?"

"No, I want my dad to meet you."

"You're sure about that?"

"I met your parents. You should meet my dad."

Hiro stands up straighter, brushes at his shirt, and adjusts his hat. I feel as nervous as he looks. "Is he going to kick my ass?" he asks, eyes wide.

"He'd have to go through me."

"Berlin?" my dad calls.

"Back here," I call back, hands shaking.

My dad notices Hiro, and his pace slows like he's happened upon a rattlesnake in the woods.

"This is my friend, Hiroku," I tell him.

Dad nods and cautiously holds out his hand. Hiro shakes it. "Nice to meet you, sir."

"You too. Hiroku, was it?"

"Just Hiro is fine."

"We went riding," I tell Dad, and then because I'm nervous, "Waterholes on the south side of the creek are full, if we want to move the herds over next weekend."

"Good. Is your… friend staying for dinner?"

"No, sir," Hiro replies. "I've got to get going. Thanks for the ride, Berlin." He pats my shoulder. "Nice to meet you, Mr. Webber."

"You too, Hiro."

I walk Hiro out front to where his bike is parked and kiss his cheek. I'd rather kiss his mouth, but I don't want my dad to come around the corner and find us making out. That's not how I want this thing to go down.

"Thanks for the hat and… other things," Hiro says with a smirk.

My eyes drift down to his groin and back, warm memories of the afternoon floating through my mind. "You're welcome."

I watch him ride off with a sinking feeling in my gut, then collect my courage. If Hiro can be honest about who he is, then I can too. When I get back to the barn, Dad has taken over putting the horses away. I fork some fresh hay into the stalls while he fills their water buckets. As we work in silence, the tension mounts, like he's waiting for me to speak.

"So that's your friend?" Dad finally asks, standing with his arms crossed. I'm bigger than my dad, but we have similar builds and hair color, the same tendency to keep things to ourselves, a Webber trait. My mother used to say that if she didn't talk, there'd be no conversation at all.

I plant the pitchfork in a pile of hay and wipe the sweat from my forehead. "Yeah."

"You guys see each other a lot?"

"Enough."

"Trent know about him?"

"Trent doesn't know we're friends." I told him that already. Dad squints at me as if trying to understand better.

"What about Coach Cross and the rest of your team?" he asks, like I need their approval.

"Nope."

He grunts, which says more than words. "You think that's wise, son?"

"Which part? Our friendship or the fact that I'm keeping it from the team?"

"All of it."

"Probably not." Like Hiro said earlier, I haven't really thought this through. I just know what I want. I couldn't stop seeing Hiro if I tried.

"Football still important to you?" Dad asks. "Getting a scholarship?"

"You know it is."

"Seems like at some point, you're going to have to make a choice."

He's talking logistics, but what I really want to know is how he feels about it. About me.

"Forget football for a minute, Dad. What do you think? About me... and Hiro, together." I swallow tightly. "More than friends."

Dad takes off his hat and wipes his arm across his forehead. "I don't know what to think, son. Seems risky. And unnatural. I mean, it'd be a whole lot easier to find an Asian girl."

Unnatural. I don't like that word. It makes it seem perverse and sinful. It's the word Pastor Craig uses. This isn't a choice I made, any more than Dad choosing to love women. It's part of who I am. Like Hiro said, a big part. Everything I've done up until now feels unnatural. Being with Hiro is the first time I feel like I'm not pretending.

"I'm not interested in someone *like* Hiro," I say carefully. "I'm interested in Hiro. Because he's a guy, not because he's Asian. Because I like guys and I always have."

My dad sighs like he's been holding on to a lifetime supply of oxygen. "What can I say? I'm not thrilled about it. I'm worried. It's tough out there for kids like you."

"Are you going to kick me out? Try to stop me from seeing him?"

Dad looks insulted as he shakes his head. "Berlin, you're my son. Part of being a man is making your own decisions and living with the consequences. I just hope you know what you're doing. And that it's worth it."

He comes over and pats my shoulder like it's any other workday and we've just finished doing a job together. Then, as if on impulse, he pulls me into a good strong hug. His embrace reassures me more than anything else. My eyes fill up with tears and I blink them away, suck back the emotions threatening to pour out. Webber men don't cry.

"It's past my bedtime," he says, clearing his throat. "I'm hitting the hay, so you're on your own for dinner. If you keep on with this Hiro kid, have him over for supper, so I can meet him properly."

I swipe at my eyes. I figure I better tell him now and get it over with. "Something else you should know, Dad. Hiro's a vegetarian."

Dad groans and throws up his hands. "Course he is."

I watch him walk toward the house. It feels like a huge weight has been lifted off my chest and I can take a full breath again, maybe for the first time in my life. I'm not hiding it anymore, at least not from my dad. It makes me want to shout it from the barn rafters. *I'm gay.* Not maybe, not possibly, but definitely, positively. Hiro's my boyfriend, and my dad knows it.

I wish my mom were here, too, so I could tell her and she could meet Hiro herself. And then I think, maybe she is.

Yeah, she is.

HIROKU

I GET Berlin's text on my way home, but I don't check it until I've docked my bike.

Told my dad I'm gay.

What?! How was it?

Good. He wants to have you over for dinner.

I'm there.

My smile feels like it's too big for my face to think Berlin has finally come out to his dad. That took guts. I knew he could do it.

I'm so proud of you.

Thanks. I had a great weekend.

Me too.

I throw a few emojis in there for good measure. My rib cage feels like it's too small to contain all the good feelings I'm having. Berlin is like, perfect. Gorgeous, strong, kind and caring. And he likes me too. I still can't believe it. If I were the gay bachelor, I'd choose Berlin a hundred times over.

I go inside and review three missed calls from my sister. My mom notices the cowboy hat immediately and wants to know if Berlin gave it to me. Then she wants to hear all about our date. I edit out the sexy times. My dad's been called into the office, so we eat leftovers on TV trays in the living room while my mom watches her soap operas. She loves Telemundo and has picked up a lot of Spanish from all the novelas she watches. Halfway through eating, Mai calls me again, and I take it up to my room.

"Tell me everything," she says. Ever since I broke up with Seth, we've become close again. I used to confide in her, but then around the time she left for Columbia, I started snorting painkillers and having to sneak around because my mom got hip to the fact that the fights I was getting into weren't happening at school.

So I tell Mai about how Berlin cooked a million vegetables for me last night, then took me horseback riding today, and how he came out to his dad this afternoon.

"He's totally getting a rose," she says with a happy sigh. "He sounds really nice, Hiroku, and Mom likes him."

"I like him too, Mai." I feel it in my chest, pride or something, that I have someone like Berlin in my life. "I wish you were here to meet him."

"I can't wait, especially after that picture."

I laugh at that. "Yeah, you're welcome."

I spend the rest of the night catching up on homework and downloading footage from the football game on Friday night. I keep coming back to the videos of Berlin. I want to create something really cool with the game footage. Something radical and different. I need more material, though, and to be honest, I wouldn't mind checking out another game. The vision will come to me. It always does.

MONDAY MORNING is the usual drill: pull into the high school parking lot, pass by Berlin like we're strangers, hit up my locker to find some hateful note stuffed inside it. Today it's *God hates fags*. This is exactly the kind of bullshit I was telling Berlin about, people using religion to justify their own intolerance, often toward a bloody, violent end.

Berlin thinks I should lay off Trent? If Berlin only knew the half of it. I crumple the note and toss it into the nearest garbage can. With the exception of gym, I keep my camera on me all day long, because I don't trust my locker. They can gay-bash me all they want, but if anyone touches my camera equipment, I'll lose my shit.

As I leave my locker, one of the football players shoves me from behind. I recover before I bust my ass completely. Jesus, if it weren't for Berlin, I'd have dropped out of Lowry by now.

In Digital Arts, I actually feel calm and safe. The kids are cool, artsy types like me, and brighter than your average Lowry Lion. It's like an island of awesome in a sea of suck. They want to see my rough cut of the football game, but I tell them it isn't ready yet. Instead I give them highlights from a swim meet, which is pretty rad because I got to use the school's underwater camera. I also added all these bubbling noises to some very atmospheric music and sped up and slowed down the tempo so the dives and laps look really cool, like an underwater ballet.

There's a guy in my class named Spencer, who I think might be gay. He's on the chubby side, with red hair and a sprinkle of freckles across his nose. Kind of looks like Ed Sheeran. He keeps going on and on about how awesome the video is. Then later, when everyone goes back to doing their own thing at their computer stations, he sits down next to me and asks what I'm doing Friday night.

"I have to shoot the game," I say. Though technically not an assignment, I'm working overtime to make the football video really special, partly for Berlin, but also to flex my chops.

"You want to hang out after?" he asks. "I know a good Vietnamese restaurant in Dempsey."

I glance over at him. I can't believe someone else knows my restaurant. My next thought: is he asking me out on a date, or just as friends? One thing about being with Seth is that everyone at my old school knew we were together, even after he graduated. When people asked me to do stuff, I always knew they weren't looking to hook up.

I study my hands resting on the keyboard. "I'm seeing someone." I don't know if Berlin and I are exclusive, but I'm not interested in being romantically involved with anyone else.

Spencer pulls up his chair and leans in closer. "Someone at school?" he whispers.

"No," I say a little too sharply. "He's older." Another lie to protect him. And us.

"Well, I'd still like to hang out," he says. "You're, like, the coolest thing to happen to the gay community in Lowry since Colton Haynes came out."

I didn't realize there was a gay community in Lowry, but it makes sense that it would have to be more skull and bones than my old school. One more friend at Lowry means one less enemy.

"You want to shoot the game with me on Friday?" I ask him. I could use a second angle. "We can go get dinner after." Berlin has his ritual barbeques anyway. We never get together until late.

"Yeah, sounds great."

I'm feeling pretty good after that. Calculus is uneventful, and then it's Team Sports with the bigot brigade. In the locker room, I always change with my back to them, in case they think I might be trying to check them out, which I never do because I'm not a pervert. But it means I'm not able to see what's going on, which makes me an easy target.

They're talking about what they did over the weekend, who hooked up with who, various girls and their physical attributes that are either pleasing to them or not. That's the polite way of putting it. It seems there is always a keg party and they're always invited. Their lives seem kind of monotonous to me, but I suppose there's safety in that groupthink, not having to make your own decisions or go it alone. Berlin never does much of the talking, something I've noticed about him. He talks more to me than I've ever heard him say to his friends, which is a shame, because he has really intelligent, insightful thoughts. Trent asks Berlin why he didn't show up to the party. Berlin tells him he wasn't feeling well, that he might have had a bug, so he stayed in all weekend. I wonder how many times that excuse is going to work.

"You keep ditching us like that and I'm going to start taking it personal," Trent says. Maybe it's my own experience with him, but to me it sounds like a threat.

Like always, once we get into the gym, Coach Gebhardt makes two guys team captains and we do the whole asinine picking teams thing. I'm never a captain, even though I'm one of the better players. The first couple of weeks of school I always got picked last, but since my teams keep winning, I now get picked midway through. Usually it's something like, "Fine, I'll take Hiroku," like I'm some kind of handicap, or in Trent's case, it's "Come on, Faggy." But I'm never picked first.

Today Coach assigns Berlin and some other kid they call Anderson as team captains. I have the uninterested thing down already. I glance at the floor, the wall, the baskets, but I don't look at Berlin. Not ever, because chances are, he's already looking at me.

"I'll take Hiro."

I glance up. Berlin picked me first, over Trent and the rest of his cronies. And he used the nickname that's only for him. Has he already forgotten our conversation about keeping this thing under wraps? I slouch over and act like it's no big deal.

"What the fuck, Berlin?" Trent says.

"Sorry, man, he's good," Berlin says by way of an excuse, because there has to be a reason to pick the gay kid. That's the crazy double life Berlin's living, and by extension, me as well. The whole situation irritates the shit out of me. With Seth and the drugs, I got good at lying, but it was never something I liked. I hate being dishonest, and here I am doing it again.

I stand there looking bored while the rest of the teams are picked. Anderson picks Trent first, even though he sucks at basketball. The kid has no mobility. I suppose that's why he always throws the ball or gives it to Berlin in a football game. I don't think he's gained five yards on his own all season.

The basketball game starts. Trent's up to his usual tricks, talking shit, using his weight to shove me around, sometimes even when I don't have the ball. He keeps trying to trip me when Coach's back is turned. Despite all of it, I keep scoring on him. If he paid more attention to the game and less on fouling me, he might be able to block some of my shots.

After a particularly pretty three-pointer, Berlin says, "Nice one, Hiro" and nudges my shoulder playfully. Trent catches it, and I can tell his wheels are turning. Meanwhile, Berlin plays on, completely oblivious. Toward the end of the game, I'm pretty stressed, which makes me irritable. With the score tied, Trent shoves me again.

Berlin points at Trent to get Coach's attention. "Foul."

"The fuck, Berlin?" Trent shouts. Berlin has broken the bro code again.

"You've been fouling him all game," Berlin fires back. "You weren't even going for the ball that time."

"Free throw," Coach yells.

Trent whispers slurs while I take aim. The rest of the guys snicker.

"Cut it out. He's on our team," Berlin says to our teammates.

"He's on your team, huh?" Trent says, insinuating who knows what. Berlin doesn't blush this time, thank God. He does look like he wants to tear Trent's head off.

I block them out and focus on the basket. I have the opportunity to get the winning shot. If I miss, it might defuse the situation, but I fucking hate Trent and I have something to prove. I take the shot and make it, winning the game for our team.

Berlin comes over like he's going to pull me into a bear hug, and I give him the look of death. He turns and congratulates his teammates instead. They all suck each other off with their ego stroking. I've had enough of this bullshit for one day.

I head to the lockers, take the shortest shower of my life, and jet out of the locker room. I think about texting Berlin, but knowing him, he'll let Trent check his phone for him.

My adrenaline is still thrumming from the game as I dial the combination on my locker. I pull it open. A hand comes out of nowhere and slams it shut.

"Hello, Faggy," Trent whispers in my ear. He's still wearing his gym clothes and he smells like BO. He skipped showering just to stalk me. What a fucking creep.

"Hello, Trent." I turn slightly and make myself look casual while taking a solid stance to have the best chance to defend myself. I got lucky in the locker room that one time. Trent's head was turned and he wasn't expecting it. Physically, Trent can overpower me in a heartbeat. Trent's left arm lingers over my shoulder. For as much as he claims to detest gays, he sure does like to get all up in my personal space.

"You like my boy Berlin, Faggy?" he asks me.

I learned how to pretend I don't give a shit with my dad and then later with Seth. I know better than to deny it. Denial implies guilt. "Yes, Trent, homophobic jocks are a real turn-on for me."

Trent moves closer, his left arm crowding my shoulder. "Why'd he pick you first today?" Trent asks me.

"You mean why'd he pick me over you? Maybe because you fucking suck at basketball. I don't know if you got the memo, but the point of the game is to get the ball into the basket." If I insult him enough, maybe he'll direct his anger at me and forget about Berlin.

"You've got a real smart mouth for a faggot. No one ever taught you any manners, did they?"

I see something then in Trent's eyes I haven't seen before, a different kind of excitement. Like he's getting turned on by this, maybe even by me. I should back off, but I never know when to quit.

"You want to teach me some manners, Trent?" I purr, dipping my head a little. I know what I'm doing. Time for him to confront his own bullshit, if that's what this is.

Trent blinks, stunned, and backs away, then slams his fist into my locker, denting it. With his knuckles. I try not to show fear, but that could have been my face.

"Stay the fuck away from Berlin," he snarls. "And keep your smart fucking mouth shut, or I'll do more than foul your ass on the court."

He stalks away, huffing and puffing, while I contemplate this whole new layer of bullshit. If Trent's wrestling with his own sexuality, it makes a lot more sense why he's so ruthlessly vicious to me. Judging from what I know about that stinking football coach, I doubt Trent's dad will be as accepting as Berlin's.

Trent's a powder keg and I'm the match. If Trent detonates, Berlin will get hurt.

The only way to diffuse this situation is to remove myself from the equation.

BERLIN

HIRO'S IGNORING me. Monday night, the same day I picked him first in basketball, he didn't answer my texts. Tuesday he said he was too busy with homework to talk. When I called him Wednesday, he was doing something with his mom. Thursday my practice went late, and he didn't answer me at all that night, then said in the morning he fell asleep, which I didn't believe for a second. Friday I see him at the football game, hanging out on the sidelines with one of the guys from his Digital Arts class.

Is he breaking up with me? I assumed we were together, but maybe he doesn't see it that way. Did I do something to piss him off? The not knowing is tearing me up to the point that I'm off my game. I miss an easy handoff in the first quarter, and then a few minutes later, I trip over one of the other team's players and fumble the ball. That type of thing never happens to me. At halftime Coach Cross is all over me about getting my head in the game and stop getting distracted by the cheerleaders. I wonder if he noticed me looking toward the sidelines. Trent is off as well. Whenever I try talking to him on the field, he cuts me off and tells me he has it under control. Third down with only twenty yards to go, I tell him to hand it off to me, but he throws a pass instead that goes wild. We end up having to kick a field goal.

"Fuck, Berlin, if you'd been a little more reliable, I'd have given it to you," he says as we walk off the field.

We end up winning, but just barely, and it's more thanks to our kicker than either me or Trent. Coach Cross reams us out because it should have been a slam dunk. After the game there's a barbeque at one of the boosters' houses, but all I want is to hang out with Hiro. I text him as I'm getting ready to leave the locker room.

"Hot date tonight?" Trent asks.

I put my phone away. "Maybe." I grin, playing along.

"Who is she?"

I'm stuck. Anyone from school is obviously out, and I can't name someone from church because we go to the same one. Our town is too small.

"Someone I met in Austin," I say.

He looks at me with disbelief. "When were you in Austin?"

"A few weeks back. Went to check out a concert."

"Which one?" he asks, like it's completely crazy to do something on my own.

"Some country band called Texas Forever." Now I'm just making shit up.

"I'll look them up," he says. "What's her name?"

"Ashley," I say, digging myself deeper, "but I don't know if it's going to work out. I think she likes to play games."

"Don't they all?" He slaps my back. His good mood is back. I exhale a sigh of relief.

My phone chimes. I pull it out to find a text from Hiro.

At dinner with a friend. Meet up with you after after.

He went to dinner with that redheaded kid? Is it like a date or something? That's messed up. I didn't call him my boyfriend or anything, but I thought it was understood. Whoever this kid is, he doesn't have a problem hanging out with Hiro in front of everyone else. That's what Hiro wants, to not have to sneak around all the time.

Damn.

"Don't stress about it," Trent says. I guess he saw my face. "Come out with us. Madison has a ton of slutty friends. They'll take care of you."

"All right. Sounds good," I lie.

I go out with Trent and the guys, but I can't eat much because my stomach is upset. I talk to the boosters about the game and keep Madison's friends at bay, but all I can think about is Hiro out with someone else and the cold shoulder he's been giving me all week. Is he bored with me already?

A little before eleven, I tell Trent and the guys I'm tired and heading home. Trent's on his way to getting loaded—he must have spiked his soda, because there's adults all around us—and he's feeling sentimental, kind of hanging on me. He's talking about this one time we were down at the Pac N Sac when we were eleven and found a stray dog wandering down the road. No tags or anything. She was a chocolate lab, sweet old girl. Probably a hunting dog that got too old to track game. Trent had always wanted a dog, but his dad wouldn't allow it, so I took the dog home with me, got her cleaned up, and took her in to get her shots. Trent named her Cookie, and she was his dog from then on, just happened to live in our barn. Trent would come over all the time to visit, just lay in the hay and let her lick his face. She was an old dog when we found her. Bad hips. We had to put her down at the end of our freshmen year. Had a funeral for her and everything. Trent was pretty tore up about it.

"Aw, Cookie," Trent says, tipping his cup to spill some of his drink on the yard in her name. "God, how I miss that dog."

"Me too, buddy." I pat his back, thinking how Cookie brought out a tenderness in Trent I haven't seen since.

"Still can't believe you kept her for me," Trent says.

"She didn't eat much." That's my dad's rule of thumb around the farm. An animal can only stay if they don't cause trouble or eat too much, even better if we can put it to work. Cookie was good at keeping the coons away from the chicken coops.

"This guy," Trent says to the rest of our friends while pointing at me with his cup. "You're my fucking Goose, Berlin."

"I'm Maverick and you're Goose," I reply. It's an ongoing feud.

"I don't care, man, so long as you've got my back." He pulls me into a hug, and I hug him back. Then I untangle myself and leave Trent in Madison's capable hands.

I'm a little late arriving at the fence. I gave Hiro the code a while back. He's already waiting for me in the grove of trees where he usually parks his bike. He sits with his knees bent, back against a tree trunk. The moonlight makes his skin glow. He gazes up at the trees and then, as I approach, at me.

Just the sight of him affects me in a way I can't control. My blood flows faster, my skin tingles, my senses become more alert. My whole body feels raw when he's around, even at school, but especially now, when we're alone, when I know I can touch him, if he'll let me.

"How was dinner?" I ask. I don't mean to sound pissed, but that's how it comes out.

"Delicious," he says in a neutral tone. He's like a vault sometimes. I'll only get in if he lets me. I decide not to beat around the bush.

"You leaving me for a ginger, Hiro?"

He snorts and glances down at the ground. "No."

I drop down next to him. I look forward to this all week long, the few hours I can be myself around him. I guess it means more to me than I even realized.

I tug at the end of his hair. "What's playing on the Hiro channel tonight?" I want him here with me, not off in his own world, but if he is there, maybe I can join him.

He lets out a long sigh and draws his finger along the ground. "It's a western, featuring a rugged, fair-haired sheriff and his deputy of undetermined race—that's in order to get the ratings up among minorities."

I smile. "Sounds good. Is the deputy a dark-haired beauty?"

"Some would say he was cast because he looks good in a pair of blue jeans, except he only wears black because he has a troubled past. I have to warn you, the writing's a bit clichéd."

I chuckle at the way he can make fun of himself. He's so damn smart and creative. "I love dark horses. What's the trouble in their town?"

"A band of bank robbers, naturally, except that before they all came out west, the sheriff and band of thieves fought in the war together."

He means the football team. He's still worried about them finding out about us. Is that why he's been avoiding me all week? "Sounds like the sheriff's loyalties will be tested. Where does the deputy fit in here?"

Hiro shakes his head slowly. "He doesn't."

I nudge him. I don't like it when he talks like we're on opposite sides of the fence. "Of course he does. The deputy is the mastermind behind the entire operation. The sheriff would be completely clueless without his brains. And lonely too, I'd bet."

Hiro frowns and crunches a dried leaf in his fingertips, then blows it off his hand. "The deputy doesn't want to be the stick of dynamite that blows the whole town to smithereens."

I reach for his hand and try to draw him out of his own head. He worries too much. "Maybe that's exactly what this town needs."

He pulls away from me and caps his knees with his palms. "I have a really bad feeling about this, Berlin. I know when some shit's about to go down. It's a sixth sense of mine. We could walk away right now without any fallout."

"There'd be plenty of fallout." My heart, for one. Hiro's the one true thing in my life. I don't want to go back to pretending to be something I'm not. Being with Hiro gives me courage and purpose. "Did something happen with Trent?" He won't meet my eyes. Maybe Trent said something or threatened him again. He's holding back, probably for my sake. "You can tell me. Whatever it is."

"Trent's going to find out about us," he says forcefully. "He's going to tell everyone. You're going to get kicked off the team, maybe even get your ass kicked. And it will be my fault. I don't want to be responsible for that."

I shake my head. He's sprinting ahead again, leaving me in his dust. "It wouldn't be your fault."

"You might hate me by the time all this is over."

"Never."

I can tell he's imagining every worst-case scenario. I'll handle Trent and my team. I know the risks already, and Hiro is worth an ass-kicking. I pull him into my arms.

"You still like me?" I ask, burying my nose in his hair and breathing him in. He nods. "That's all that matters to me. Forget about everything else. You're good for me, and I think I'm good for you too."

He relaxes against me, which tells me I'm winning the argument. I rub his back and nuzzle his neck. He smells so good.

"Just remember this moment," he says softly. "Remember that I warned you."

HIROKU

I SPEND the weekend working on my football video. Turns out all I need is the right music. Beethoven's Fifth Symphony has exactly the right tempo and mood to keep up with the action of the game. I also mess with the speed and timing of the runs, slow down some of the best parts to really capture the football players' athleticism, especially Berlin's. This happens to me from time to time, where I kind of fall in love with my subjects. I even find myself feeling less hateful toward Trent. That's the power of art; it makes me soft.

I send the link of the final cut to Berlin. His response is immediate. *So cool!!! You're such a talented artist.*

I smile because I like thinking of myself that way. When others say it too, it makes me feel like I'm not just making all this up in my head. Maybe I can make something of myself doing the kind of work I love.

We text for a little while longer, and I make the video public the same night. When I get to first period the next morning, my classmates all compliment me on it, Spencer especially. "I've never looked at football quite like that." He waggles his eyebrows a little. I'm not sure if he means there are sexual overtones or what. If there are, it's accidental. I really just want to highlight the beauty and grace of the game, slow it down a little to really appreciate it, maybe even subvert it a bit to give a fresh perspective, like I did with the cheerleading video.

"You liked it, though?" I ask him. "It was your footage too. I hope you're okay with what I did with it."

He squeezes my arm. "I loved it. You're a mad genius, Hiroku."

I'm feeling pretty good going into third period. As I'm changing in the locker rooms, one of the guys, Anderson, mentions the video to Trent, who hasn't seen it. Anderson pulls it up on his phone. I take a deep breath, thinking maybe this is an opportunity to make peace with the bigot brigade. The video definitely shows Trent in a flattering light. I left out all the interceptions and wild passes. I still hate the guy, but for Berlin's sake, I want the feuding to be over.

I finish dressing and turn around to put on my tennis shoes, keeping my head down so they don't think I give a shit what they think.

"What the fuck is this?" Trent shouts. He still has Anderson's phone in his hand. I can hear the music coming out of the phone's shitty speakers, tinny and weak. "Who did this?" he roars. I glance up. What the hell is he so worked up about? I swear he must be on steroids to have so many raging hissy fits all the time.

Anderson nods in my direction and Trent steps to me. I stand up to face him, feeling a spike in my heart rate. "Take this shit down, Faggy," he demands, squaring his shoulders and puffing out his chest to intimidate me. I feel like a wild animal when confronted by Trent—a powerful cocktail of adrenaline, hatred, and fear.

"Fuck no," I say. "What the fuck is your problem now?"

"Take this shit down or else." He raises one fist like that's supposed to change my mind. He's such a tiredass cliché.

"Why? Because I made it?" I'm truly confused.

He snarls. "Don't play dumb with me. You made us look like faggots with the music and the ballerina shit." His eyes narrow, daring me to say something. I'm not going to out him in front of his friends, for the same reason I didn't break his throwing arm when I had the chance. Because even though I hate him, there are basic laws of human decency I live by, though I'm pretty sure he doesn't abide by those same rules.

"You're saying Beethoven is faggy music?" I say to him. "Jesus, are you inbred?"

"You know what you fucking did, you little shit."

What the fuck ever. He can be a raging homophobe all he wants, but he's on my turf now. "Listen, Trent, I don't tell you how to throw interceptions, so don't you tell me how to make videos. Fuck you and the rest of your bigot brigade. I'm not taking it down."

His face screws up like a tantruming child, and he raises his fist higher, like he's going to clobber me over the head with it, like Donkey Kong.

"No way I'm going to let you disrespect me in my house, you smart-mouthed son of a bitch."

I'm so fucking sick of his bullshit. And I'm not going to back down from his threats. If he wants to kick my ass, then he can fucking do it. Spencer told me over dinner that Trent used to torment him too, and still does from time to time, that it only stopped when I came to Lowry. That's one plus to me being the gay whipping boy of Lowry High School—it allows Trent to funnel all his hatred for himself at me. Whatever, I can take it.

"Just think, Trent, all those guys bent over wearing tight pants," I say, "asses in the air, grunting, waiting for you to make the call. Maybe it's football that's faggy—"

Trent takes a shot, but Berlin comes from out of nowhere and jumps between us, taking Trent's fist in his shoulder. Berlin pushes Trent backward and spreads his arms wide, using his body to both block me in and shield me.

"Get the fuck out of the way, Webber," Trent shouts. His rage reverberates throughout the locker room like a war cry. The other guys feel it too, shuffling around nervously. If we were alone and there were no witnesses or evidence, Trent would probably kill me.

"Get him out of here," Berlin orders his teammates. I hear some scuffling and glance over Berlin's shoulder to see them shoving Trent out of the locker room. A wall of flesh. His own linemen are using their blocking skills against him. Trent probably hates me even more for it.

Trent points his finger at me like it's a gun. "You're fucking dead, you little faggot." Maybe I'll be scared later, but in that moment, I want him to fucking try it.

My heart feels like it's going about a million beats per minute as they leave. I could lift a car if I had to. Berlin is silent, shoulders heaving, hands clenching and unclenching.

"Was that necessary?" he finally asks.

Another wave of fury rolls through me, that those are his first words to me. I feel like punching Berlin, but I won't.

"Are you saying that was my fault?" I hiss.

"No, I'm saying you didn't have to rile him up like that."

"Fuck, Berlin." I push him away from me. "I don't need your fucking protection. Go join your bros, maybe even get some gay-bashing in for good measure. I'm fucking done here."

I stalk out of the locker room, ignoring his calls for me to come back and be reasonable. Jesus fucking Christ. Reasonable? There are no rules of engagement when it comes to Trent and his posse. The fight is rigged.

I am so fucking done with Lowry and its small-minded bullshit. Berlin is just as brainwashed as the rest of them. If he wasn't gay himself, he'd probably be joining in their antics. The thought makes me sick to my stomach. The strong and the weak, the predator and the prey. It's the reason I left Seth in the end, because I was so sick of him winning all the goddamned time.

I grab my camera and head out to the parking lot to get my bike. I'm taking a personal day.

BERLIN

BASKETBALL IS a shit show, with everyone out of sorts and missing baskets after Trent and Hiro's fight. The guys on our football team keep glancing between Trent and me, trying to figure out whose side to take. Trent won't even look at me. I might get my ass kicked before the day is over. I don't care about my team's loyalty as much as I care about protecting Hiro. If I hadn't been there, Trent would have destroyed him.

I try texting Hiro during lunch but get no response. Out in the parking lot, I see his bike is gone, which means he must have left school. I know Trent will be all over me about interfering in the locker room, so I eat my lunch on the tailgate of my truck, hoping to see Hiro pull in at some point. No such luck.

Practice that afternoon sucks. Trent doesn't say two words to me, but I can feel his rage simmering just beneath the surface. It messes up his game too. Coach calls us off the field midway through and demands an explanation. Neither of us says a word, so he makes us run laps for the rest of practice. Trent stays just ahead of me on the track, which is fine by me. He was such an asshole. There's nothing gay about that video. Trent was just picking a fight.

I text Hiro again that night but get nothing. I think about driving over to his house, but I don't want to cause a problem with his parents. It seems I've done enough damage already.

I hope it will blow over, but both Trent and Hiro ignore me for the rest of the week. My texts and calls to Hiro go unanswered. He also doesn't show up to Team Sports, though I see him elsewhere during the day. He must be skipping third period to avoid Trent.

Or maybe it's me he doesn't want to see.

On Thursday I can't handle the silent treatment anymore. I drive over to his house after practice and knock on the door. Mrs. H. opens it and glances behind her at the stairs. Hiro must have given her instructions, but she seems torn.

"Please, Mrs. Hayashi, I just want to talk to Hiro for a few minutes."

"Hiroku," she calls from the door, then goes to the base of the stairs and calls again.

"Come in," she says and points to the living room, then heads upstairs. A few minutes later she returns.

"He'll be down," she says with a smile and offers me tea.

"No, thank you, ma'am." I stare at the stairs until, finally, Hiro slouches down. His face is expressionless, but I know he's still pissed at me. How much? If there's any way to make it up to him, I want to try.

"Come on," he says glumly and leads me out to his backyard. He sits on the back steps, and I stand on the ground in front of him so I can see his face. Apologizing seems like a good place to start.

"I'm sorry for what I said the other day in the locker room and for the way Trent's been treating you. It's messed up and I know it. I wish I knew how to make him stop."

"Okay." He studies his hands and says nothing else, always a puzzle.

"What does that mean?"

He sighs like he's bored, but I know it's only a front. Hiro cares the most when he acts the least interested.

"It means I heard you," he says.

"And?"

"And nothing. I appreciate your apology, but it doesn't change the situation. Living in this town is hard enough without Trent's bullshit. I'm out of Team Sports. I changed my schedule. I'm staying the hell away from Trent, and you should too. He's a live grenade."

This isn't fair. Trent gets his way again, but I've been telling Hiro all along to back down too. I'm just as responsible. "You shouldn't have to do that," I say miserably.

"Yeah, well, I don't think Lowry will be flying the rainbow flag anytime soon, so until then…." He drifts off, grinding his fist into his open palm.

I should just suck it up, come out to Trent, and deal with the consequences myself. Hiro shouldn't have to take this abuse. And at least if Trent knows about me, he'll have a new target.

"I'll talk to him," I say.

He glances up with a frightened expression. "Don't, Berlin."

"Why not?"

He presses his hands together and rests his lips against them like he's trying to stop himself from saying anything more.

"Talk to me, Hiro. What is it?"

He shakes his head, so I urge him again, gently, though. With Hiro, you get more with sugar than vinegar. Finally he looks up at me. "Ever wonder why Trent goes off anytime someone calls him gay?"

I'm not sure what he's getting at. "What do you mean?"

"Sometimes, when he thinks no one is watching, he looks at you, Berlin. The way you look at me."

I swallow. Trent looking at me? Like that?

"No way," I say.

Hiro nods but doesn't say anything more about it.

I step back from the situation and try looking at it as an outsider. Trent does tend to get affectionate with me after a few beers. He also talks all the time about his exploits with Madison, almost to the point it seems like he's trying to prove something. "You think Trent's *gay?*"

He shakes his head. "I don't know."

I bet he does know; he just doesn't want to say it. "You knew about me."

"That was different. But imagine if Trent is gay, and how dangerous it would be if that got out. Trent would want to silence anyone who suspected it. This is a land mine we're walking on."

"I'm not afraid of Trent." He might end our friendship and get me kicked off the team, but if he stepped to me, I'd destroy him.

"Maybe you should be."

I honestly don't give two shits about Trent right now. All I care about is whether or not Hiro is still mad at me. I lay one hand on his arm. "What about us?" Hiro shakes his head, and I worry he's going to try to end it with me. "Come over this weekend. Please? I'm dying over here."

He stands. "I've got homework to do."

"You'll come over, though?"

He gazes across the yard, avoiding my eyes. "I'll think about it."

I nod. I don't want to push him. "Okay."

The next morning Trent resumes his before-school post on the tailgate of my truck. I greet him with a nod and he does the same. We're stiff with each other, and silent. I keep thinking about what Hiro said, reviewing all the awkward moments in my friendship with Trent over the past few years, unsure if it's just typical best friend behavior or if it's something more.

Trent chews his tobacco like cud and goes over the plays Coach wants us to execute at tonight's game. We strategize about which ones might work against the Cavaliers' defense.

Hiro pulls into the parking lot, and I try not to notice.

"Haven't seen Faggy in class," Trent says like he doesn't care about it one way or another. Like he's baiting me. I could act like I don't know anything about it, but I'm still pissed about Trent's bullshit and Hiro having to drop Team Sports because of it.

"He switched classes." I don't say *because of you*, but that part is obvious.

"How the fuck do you know that, Berlin?" he asks, his face all pissy. When did he become so angry all the time?

"He told me."

"I didn't know you guys were so close."

I shrug. "We're friends. I didn't know I had to ask your permission."

"Friends, huh?"

I say nothing, and Trent spits again, a squirrely look in his eyes. "You a fucking faggot, Berlin?"

I decide to put it back on him, see how he likes the question himself. "Are you, Trent?"

He gets real quiet then, his eyes focused on Hiro's back as he puts away his helmet. I don't like the way Trent's looking at him.

"Fuck, no," he spits. The hatred in his voice makes the hairs raise on the back of my neck. "Now, how about you?"

Here's my moment of truth. If I admit to Trent I'm gay, I can forget about finishing the football season, and with it goes any chance for a scholarship, which means I'll be going to community college, if my dad can afford it. No more football practices or games, no more hanging out with the team. I don't want to give that up just yet. If I wait a few more weeks, I know I'll get recruited. Scouts are already showing up to our games. All I need is a little more time.

I straighten up. "I'm not gay, and not everyone who pisses you off is a faggot. Sometimes you're the asshole."

Hiro passes in front of us with his eyes straight ahead. I know he's seen me with Trent, and that must bother him. My loyalties are being tested just like he predicted. Even though I know which is the right side, I can't join him there. Not yet.

"Sure about that?" Trent asks. "If I find out that you're lying to me, there'll be hell to pay." He spits a tar-blackened loogie at my feet.

I hop off the edge of my truck. "Don't threaten me, Trent. That shit may work on other people, but it doesn't work on me. I'm not scared of you. If you've got something to get off your chest, you know where to find me."

As I walk away, I realize Trent is reminding me more and more of his dad every day.

I'm really starting to hate him.

HIROKU

CHANGING MY schedule around was a major pain in the ass. It meant I had to drop Digital Arts, the best part of my school day. Having to drop Team Sports also sucked, because it was my only class with Berlin. Even though we couldn't really acknowledge each other, it was guaranteed time together.

When Mrs. Potts asked me why I wanted out of Team Sports, I told her Trent Cross and I weren't getting along.

"I see," she said, and that was all. I expected her to ask more questions, really get to the bottom of it, but from the expression on her face, it seemed that was all she needed to know. It pisses me off. It's like everyone at the school knows Trent is a homophobic psychopath, and they just let it slide because he's quarterback for the football team. And not even a good one.

Whatever. By my estimation, I'll be dual enrolling by the end of this semester anyway, which means I can give Lowry the one-finger salute. That thought alone is what keeps me going for the rest of the week.

When I see Berlin palling around with Trent on Friday morning, I suspect their little spat is over, which is irritating, but also a relief. If they're chummy again, then Berlin is still in the closet, and safe, which means the situation has deescalated, at least for now.

I skip the game Friday night, but I can't resist texting Berlin after it's over, because I miss him like crazy and still want to be with him in spite of everything.

Score any goals?

We lost, 17-7

There's a long pause then, and I wonder if he's going to ask me to meet up with him. I hope he will.

Want to make me feel better?

I smile, feeling the familiar flush I get whenever he says something the least bit suggestive. With Berlin, I thrive on subtext.

Yes.

Meet me at the fence in an hour.

Don't you have a barbeque?
Change of plans.

I shower and shave even though I don't really need to. I pick out my favorite black shirt, the one with hot pink lettering that says "Save the drama." It's actually my second-favorite shirt. Seth stole my first favorite, an original Petty Crime band shirt that I designed when they were just starting out. Suddenly I realize I don't give a shit about the shirt anymore. Seth can have it. He's in the past where he belongs. Berlin is the present, and maybe even my future.

I tell my dad I'm going out, and he grunts from behind the computer in his study. I kiss my mom good night.

"Are you meeting Berlin?" she asks with a smirk.

"Yeah," I say, my chest expanding a little.

"He makes you smile," she says to me in Japanese, so I scowl at her for good measure.

I hop on my bike and ride over. My palms are sweaty on the handlebar as I arrive at Berlin's property. My heart is kind of fluttery in my chest, the way I always get at the prospect of seeing him. Usually he's there already when I arrive, but it looks like I've gotten here first. I punch in the gate code, roll my bike inside, and pull out my phone to text him. I smell something like charcoal burning and figure he has a bonfire going somewhere.

Here now. You?

I'm about to hit Send when I hear footsteps galloping toward me. I spin around and someone slaps my phone out of my hand. My cheek explodes with a force that lifts me off my feet and makes my head spin. I land on my ass in the dirt, pain rocketing through my jaw, and grasp at my face to make sure it's still a face. I'm dizzy and disoriented from the blow. I've never been hit that hard in my life. I paw at the ground, trying to work up the balance to stand and get away from the fuzzy, hunched shadows surrounding me.

A million hands grab me, clutching at my wrists and ankles, pinning me down. I try to curl into a ball, but they force my limbs apart. *I'm an open target*, I think as terror rips through me. A boot descends on my chest, one that could crush my rib cage or my skull. I go wild, fighting against their vise-like fingers. I finally get my hand free, grab the booted ankle, and yank, hard.

"Hold him down," a voice commands. Trent's voice. Someone else slams my wrist back to the ground and leans on it with his full weight. I know then that Trent—the whole team, probably—is going to break every bone in my body. I scream for help. I sound like a wild animal.

Someone stuffs a cloth into my mouth, jams it so far down my throat I gag. I feel the shirt being ripped off my back, then wrapped around my face so I can't see them. I smell the charcoal again, a sooty, smoky odor, then hear something hiss as I feel heat, like from a fire. I scream into the gag, choking on my own fear and panic.

"Better bite down on that jockstrap, faggot," Trent says calmly. "This shit is going to hurt."

I scream again, twisting as something burning hot plunges into my chest—a red-hot iron poker, the fucking pitchfork of the devil himself. They're carving out my heart with a razor and setting me on fire at the same time.

I scream incoherently into the gag, delirious, my mind exploding from the pain. I must black out then, because when I come to, I'm being dragged across the ground by my wrists. I can only feel one hand. My chest is on fire. I can't catch my breath or hear anything above my wild, beating heart.

"Tie him to the fence post," Trent tells someone, then thumps me on the shoulder. "What's the password to your phone, Faggy?"

I'm still blindfolded as my head slumps forward. Waves of dizziness and nausea come over me as my hands are clamped behind a wooden post. I hardly feel the rope cutting into my wrists. The pain from the burning hole in my chest overrides everything else. I'm going to pass out again.

"What's your password?" Trent shouts.

"Fuck you," I moan into the gag. Someone rips it out of my mouth and punches me in the gut. My legs finally give out and I fall back against the wooden post.

"Tell me your fucking password or we'll brand your ass too," he says.

It takes me a second to process his words. They *branded* me? It has to be a joke—a sick, twisted joke, but the pain in my chest is unlike any I've ever experienced before, an ungodly burn. I can smell it too. Burnt flesh. *My* burnt flesh.

"Your password," he says, and follows it with a blow to my temple.

"Fuck you," I say weakly and give it to him.

"Text Berlin from Faggy's phone and tell him where to find his boyfriend," Trent says to someone else. I feel his breath, hot and foul on my neck as he whispers in my ear, "This here is what we do to faggots."

For once I have no clever comeback.

BERLIN

AFTER THE game, which we lost thanks to Trent throwing a record five interceptions, I'm more relieved than disappointed when the team barbeque gets cancelled. Hiro agreed to meet me and I can't stop thinking about it. Driving home from school, my truck starts pulling to the right, then the ride gets rough, and I realize I have a flat. I get out and inspect the tire to find a nail sunk in deep. Just my luck.

It takes me about half an hour to replace the flat with the spare tire I have stored under the back of my truck. Right when I'm about to text Hiro that I'm running late, I get a strange message from him.

Come get me at the fence post, you fucking faggot.

I stare at my phone, then scroll back to read our earlier texts, trying to figure out what's going on.

Trent.

He must have stolen my phone while I was in the showers after the game and guessed at my password, my mother's birthday.

I'm white-knuckled the whole drive to the fence, dreading what I might find. My breath catches when my headlights hit Hiro. Tied to a fence post, his head covered with a black cloth, shirtless and slumped over like he's....

"Hiro!"

I slam it into park, fall out of my truck, and sprint over to him. He lifts his head and I can't help praying, *Thank you, God.* Whatever Trent's done to him, he's alive.

"Hiro," I call again. My voice cracks and I can hardly get out his name. The panic and terror have cut off my breath.

"Don't come any closer," Hiro shouts, his voice muffled by the cloth. I slow my pace, confused. "Give me your knife," he says, his voice raspy and low. "Put it in my hand, then get the fuck out of here."

"I'm not leaving you. I'm going to kill them. All of them." My mind feels like it's exploding. All I can see is my fists on their flesh, beating the living shit out of them.

"Please listen to me, Berlin." He sounds like he's on the verge of tears.

I pull out my pocketknife and approach him cautiously. Instead of handing the knife over to him, I grab on to his hands, squeezing to reassure him and me too. He pivots on the fence post so that his back is to me, maybe to give me a better angle to cut him free. I don't want to accidentally slice him, so I gently saw away at the rope. As soon as his hands are free, he yanks the cloth off his head and grips it to his chest.

"Give me your shirt," he shouts hoarsely. My hands curl into fists as my head swivels around to make sure no one is hiding in the bushes. I dare any of them to step to me now. I should have known they'd come after Hiro. That Trent would hurt him to get to me. Because Trent's a coward and a piece of shit.

This is all my fault.

I pull off my shirt and hand it over to him. He gingerly puts it on, then doubles over in pain. I rush over and grip his shoulders carefully to help him stand.

"Is it your ribs?"

"Yeah," he utters through clenched teeth. They must have bruised or broken a rib for him to be in that much pain. His arms and legs look okay, thank God.

Hiro stays hunched over for a minute, then slowly rises to a standing position.

"You're hurt. Let me take you to the hospital. We can call the police from there. Trent's not going to get away with this. This is a hate crime."

Hiro shakes his head like he can't believe I suggested it. Then he starts laughing. It sounds a little unhinged.

"This isn't a hate crime, Berlin. It's just boys being boys." He copies our country accent. "Just a little *smear the queer*. A little rough-and-tumble after the big game."

I edge in closer. I should have settled this thing with Trent myself a long time ago, but I was selfish, a coward. And now they've hurt Hiro to punish me.

"That's not what this is. Come on. I'm taking you to the hospital."

Hiro shakes his head. His left eye is swollen and his lip is cut. I'll do so much worse to Trent and whoever was with him. But first I have to get Hiro to a hospital.

"I'm done." His voice is empty. He curls inward, protecting his ribs. "The fucking bigot brigade wins again."

Hiro straightens up and walks stiffly toward his bike. I follow behind, not knowing what to do. I don't try to touch him even though that's what I want most of all, to just hold him.

"You shouldn't be driving," I say. "Please, let me take you to the hospital so they can look you over. Your parents can meet us there. We don't have to go to the police right away."

He shakes his head. "Don't you get it? We're not going to the police, ever. You don't even know your own privilege. Jesus, you're just like the rest of them."

"I'm not," I say weakly. I'd never do this to another person, but I've also never done anything to stop Trent. Hiro isn't his first victim. There were others Trent has bullied and intimidated over the years. I stood by and watched it all.

I lift Hiro's motorcycle from where they kicked it over. "Please come with me." I grab for his hand, but he tears it away.

"Go home, Berlin."

He dons his helmet, climbs onto his bike, and kicks on the engine, drowning me out with the roar of his motorcycle. He disappears into the night in a cloud of dust.

I run back to my truck, thinking I can at least follow him to make sure he gets home safely, but by the time I'm on the road, the sound of his motorcycle is a distant hum, and he's gone.

HIROKU

ADDICTION IS a mind game. When I was in rehab, it was easy to stay clean, because the pills they had me on made me feel dead inside and there was no easy way to get my drug of choice. Snorting antidepressants just isn't the same.

In Lowry, it was harder because I knew I could drop in to Austin in an afternoon and be high within the hour, but I kept thinking of my mom visiting me in rehab, how sad and tired she looked, how patient she'd been with me, how unconditional her love, even when I was fucking up left and right. I thought of my sister Mai when she graduated from high school and how I wanted to be someone worthy of her company. I thought of my father and hoped that someday I'd be able to turn this ship around or bail it out enough to have some kind of relationship with him.

I thought of Seth and how if I let my addiction get the better of me, then he'd win. Anger is a strong motivator—at least, it is for me—and I was fucking pissed. But in all those scenarios, the reason I was able to stay sober was because I wanted it. Because I still had some small shred of hope that if I could just get away from Seth, my life would be better. That I might even be happy, or at least not so fucking sad all the time. I'd find those highs naturally, through my art or in sports, maybe even with another guy.

There is no future for me in Lowry. Berlin suggested I go to the cops. What a joke. They aren't going to do shit about it, not even with the proof of Trent's hate crime on my chest. A queer kid versus the high school quarterback? Berlin is delusional if he thinks Trent is going to be punished for what he did to me, and I can't be drawn into his fantasyland anymore.

What I want now more than ever, to deal with the pain and degradation, the fucking hopelessness that is my situation, is to get high as fuck. To fucking forget Lowry ever existed, wipe it off the map completely. Drugs treat the symptoms, Dr. Denovo warned me, not the problem.

The problem is beyond me, and when faced with the choice, I'll take the devil I know.

I head for Seth's apartment.

IT'S NEARING eleven when I arrive at Seth's place, the Berlin hour, as I've come to think of it, when he'd text me after practice or when we'd meet. But those days are over. The stick of dynamite has blown the town to smithereens, and with it went the fair-haired sheriff and his deputy.

I stand outside Seth's door and lean my forehead against it, debating with myself. I can still walk away. I can go home, sleep it off, and start over tomorrow morning. I'll take online school. My mom will let me if she sees what they've done, but I don't want her to know. Her son has been branded for being a faggot. She'll blame herself for coming to Lowry, even though it was my fault we had to leave Austin in the first place. Some part of me wishes they'd just killed me, so I won't have to live with it. Every time I look in the mirror, I'll see it. Every time I'm with someone, they'll see it. Jesus Christ, it feels like the walls are closing in on me.

I hit Seth's door with the palm of my hand, once. He probably isn't even home. Then what will I do? Get on my motorcycle and fucking ride. The idea appeals to me. I can get lost out west, just disappear altogether. Dip behind the horizon like the setting sun.

I turn away from the door as it opens and Seth appears, shirtless, a glazed look in his eyes. He's either just gotten high or gotten off, maybe both.

"Hiroku," he says like we're both trapped in the same dream. He reaches out one hand to touch me, but I step back. He doesn't like that, but he tempers his expression. He was never good at hiding his feelings. "You're hurt." His eyes turn soft and misty like he's going to cry. It annoys me, mostly because I'm mad at myself for coming here and saddened by how badly I need him to want me. Despite everything, he did make me feel as essential as the air he breathed.

Seth steps back into his apartment, narrows his eyes, and says to someone unseen, "Leave."

Seconds later, a pretty young thing stumbles through the doorway, barefoot, holding his shoes in one hand and clutching his shirt to his chest. Of course Seth hasn't been celibate in my absence. Still, it never feels good to meet your replacement.

Seth doesn't say anything more to me, just opens the door wider and steps aside so I can enter. He closes it quickly behind us and deadbolts it from the inside. He'd probably padlock it if he thought that would keep me here.

"What are you wearing?" he asks. He creeps closer and sniffs the shirt. It smells like Berlin, the forest after the rain. Seth knows it isn't my smell. His shrewd eyes narrow.

"I need a shower." I haven't assessed the damage they did to my chest, and my face isn't feeling too great either. I have a high tolerance for pain, but this is in another stratosphere. I hope the pain is worse than the injury itself, but somehow I doubt it.

Seth motions to the bathroom, even though I know where it is already. Not much has changed since I left him. Unlike me, he didn't feel the need to clean house. The apartment has the same brothel atmosphere, with lots of curtains and moody lighting, floor cushions and plush pillows set up in different areas. Perfect for blowing your mind with drugs, then blowing each other. I cringe to remember all I did in this apartment with him, for him, at the pleasure of his company, the way he'd trot me out like a doll and manipulate me in front of others. I had to be high to withstand it.

I head to the bathroom and lock the door behind me. My mind is fuzzy from being in his apartment. Seth's everywhere all at once, a barrage of sensations. All those memories I've scrubbed clean from my psyche are swirling back now, filling my head with conflicting emotions.

I turn on the shower to drown out the sound of my whimpers as I peel off Berlin's T-shirt. My mangled flesh has fused with the cloth, and it hurts like a bitch getting it off.

"Fuck me," I utter when I see the brand in the mirror. I grip the counter to keep myself from passing out, splash some cold water on my face, and convince myself to look again. It's hideous, a fist-sized lesion on my left pectoral, directly over my heart. I wonder if that was Trent's intention or if he just got lucky.

What remains of my flesh is gooey and bloody, with areas of blackened, charred skin. I look like a piece of meat. I can't catch my breath, so I grab a towel and stuff my face into it, trying to calm myself down.

"What the fuck is that?"

Even though I locked the door, Seth is there at my shoulder, a horrified look on his face, which freaks me out even more. He drops the towel and clothes he was carrying and grabs my shoulder to see the wound better.

"Don't fucking touch me," I snarl and tear myself away, stretching the tender, broken skin in the process.

"Did that redneck do this to you?" he demands. His eyes are wild. Is it because he truly cares about me, or is it because someone else has ruined his property?

"His friends."

"Shit, Hiroku, where the fuck have you been?"

"Hillbilly hell." I point to the bathroom door. "Get the fuck out, Seth."

He glances again at the mirror, where my hideous flesh is still on display. It looks like a zombie tried to eat out my heart. I look fucking disgusting. I want to die. But first I want to get high.

"Should we go to the emergency room?" he asks hesitantly. "Or the police?"

"No, I'll handle it. Go do what you do best." He studies me again, almost like he doesn't recognize me, then bows slightly and backs out of the bathroom, leaving the door open. I wonder if it's on purpose, so I'll know who's still in charge.

In the shower, I finally let go and cry, shaking with rage and digging my fingers into my arms to keep my mind from deserting my body. I stand with my back to the water because the sting of it on my chest is too much, even for me. After I've cleaned the filth and sweat and fear off my skin, I climb out of the shower, dry myself gingerly, wrap the towel around my waist, and locate Seth's hydrogen peroxide and bandages.

"I can do that for you," he says. He's back in the bathroom, looking for any opportunity.

"I got it." I unscrew the lid and douse my wound with peroxide. It hisses back at me like a snake, foaming up something vicious. I grit my teeth as a fresh burn eats away at my flesh.

"Fuck, Hiroku." Seth covers his ears with his hands and squeezes his eyes shut. He used to do the same thing after we fought. Like he can't handle my pain, even when he's the one to inflict it. I thought it was because he felt guilty, but maybe he truly feels it himself. He does tend to make everything about him.

After it airs out a bit, I slather it with Neosporin. Only then do I realize what the mark is, a semicircle with a *W* cradled inside. Webber Ranch, the same mark I've seen on Berlin's cattle. Trent thought this through. If I go to the police, he'll say it was Berlin who did it. It happened on Berlin's land, and Trent made it look like Berlin set me up. I can't even swear Berlin wasn't there, since I didn't see anyone's faces.

Thank God Berlin wasn't there. Thank God Trent didn't think to make him watch. I shake my head to rid myself of all their sadistic faces.

"I fucking hate Lowry, Texas," I spit at my reflection, then bandage up the massacre of flesh on my chest. I can't bear to look at it anymore.

"I'm so sorry, Hiroku," Seth says miserably.

Which part is he sorry for? The drugs? His cruelty? My banishment? Or is he simply sorry that I'm suffering? I don't ask him, though. I can't handle another confrontation tonight. He comes up behind me and rubs my shoulders. I let him because I'm weak and it's inevitable, the two of us. My willpower is shattered. The shirt he laid out for me is my favorite Petty Crime shirt. I pick it up but I don't put it on because I don't want anything tugging at the bandage.

"I knew you had my shirt, you bastard."

"It's all I had left of you," he says pathetically, probably to make me feel bad. It almost works.

Seth kisses the side of my shoulder, letting his lips graze across my skin, sending a shiver down my spine, part pleasure, part revulsion. I shouldn't be here, but I have no other place to go. He trails one fingertip down my arm and appraises me. I know he likes what he sees, aside from my recent defacement. I need that right now, to feel beautiful in someone's eyes.

"I missed you," he says, his voice dripping with desire. He leads me out to the living room to a soft, velvet chaise fit for a prince. On his glass coffee table are three pretty white lines waiting for me like virgin brides.

"Feel better, baby," Seth whispers like the devil on my shoulder, but the devil is inside me, a sleeping dragon stirring awake.

I snort all three lines and sink back into the plush cushion, which is a cloud, and I'm floating up and away from all of earth's bullshit. I'm an angel with wings, a fucking supernova. My powers are limitless and the bigots way down on earth are ants. I crush them with my mind, and my magnificence outshines the stars.

BERLIN

I DON'T remember driving to Trent's house. My mind is still reeling with what I just witnessed, my worry over Hiro, my fury at Trent and the guys I once considered my closest friends.

I barrel up to the Crosses' front door and pound the solid oak with both fists. With a fiery rage coursing through my veins, I could have ripped the door right off its hinges. Coach Cross answers.

"Webber," he says with a sneer on his face, a cold beer in his hand. "Is it true, then? You a fucking faggot?"

"Where's Trent?" I blame Coach Cross too. He made it the standard to hate on gays by calling us pussies and faggots and demanding that we prove our manhood in stupid ways. His homophobia is a cancer that's diseased the whole team.

"Trent's busy," Coach says to me with a cold, hard look in his eyes.

"Tell him I want his ass on the front lawn or I'll smash his window. He can come face me like a man."

"Is that what you are?" Coach asks me, his lip curling in disgust. "A man?"

I come in close to him. I want him to see the fury in my eyes, feel the rage rolling off my skin. Violence is a tang in the air, and my fists are clamoring for a fight. "I'm more of a man than you'll ever be, Coach."

I dare him to come at me with his fists the way he's done with Trent his whole life. I double-dog dare him. I've been hoping for a reason to lay him out ever since I saw Trent's first black eye when we were eleven. The beatings only stopped when Trent grew to be bigger than him. But like a true coward, Coach Cross doesn't start fights unless he knows he can win them.

"It's too late for this shit," he says, then slams the door in my face. I pace their front lawn, clenching and unclenching my fists, thinking about what I have in the back of my truck that can break a window. The door opens and Trent comes stumbling out on the lawn, rubbing his eyes like he's been asleep. What a fucking liar.

"All these years we been friends," I say to him with my finger in his face. "I've had your back the whole time because I felt bad for you because your dad's a meanass man. But no more, Trent, and never again. We are fucking done. You're a sick, twisted fuck, and I'm goddamned ashamed to say I ever considered you my best friend."

Trent screws up his face like he's unimpressed, the same cruel sneer as his father. "You've got a whole lot more to be ashamed of than that, Berlin. You like the treat we left for you?"

"I'm going to the police. I'm going to tell them what you did. They'll arrest you. You'll get kicked off the team, and you'll fucking deserve it."

"I've been here all night." He spreads his arms like he doesn't give a fuck what I say.

"There are boot prints and tire treads all over my property." I'll make sure the police see the proof.

"I'll tell them it was your idea. After all, it was your brand."

I don't understand what he means by it. My brand? Then I remember the way Hiro had slumped over, the pain he was in, how he leaned to one side so that his shirt didn't touch the skin. I thought it was his ribs.

He didn't want me to know what they did to him.

"You branded him?" My voice is shaking, and so are my hands. The ground tilts, and I feel like I'm going to puke.

Trent hoots and slaps one knee. "Boy, was he a scrapper. You should be proud of your boy. Took it like a champ."

I can't control my hands. They shove Trent backward, and I tackle him to the ground. We're about the same size, but I'm a lot stronger, plus I'm furious. We wrestle like we did when we were coming up, but there's nothing playful about it now. I want to pound his flesh with my fists. Make him bleed. Fucking destroy him. I pummel his ribs, and he grunts in pain. I cross his face. His head snaps to the side from the force of the blow, and his mouth spews blood like a fountain. It's not enough.

A gunshot rings out, startling me. I pin Trent to the ground and find Coach Cross aiming his shotgun at my chest.

"You touch my son again, I'll kill you and call it self-defense."

I slowly unclench my fists and stand to face Coach Cross. "It's your fault he's such a hateful son of a bitch," I shout. "You beat this into him over the years. You twisted him into this spineless piece of shit. He branded another human being tonight, Coach. The football team helped. You proud of that? You proud of the hate and fear you've brought down on your team?"

Coach angles his shotgun at my face. "Get off my property, Webber. And in case you don't already know, we don't let faggots on the football team."

"Fuck you and your football team," I spit. I love football, but I've seen the depths of their hatred. I don't want any part of it. If that means walking away from my passion, I'll live with that. "You'll get what's coming to you," I say to Coach. I glare down at Trent on my way out. His face is a mess, and he doesn't look so cocky anymore. "You too, motherfucker," I growl at him. "This isn't over."

I storm off to my truck, climb in, and head for Hiro's house. What can I even say to him? To his mother? There's nothing I can do to fix this, but I have to make sure he's okay.

They branded him like an animal. There will be justice for what Trent did to Hiro. I'll make sure of it.

HIRO ISN'T at his house when I get there twenty minutes later. His mother answers the door, a worried look on her face. She invites me inside, sits me down, and offers me tea. Mr. H. joins us. My knuckles are bloody and swollen, and Mr. H. keeps asking me questions. Rapid-fire. I don't know what else to do, so I tell them what happened. His father interrogates me while his mother keeps pouring tea, and I keep drinking it to have something to do with my hands. At one point she starts to cry, and Mr. H. quietly lays his hand over hers. I excuse myself to use their bathroom and wash the blood off my hands. When I come back, they're looking at their phones and speaking to each other softly in Japanese. I stand in the doorway to give them privacy, though it doesn't matter much because I don't know what they're saying.

"We have to go to the police," I say from where I stand. "We can't let Trent get away with this."

They glance over at me, then speak again to each other. I wait. It seems to turn into an argument.

Mrs. H. stands, snaps at Mr. H., then comes over and lays her soft hand on my wrist. "It's late, Berlin. You go on home. We'll wait up for Hiroku."

"You know where he is?" They exchange a look. "Are you going to call the police?"

"We'll handle it," Mr. H. says in a tone that leaves no room for argument.

"I should be here for the report." Hiro needs someone to back up his story, and he needs a friend. "Where is he?" I figured he'd gone for a ride, but this seems too long, even for him. I think of the quarry, and my stomach drops. What if he went there?

"You go, Berlin," Mrs. H. says again and pulls me gently toward the door. I let her see me out, then stand behind the closed door like a dog that's been put outside. I get back in my truck and ride out to the quarry while imagining the worst. I don't see his bike, so I jump the fence and poke around, calling out for him. He isn't there, which is a relief, but then I wonder where else he might have gone. Maybe to that redheaded kid's house?

I drive back to Hiro's, figuring I'll wait it out. Their garage door is open and his bike isn't inside it, so I park on the street. I don't care how late it is; I want to be here when he gets home. He has to know I'm on his side. I should have been with him the whole time instead of trying to defend Trent's behavior and point out his good qualities. For the life of me, I can't remember any of them now. This is worse than a mistake. I chose to be ignorant, even when the facts were staring me in the face, even when Hiro was pleading with me to acknowledge what we were up against.

I slam my fist against my steering wheel, then pound my chest a few times. I should have been there. I could have done a million different things, and instead I did nothing.

I keep imagining Hiro's face—his big, sad eyes, the tilt of his head when he's thinking on something, and his smile. With all that he's been through with his addiction and Seth, he needed someone to protect him, and I failed him in the worst possible way.

If he hates me, I can live with it. I just pray he'll come home safely and soon.

HIROKU

THE FIRST hit is always the sweetest.

I sink back into the chaise in Seth's living room, floating on clouds, drifting farther away from reality, my body feeling good in the most glorious way, my mind not giving a shit, at least for now. Meanwhile Seth makes promises. It's something he excels at. Sticking to his word, not so much, but in making promises, he's aces.

"In two weeks the band's going out to the desert to record our next album," he says in his melodic voice, his instrument of seduction. With his words he spins a silken cocoon for me to nestle deep within. I need a place to hide. "You can come with us, film the band, write a few songs, maybe shoot a few videos. Whatever you want, Hiroku. You don't have to worry about money. I'll pay for everything."

What he doesn't say is what my payment to him will be—my body, for one; my creativity; my freedom. The details of our arrangement are somewhat irrelevant. Seth changes the rules to fit his mercurial wants and desires. There's no use in negotiating with him up front.

"When you posted those pictures on Instagram, were you hoping I'd see them?" I ask.

"Yes," he says without hesitation. "I wanted to make you jealous so you'd come back. Then I started hooking up with guys who looked like you to see if I could get over you. That didn't work either."

Seth can admit things like that. He's truthful in many ways. He tells me every little demented thought in his head.

"I guess you were hooking up with that hillbilly by then," he says.

He assumes I behaved the same way after our breakup. For me, it was the opposite. I lived like a monk the whole summer. Rehab helped with that. I know Seth's waiting for me to confirm or deny my relationship with Berlin. I used to get off on making Seth jealous, but that was with guys I didn't care about. Berlin feels sacred. I don't want Seth to wrap his dirty mind around him. Lowry is an inbred, two-bit town anyway. I'm already speeding away from it. Like it or not, that means Berlin too.

"No comment, huh?" He takes another hit from his bong. The weed is to help stabilize his mood. Xanax for anxiety. Alcohol to help him decompress at night, and an occasional upper to get him through a show. Not too much, though, or he starts singing faster than the beat. Painkillers are for pleasure and to ward off withdrawal. He's a walking medicine cabinet. He's careful about dosage, though. It's me who needs portion control, which is why Seth always holds the drugs, so I don't overdose. Last spring I wanted to get back at him for hooking up with another guy, so I snorted the rest of his stash and woke up in the hospital.

"Did you know I was in rehab?" I ask him.

"Sabrina mentioned it. Made me feel like shit."

"Really?"

"Of course. Rehab fucking sucks."

I chuckle darkly. I can't help it. Rehab did fucking suck.

"Thank God your funny bone's not broken," he says and nudges me with his bare foot. Then he gets quiet. "It'll be different this time, Hiroku. I hated you not being here, but I thought a lot about the way I treated you, the way I should have treated you. You were always too good for me. I want to be better, for you."

I glance over at an old couch sitting in the corner of the room. It's from the garage where the band used to practice, evidence of Seth's sentimental streak. So many of my firsts happened on that old couch. The dreamer in me wants to believe that Seth's changed, but the realist knows he's just saying whatever he needs to get me back on the line. I think back to earlier that night when he coldly dismissed his latest hot dish. He can turn that same cruelty on me in a heartbeat, only it won't be so cool or indifferent.

I don't need any of Seth's promises or bullshit stories. His actions will prove himself one way or another. And maybe if I disappear, Berlin won't get kicked off the football team, and he can still get that scholarship and get the fuck out of Lowry.

"I'll go with you to the desert," I tell Seth. "I can't wait two weeks, though. It's got to be sooner." I'm not going back to school. I don't want to face the bigot brigade again on Monday. If I ever get to feeling sentimental, I have this huge fucking atrocity on my chest to remind me.

"We can leave tonight," he says. His eyes glow with anticipation, like some cartoon villain, Jafar from Aladdin.

"I need to say good-bye to my mom." Somehow I know this isn't going to be a short trip, that if I come back, things won't be the same.

The nail in my coffin, as it were. My mother's heart will be broken all over again. What small shred of familial regard my father has toward me will be severed. Mai will be pissed at me for being weak and selfish and putting our parents through hell again.

"Monday morning," I tell him. I'll have the weekend to hang out with my mom. I'll take off after they go to work, leave a note so they'll know I haven't been kidnapped or anything. I don't want any needless drama.

"Monday morning," he says. "I'll let the band know we're getting there early to set up. I should tell you, though, I want it to be as more than just friends." He lays his hand on my knee, and his eyes search mine. The terms are implied already. He's testing me to see if I'll submit.

"Were we ever friends, Seth?"

He shakes his head slowly. His lips curl into a smile. "My sweet Hiroku, I think we've been everything but friends."

In my drug-induced haze, I see Berlin, my light at the end of the tunnel. Only I'm heading in the opposite direction and the light is getting dimmer.

BERLIN

I STARTLE awake in the cab of my truck to the keen of Hiro's motorcycle. It's the middle of the night, and I stumble out of my truck and catch up with him as he's rolling his bike inside the garage. The shirt I gave him is gone, replaced by a Petty Crime T-shirt. There's only one place besides his closet he could have gotten a shirt like that.

"What are you doing here?" he asks me. He doesn't seem angry, just exhausted.

"I wanted to see how you were." He looks as stoic as ever, but I can tell from the way he's walking he's in a lot of pain.

"Fantastic."

"I know what they did to you, Hiro. I'm so sorry. I should have done something. I should have—"

"It's late," he says, and holds up one hand to silence me. I reach out to him, but he shrugs me off, then winces in pain. It should have been me, not him. I should be the one with the brand on my chest. I'm the coward, not Hiro. "Did you say anything to my parents?" he asks quietly.

"They kept asking questions." I only wanted to help.

He raises both arms in the air, then slumps forward, placing a protective hand over his chest.

"Jesus, Berlin, how do you think my mother's doing right now, knowing a pack of ignorant rednecks attacked her son and fucking branded him? I never wanted her to know, and now you've taken that from me too."

He's like one of his mother's impossibly delicate bowls, and I'm trying to hold him without breaking him. "How would you even hide something like that?"

"Like everything else. By not fucking talking about it."

"I'm sorry," I moan, feeling stupid and useless. The last thing I wanted is to make it harder for him.

"Stop apologizing." He glances away, then back at me. I see the pain in his eyes, the loss, like he's given up. I want to ask him about Seth and the glassy look in his eyes that tells me he's been using, but I don't want to kick him while he's down.

"Can we talk tomorrow?" I ask. I hate leaving things this way between us, but I know he's had a horrific night.

He shakes his head slowly. "No, we can't. Just forget you ever knew me, Berlin. Whatever we had, it's over. I'm sorry, but your friend Trent killed it."

He climbs the stairs to his house and shuts the door quietly behind him. I shuffle back to my truck with my tail between my legs.

I might never be able to make it right, but I'm not going to give up without a fight.

I CALL Hiro the next day and again on Sunday, but my calls go straight to voice mail. He ignores my texts too. The Crosses aren't at church on Sunday morning, and I hope it's because Trent is still hurting from the ass-whooping Friday night. On the way home from church, I tell my dad everything—Trent, the branding, the fact that Hiro and his family didn't go to the police.

"What should I do?" I ask.

"Give him some space. He'll come back around when he's ready."

"What about telling the police? It's a hate crime. Trent can't get away with this."

"You want me to talk to Hiro's parents?"

Hiro was so angry when he found out I'd spoken to his parents. "No, I don't want to make it worse." My mind goes in circles thinking about what happened, what I should have done, and what I can do now to make things better for Hiro.

"I beat Trent's ass Friday night," I tell my dad as an afterthought. "And I quit the football team."

"We'll figure out another way to get you to college," he says, which is the least of my concerns right now.

On Monday morning, Anderson's truck is parked in my space, and he and Trent are sitting on the tailgate. He can have it—my parking spot, Trent's friendship, my starting position—all of it. I want nothing to do with them or the rest of the football team. Trent taps a baseball bat against his open palm, no doubt trying to intimidate me, and Hiro too. Hiro isn't here, though. Who knows if he'll ever come back?

"What are you looking at, faggot?" Trent says as I pass them in my truck. His right eye is still swollen and there's some bruises on his face. I wish it were worse.

If Trent comes at me, I'll fight back, but I'm not going to egg him on—he'd enjoy it too much. I find a spot in the underclassmen parking lot and arrive late to first period.

In the hallways everyone is staring at me and whispering, and not in a good way. No doubt they know I'm off the football team. I can't speculate beyond that. Kayla finds me after second period and asks if I'm coming to church that Sunday. I'm so grateful to have someone speak kindly to me that I practically sing out, "Yes."

"Good," she says brightly, "because I spoke to Pastor Craig, and he wants to meet with you after services." She gives my shoulder two quick pats, then pulls her hand back.

"About what?"

"Oh, you know." She pauses and looks at me with intention. "Things." She smiles awkwardly and hurries away.

Does Kayla know I'm gay? Does Pastor Craig? The whole school? My sexuality is my business, not my church or my classmates. I want some say over who knows it, but Trent has ruined that for me, the same way I took the story of Hiro's assault away from him by telling his parents. Shit.

In Team Sports I find my gym clothes in one of the shower stalls, soaking wet. I can't dress out and play soccer, the new sport, so I sit on the sidelines in my jeans and boots and get a sunburn. I don't bother telling Coach Gebhardt about my clothes. He didn't do anything when the same thing happened to Hiro.

I eat lunch alone on the tailgate of my truck. I think about skipping, but I'm not going to punk out so soon. Hiro endured this abuse a lot longer than half a school day. When I go to get my books for fifth period, someone has scrawled *FAGOT* in bold black letters across the top of my locker. Probably Trent, since he can't spell for shit. I try to erase the word with my shirt, but it's some kind of permanent marker. Behind me, people are snickering. One of the linemen shoves me into the lockers as he passes. I don't react. In a way, I deserve it. All the times I stuck up for Trent, all the times I told Hiro to back down—how shitty that must have felt for him. As to finding out who my real friends are, it's zero.

Since I no longer have practice after school, I head straight for my truck, only to find the windshield is cracked and my tires are slashed. Trent and his baseball bat.

"Dammit," I shout in frustration. I kick the rim of one of the tires so hard it feels like I broke a toe. When I report it to the school's resource officer, he says there's not much he can do about it, since all I have is a hunch and no witnesses. He'd probably try a little harder if it weren't Trent Cross I was accusing. I call a tow truck operator who's a family friend and sit out in the parking lot stewing in my own juices until he shows up. I think about heading down to the football field to confront Trent and the rest of the team, but I'm outnumbered and outgunned.

"Looks like you got on someone's bad side," the driver says to me as he's loading up my truck. "Cheat on your girlfriend?"

"It's a long story." And one I don't want to tell to a friend of my dad. Then I realize I'll have to tell my dad about this. I dread it. I wish I could just have it fixed without him knowing. Then I think of Hiro and his mom and how I screwed everything up for him. I pull out my phone and try calling him, but get his voice mail again.

I leave another message.

HIROKU

MY MOM wants to go to the police about the assault. We argue into the early morning over it. I lay out all the reasons why it won't work. When that doesn't convince her, I tell her that if she forces me, I won't talk. The same thing happened with Seth. She wanted me to press charges, but I wouldn't, because I didn't want Seth to get in trouble. This time it's different. I don't think it will matter. And I don't want a bunch of strangers poking and prodding me, asking me questions, getting all up in my business and making me defend myself.

I don't want to see Trent's face or relive it. To press charges would mean having to experience that pain and humiliation over and over again with no guarantees he'd even be punished for it.

And what if Trent tries to put it on Berlin?

I tell her I'm tired and I need to go to bed. It takes forever to fall asleep because the drugs are wearing off and the pain in my chest is back, and I can't stop thinking about Berlin's face when I told him it was over. Ending it with him was my only option, but I don't feel good about it.

I gave in to my addiction. I went running back to Seth.

My mother wakes me up around eleven in the morning with tea and breakfast in bed. She wants to see my chest. I lie and tell her it isn't that bad, that Berlin overreacted. My dad seems to know what I'm shielding her from and tries to calm her down. It's one of those rare moments when he and I are on the same side. My dad tells her to respect my privacy, and at last she lets it go.

Later, when my mom's gone out food shopping, my dad comes up to my room. I'm backing up my footage in preparation for my departure. I want to make sure I can access my work from wherever I end up. There's no telling what my dad will do with my setup once I'm gone.

"I thought this move would be good for you," he says stiffly, but I know how to read between the lines with my dad. This is his way of apologizing. Maybe he feels guilty, like if they had stayed in Austin and just sent me to a different school, it would have been enough. But I know it wouldn't. The temptation is too great.

"You did what you thought was best," I say, which is my way of accepting his apology. "I'm not going back to that school."

"You need to finish out the semester. Then you'll have enough credits to dual enroll."

"I'm not going back," I say again. Even though this fight is pointless, I'm not backing down. My dad has been trying to run my and Mai's lives since birth. She obeys. I rebel. But on this matter, there's no negotiating.

"You don't want to ruin your transcripts, Hiroku."

"Fuck my transcripts, Dad." I'm in survival mode, and I need another hit soon or the withdrawal will start kicking in. My transcripts are the least of my concerns. I expect Dad to get on me for my language, but he just presses his lips tightly together and takes a deep breath through his nose. I think Mom made him go to some kind of anger management counseling after our blowup last spring.

"We don't have to decide anything right now," he says, still not relenting. It seems he doesn't grasp the depth of my hatred for that school, and vice versa. Maybe he needs to see my chest in order to better understand what I'm dealing with.

I'm not going to show him, though. I don't want anyone to see it, ever. "I've already decided, Dad. I'll fucking kill myself before I go back."

"Don't say things like that, Hiroku. What would your mother say?"

"I wouldn't say it to her, but I'm telling you."

He takes a few deep breaths, exhaling through his nose, and I wait.

"Very well. We'll figure out another situation. But Monday morning, your mother's taking you to the doctor."

"Can you do it? I don't want her there."

"Fine. I'll leave work early. We'll go in the afternoon."

Seth better not be late.

My dad comes over then and lays a hand on my shoulder. I almost flinch. I can't remember the last time my dad touched me. "I love you, son," he says.

He squeezes my shoulder, and my eyes kind of sting for a second. It sucks that I have to endure something like this for him to say it. Still, it's nice to hear. "You too, Dad."

If I don't argue with him again before I leave, then this will be our last conversation.

I can live with that.

MY PARENTS aren't going to force me to go back to school. I can stay with them and dual enroll in the spring, carve out some half-realized existence for myself in Lowry. But Seth has an ace in the hole. When I left him Friday night, he sent me off with one more dose for Saturday, just enough so that by Sunday afternoon, I'm feeling restless and moody. By nighttime I'm climbing the walls, needing more. I barely sleep that night. By Monday morning I'm getting chills and body aches, sniffles and a runny nose. I tell my mom it's just a cold and convince her to go to work. I have a doctor's appointment that afternoon anyway.

I keep looking at the clock. Seth is late.

He finally arrives around noon, comes inside just long enough to get me high and comment on how ugly our new house is. His eyes rove over my bedroom, perhaps looking for some remnant of my relationship with Berlin, but there is nothing except my black cowboy hat, which I've strung to one of my duffel bags. If Seth asks about it, I'll tell him I bought it myself.

Seth nods to my phone. "Better leave that here." My parents will be able to track me with it, but it's also my lifeline. If I leave it behind, it's one more way I'll be dependent on Seth. I scroll through my contacts until I find Spencer.

Check in on Berlin Webber for me, I text him. If Berlin and Trent don't make up, Berlin's going to need a friend, and Spencer has a direct line to Lowry's gay community. Then I find Berlin's number and memorize it. I'll check in on him in a couple of days.

"We'll get you another one," Seth says, perhaps noticing my reluctance to let it go.

I clear out my phone and leave it there on my desk, next to the note for my parents. Seth helps me load my video gear into the back of his van. He wants me to leave my bike, but there's no way in hell I'm going without it. I need an exit plan this time. Standing in the doorway to the house, I have second thoughts. It's easy to do now that the drugs are coursing through my veins. They offer me the luxury of choice, but only until they leave my bloodstream. I'm tossing the dice with my addiction, but I'll be creating the kind of art I want again, and there will be moments of sheer fucking bliss. Isn't that enough?

Besides, I don't want to try so fucking hard anymore. To stay off drugs, to keep away from Seth, to blend in to whatever the local norm is. Berlin was doing well enough before I arrived in Lowry, and after the dust settles, he'll be better off without me.

I'm the stick of dynamite that blew Berlin's world apart.

BERLIN

HIRO DOESN'T come to school that whole week, and he never answers his phone. I know his parents are strict, but it seems unfair they would ground him. Maybe they're letting him take online school, or they've left town completely. I head over to his house on Friday afternoon to see what's up.

Mrs. H. answers the door. She must have stayed home from work today. Her eyes are red, and she looks like she hasn't slept much that week. When she sees me, she just shakes her head sadly, and I know something god-awful has happened.

"Oh, Berlin," she keeps saying over and over.

"Where's Hiro?" I ask, trying to see if I might catch a glimpse of him somewhere inside the house.

"He's gone, Berlin. He left with that terrible boy."

Seth.

"Where did they go?"

She shakes her head. "We don't know. The police say he's too old now for them to go looking. He hasn't called or e-mailed. He left his phone behind. Five days. Nothing."

"He ran away?" I still can't believe it. Hiro's been gone all this time? With Seth? There's no telling what Seth might have done to him by now. He could be lying dead in a ditch somewhere. I don't say that, though, since Mrs. H. is probably already thinking it.

"Did he take his bike?" She nods. She looks like she might start crying at any moment. "That's good. That means he can come home."

She starts to sway on her feet, so I kind of hug her to me. She's a tiny woman with bones like a bird. Her hair smells like Hiro's, and I'm filled to the brim with regret. "I'm so sorry, Mrs. Hayashi." I shouldn't have told his parents or pressured Hiro to go to the police. I should have come by over the weekend to check on him. I should have done *something*.

She leans back to look up at me. "This isn't your fault, Berlin. You'll tell me if he calls you, won't you?"

"Of course. Will you tell me?"

She nods and wrings her hands together. "I'm so worried about him. That boy is dangerous."

After we say good-bye, I walk to my truck in a daze and sit there for a few minutes hunched over the steering wheel. Hiro didn't even take his phone? Does that mean he isn't coming back? He must know his mother is worried sick about him, and he still won't call? What if he's locked up somewhere or strung out on drugs and needs help?

Unless he reaches out to me, I might never see him again.

I DON'T want to go to church on Sunday, but my dad thinks it'll be good for me to get out of the house. He's not used to having me around all the time. Now that I don't have practice or football games, we've been seeing a lot more of each other. I spend a lot of time outdoors doing chores. It keeps my hands busy and my mind off the guilt and shame over what I let happen to Hiro. I keep my phone close, though, just in case he decides to call. I miss him pretty bad.

Walking down the church aisle on Sunday, I feel everyone's eyes on me. Folks whisper; some point. It isn't much different from walking down the hallway at school. And there's Trent sitting at the edge of the aisle, whispering "faggot" to me in the house of the Lord as I walk past him. He tries to trip me, but years of football have trained me to watch out for shit like that. I kick his ankle for good measure. I don't give a rat's ass how he treats me, but I feel bad for my dad, since he has to suffer right alongside me, now that the whole town knows I'm gay.

Pastor Craig's sermon is about the importance of family, about honoring your parents and honoring yourself. I'm only half listening, because I can't get comfortable with all the side-eyeing going on. Then Pastor Craig starts talking about what it's like to be an adolescent, what a confusing time it can be, made even more so by the Internet and television and peer pressure. He talks about how we all make mistakes and even when we do, God still loves us and wants us to make the right choice the next time. Pastor Craig keeps looking at me, and I wonder if he knows about Trent's assault on Hiro. Probably not, since no one at school is talking about it. I can't believe Trent has managed to keep his mouth shut about it.

At the end of every sermon, Pastor Craig stands outside the church and greets everyone as they leave. I want to go out the side door, but my dad likes to shake his hand and offer his gratitude. I suppose I'll have to face Pastor Craig sooner or later. I trail behind my dad, hoping to get away before I have to talk to anyone from school. As soon as Pastor Craig shakes my dad's hand, he looks at me. "Mind if I give Berlin a ride home? I'd like to talk a few minutes alone with him."

Noooo! I want to shout, make a few tackles, and sprint for the truck like it's the end zone, but my feet are cemented to the pavement.

"You can have him for a few minutes, Pastor," Dad says. My heart sinks into my shoes.

I stand a few feet away as Pastor Craig finishes shaking hands. Several of the men and women eye me up and down. I'm not sure what they're expecting to find. Proof of my sexuality? If they didn't see it before, they aren't going to see it now. A few of the men glare at me with hostility. Trent's dad looks like he'd like to spit on me.

"I sure hope you can make a man outta him, Pastor Craig," Coach Cross says loud enough for me to hear. "Lord knows, we could use a good running back."

I step forward. "I'm never playing for you again." I'll play for another high school, but I'll never be under Coach Cross's thumb again.

Pastor Craig lays his hand on my shoulder like I'm the one who's out of line.

Trent comes forward and whispers so only I can hear, "Looks like we ran your faggy boyfriend out of town."

If we were alone I'd knock his ass out. It takes all I have in me to pretend I didn't hear him. Trent's dead to me. The whole football team is.

After finishing with the congregation, Pastor Craig leads me inside the church to where he has a suite of offices, one for him, one for his secretary, and one for the programs director. I've spent a lot of time with Pastor Craig over the years. Whenever there was a chore in need of a strong back—moving furniture, building pews, that sort of thing—I always volunteered.

"So, what's new, Berlin?" he asks me once we're settled in his office. The happy-go-lucky look on his face bothers me. It feels false and besides, I suspect he knows already. News travels fast in our town, and Kayla indicated as much. But does he know the full story?

"What have you heard?" That might be the best place to start.

"I hear there's been some friction between you and the Cross men."

"Coach kicked me off the team. Or I quit. I'm not sure which came first."

"Why's that?"

I sit back and cross my arms, look him dead in the eye. "Trent and some of the other football players branded a friend of mine."

Pastor Craig raises his eyebrows. "They *branded* him?"

I'm right, then. He didn't know that part of it. Maybe Trent and Coach Cross are worried they might get into trouble after all. "They did it with my brand on my property to get back at me. My friend ran away from home because of it. His mother's worried sick about him."

Pastor Craig says nothing. He looks a little ill, like the conversation isn't going the way he planned. "I'm truly sorry about your friend, Berlin. Tell me his name and we'll pray for him."

"Hiroku," I say, though if it's souls in need of redemption, we should probably be praying for Trent and Coach Cross.

We bow our heads and Pastor Craig says a prayer. "Amen," I whisper. Pastor Craig lifts his eyes to meet mine.

"Did any of my sermon today speak to you?" he asks, which is disappointing. I suppose that's all we're going to say about Hiro and what he suffered at the hands of the intolerable bigots in Pastor Craig's own flock. To me prayer isn't supposed to be the end of a conversation, but the beginning.

"I liked the part about honoring your parents and yourself," I say, giving him the benefit of the doubt.

"Do you feel like you've made any mistakes in the past few months?"

I shift in my seat. I get the feeling he wants me to say being gay is a mistake, but I don't like the way he's going about it. And it doesn't feel like a mistake to me. More like a revelation. I'm not ashamed of anything I've done with Hiro, except for lying about it and my cowardice.

"I should have come out to Trent and my team sooner," I say. "Instead, I let Hiro take the fall for it."

"I see." Pastor Craig makes a steeple of his hands and presses his lips to his fingertips. "You know how our church views homosexuality, don't you, Berlin?"

"Yes, sir." I watched a lot of porn last summer. Perhaps to make myself feel better about it, I also spent a lot of time researching the Bible's take on homosexuality. Jesus didn't say anything about it, despite what the church pamphlets claim.

"Do you agree?" he asks.

"I don't think it's a choice, if that's what you mean. I didn't choose to be attracted to boys." *And men*, I add silently. "I've been this way as long as I can remember."

"You've always had sexual feelings toward other boys?"

"Yes, sir."

"Do you think it may have been the influence of another man who made you feel this way?"

Maybe he thinks I was molested or something. That's one of the many theories floating out there as to why a person might be gay. A dysfunctional relationship with your father is another. They play into the whole *unnatural* thing. None of those scenarios apply to me. "No, sir."

"Do you think your mother's death might have something to do with it?"

"I'm not sure what that could be."

Pastor Craig sits back in his chair and studies me for a moment. I glance toward the door, hoping I can still catch my dad before he leaves.

"Do you want to be healed, Berlin?"

"Healed from homosexuality?"

He nods gravely. He makes it sound like pneumonia. Maybe that's how he views it. Not me. If anyone has an illness, it's Trent and Coach Cross. The hatred in their hearts is a disease and it's spreading.

"With all due respect, sir, I don't think I need healing. I know you believe prayer can turn a person straight, but I've prayed plenty already. I think as long as I'm a good person, neighborly and whatnot, God will forgive me."

"I'm not so sure about that." Pastor Craig looks at me with concern. He's worried about my immortal soul. I don't think much about life after death, except when I think about my mother. My dad always taught me it was more important to treat people with kindness on this earth and leave the sorting to the man upstairs.

"I'd like to talk with you more about this, Berlin. Could we start meeting regularly? Say, Tuesday afternoons?"

I blow out a long breath. The thought of having these conversations with Pastor Craig on a regular basis makes my stomach turn. My being gay isn't hurting anyone. There's nothing in the Ten Commandments about it either. *Live and let live*, as Hiro once said.

"I don't think so, sir."

"You aren't available then?"

I stare at the smooth finish on his desk. I don't want to be disrespectful, but I figure honesty is the best approach. I owe it to Hiro to own my sexuality, even if that means making other people uncomfortable. Even if that means people calling me names or treating me poorly. Now that I'm out, I'm not going to hide it. Hiro figured that out a long time ago— it's better to be yourself than to pretend to be somebody else. Maybe if I'd tried that sooner, he'd still be here with me.

"If you're going to counsel me on how not to be gay or try to convince me that homosexuality is a sin, then I don't think I'm interested."

He studies me like I'm a lopsided cake.

"I have a colleague who runs an excellent program just outside of Dallas. I think you'd really like it." He reaches into his desk drawer and pulls out a brochure, passes it over to me. I read the front of it aloud.

"*A Man's Journey.*"

"Check out their website. I think they offer exactly what you're looking for."

Unless the website has the location of where Hiro has gotten off to, I doubt it's what I'm looking for. I fold the brochure in half and stuff it into my back pocket. Pastor Craig rises to shake my hand. "I hope you get the help you need, Berlin."

"Yes, sir." I keep my head down as I walk out of his office, then remember I need him to give me a ride home. Maybe I'll just hoof it. I'm about to head for the side door when someone calls my name.

"Berlin."

My dad's sitting in the front pew with his hat in his lap. He waited for me.

"Thought you might want to ride back with me," he says simply.

I nod, relief flooding me.

"Yes, sir, I do."

HIROKU

SETH AND I head west to Allister, Texas, a six-hour drive from Lowry. The town is on the edge of the Chihuahuan desert, a tiny place sandwiched between two small mountain ranges. Coming into it on Hwy 90, the views are breathtaking. From the yellows, browns, and greens of the desert grasses and cactuses to the blues and violets of the mountains to the corals and pinks of the painted desert sky at sunset, all the colors of the rainbow are present in one landscape. While Seth fills up the van with gas, I pull out my camera and snap a few pictures. I wish Berlin could see this.

"I knew you'd like it," Seth says to me.

"How'd you find this place?"

"We were doing a show in San Angelo. This guy gave me his card and told me he had a recording studio here in town. We checked it out and heard good things. The band liked the idea of getting out of Austin. Too many distractions, you know?"

Seth makes it seem like the band's idea, but I wonder if it's him needing to get away as well. There's a lot of temptation in Austin for someone looking to live it up like a rock star. Seth told me over lunch he's been having trouble writing lyrics ever since I left, probably because I wrote most of them with him, sometimes just a line or two, sometimes the entire song. Seth always called me his muse, but we both know I'm more than that.

Our first night in Allister, we stay in a cheap hotel. Seth gives me another bump of painkillers, and I work up the nerve to clean and re-dress my wound. It's starting to scab over in places where the blisters have popped. The burning has subsided, and now it feels like a really bad road rash. I can only stand to mess with it when I'm high, more because of the way it looks than the pain. I douse it with hydrogen peroxide, and then when it's dry, I slather it with aloe vera gel, then cover it up because it looks uglier every day.

The next day we go nosing around town for a longer-term place to rent. I want to stay in town so I'll have something to do while they're recording, even though Seth says he wants me there for all of it. "I work better with you there," he says more than once. It's his money, so I don't feel like I can demand much either way. We end up finding a guy who'll rent us a trailer a couple of miles out of town. Seth likes it because it's secluded. I like it because the views of the mountains and the desert go on forever.

Seth wants to catch me up on everything I missed while we were broken up, every show they performed, every band they met, which ones sucked and which ones rocked, the different cities they toured, the fights they got into and what they were about. Seth always diminishes his own role in the conflicts between him and his bandmates. I have to form a more complete picture from the clues he gives me. If he says, "Sabrina was being such a bitch about it. You know how she is about keeping a schedule," that probably means Seth showed up late to a show and might have been wasted as well.

He even tells me about some of the guys he hooked up with, the ones he can remember, at least. Most of their names he's forgotten, which is kind of sad. Even though he's trying to make the tour sound like it was some epic adventure, it seems kind of lonely. I feel bad for him. I even feel bad for leaving him.

On our third night together, he asks me to help him with the lyrics to one of the songs he's written. He plucks at his guitar strings and hums the melody. He tells me he wrote it right after we broke up. It reminds me of some sadass country song, so I suggest a line that seems befitting of the mood… *my broken heart is a melancholy tune, the minor chord of me without you.*

"That's brilliant." He scratches it down on a piece of paper. I think it's a little over-the-top, but he seems to like it. "I fucking love you, Hiroku."

I kind of go quiet and still, concentrating on the grain of fabric in my jeans. I hope my silence will go unnoticed—it wasn't a proclamation of love exactly, more like collegial appreciation—but I can feel his eyes boring into me, waiting for me to respond in kind.

"You're not going to say it." He sounds hurt, and I try to not let it get to me. He knows how to prey on my sympathies. He sets aside his guitar and I hunch forward, avoiding his gaze.

"You don't feel the same?" he asks.

I shrug, not wanting to answer. I do love him, I probably always will, but something has changed since we were together before. I used to think I couldn't live without him, like I'd die if he ever left me, but I had a taste of life without Seth, and despite the bullshit of Lowry, it wasn't so terrible.

Because I had Berlin.

"Are you punishing me?" he asks.

"Maybe." I haven't said it because it doesn't feel right, probably for a lot of reasons.

"Do you love him?" Seth looks like he's holding his breath, which kind of surprises me. In all the tales of his exploits, I never uttered a word about mine, even though he left the door wide open. I'm not going to bring Berlin into any conversation with Seth, because there's no telling how he'll twist it and throw it back in my face later.

"Do you?" he demands.

"I'm not going to talk about it." Not *him*, but *it*. The subject of Lowry is off-limits, and Seth knows that. It's probably eating him alive.

"Was the sex good?" he asks, ignoring my request for privacy, or maybe asking because of it. I draw a line in the sand and he erases it.

I stand and stuff my wallet and keys into my pockets. "I'm going to get a pack of cigarettes." I've started smoking again. It's a nasty habit, but it gives me a reason to get out of the trailer, and at times like these, away from Seth. "I'll be back in a few minutes."

"A few minutes, huh?" Seth plucks a few ominous chords. He doesn't like it when I go off on my own for long stretches of time. He was controlling when I lived with my parents, but out here, his possessiveness borders on paranoia.

"Maybe a little longer than that." I'll come back when I feel like I can breathe again.

I head out into the dusk and mount my bike. There are only two roads that lead to Allister. They connect it with two other tiny towns to form a triangular loop that takes about an hour and a half to ride. I do that circuit, thinking about Berlin the entire time, feeling bad for leaving without telling him good-bye. Is he still chummy with Trent, or has the bigot brigade turned on him too?

There's one pay phone in Allister, and I think about giving Berlin a call, but I don't know what I'd say to him, and I don't want to be selfish and screw with his emotions. I stop at a gas station instead and pick up a pack of cigarettes, even though I still have a full pack, and then, because there's nothing else to do, I drive back to Seth.

He isn't there, so I watch some television until he gets in around midnight, totally wasted. I'm not sure how he managed to get home without wrecking the van, except that the roads out here are pretty deserted. He reeks like cheap cologne, and I figure he went out and got a piece of ass just to spite me. I don't ask him about it. I don't want to give him the satisfaction of knowing I care.

"Don't you want to know where I've been?" he says to me after a minute. He looks unsteady on his feet, and he's blocking the television.

"Not really." I glance around him so I can watch my show, even though I've already lost interest.

"I went to a bar and drank myself under the table, then bought some aftershave at a gas station and put it on so you'd think I'd been with someone else."

I stare up at him. I actually believe him. This town is tiny, and even with his good looks and charisma, it'd take him more than one night of carousing to figure out who around here is gaytastic.

"So, did it work?" he asks me.

"Yeah, it worked."

"Did you care?" He throws out both arms as if this answer means everything. His muscles are taut and a little menacing. His eyes look desperate and sad. He'll do anything to get a reaction from me, even something as batshit crazy as this.

"Yeah, I cared." It's the truth.

He nods like it's the right answer. "Show me your chest." He points at me, his finger wobbling a little. In the time we've been together, I haven't taken off my shirt in front of him or showered with him. I change with my back turned. I don't want anyone to see it.

"No." I cross my arms over my chest.

He drops down in front of where I sit on the couch, spreads my knees far apart, and undoes the button on my pants, yanking the fly wide open like he owns me. He liberates my cock and strokes me a few times. It doesn't take long for me to answer the call. My body always arrives at his doorstep before the rest of me.

"Please, show me," he coos in the same sultry bedroom voice he uses on his adoring fans. His voice is a weapon of seduction, and as he tugs at my cock lovingly, I feel my resolve crumbling. "I love you, Hiroku, and even if you don't say it back to me, I know in your heart you love me too. I want to make your pain go away, but how can I if you don't share it with me?"

I glance away, feeling intensely sad and aroused at the same time. Seth's magic is a strange brew. I know he won't give up on this, and I don't have the strength to refuse him right now. He knows all my weaknesses. I pull off my shirt and slump back against the couch, letting him ogle me. The bandage is off to let it air out. Seth stares at it and looks strangely fascinated. With his free hand, he traces a circle around it, still scabby in some places, pink and tender in others. I wish I could scrub it off my body altogether.

"W," he says. "Was that his name?"

I shut my eyes and lean my head back against the couch, covering my face with my arms, trying not to think about that night. I want to keep the two things separate—my feelings for Berlin, and the anger and shame that overwhelms me whenever I think about what his friends did to me. Even worse is the fact that I let them get away with it. I hate myself for being weak and running away. Another win for homophobia.

"You still think about him," Seth says in an accusing tone, gripping my dick tighter, taking me to the edge of pain. I cringe, my muscles tense, but still I say nothing.

"I'm going to make you forget all about him," he promises.

He swallows my cock and sucks me off like a man who's been around the block once or twice. Then he lays out some lines for us to snort. We spend the rest of the night in a drunken, dizzy, lustful haze. I give him his pound of flesh and more, but I'm not entirely present for it. With Seth, I cease to exist as a person. I'm his vessel for pleasure and for pain.

But the next morning, when I go outside and see dawn's light pouring over the land, painted pretty as a picture, I think of something Berlin said about the hand of God, and I wonder if he still has that solid, unshakable faith. I imagine him coming up over the rise in his beat-up pickup truck and motioning with his one hand out the window like he used to for me to climb in.

In my mind, I go.

BERLIN

I ALWAYS liked school—the routines, the people, my teachers, even some of the lessons—but since coming out, school has become a nightmare. A nightmare that gives me stomachaches.

My mom used to warn me if I didn't open up and talk about my feelings, I was going to get ulcers. Now I wake up every morning with an upset stomach. Most mornings I can barely get down a glass of milk for breakfast. I have trouble eating at school, too, because I stress about when the next attack will come. One of the football players shoving me into a locker or socking me in the gut as they pass by in the hallway? Trent calling me a faggot in gym class or getting the other guys to go in with him on some stupid prank? Maybe they'll empty the contents of my locker into a trash can or leave dog shit in my gym shoes or spray-paint slurs on the side of my truck.

In football, I could navigate the field, and when I got knocked down, I'd get back up again. I was never alone. My team was there to cheer me on. We were in it together. Now I'm completely alone, and the guys I used to rely on for backup are the ones coming after me.

Ever since I stopped going to church, even Kayla avoids me.

Most days I carry all my books on my back like a pack mule so I won't have to go to my locker. I eat lunch alone on the tailgate of my truck. I keep my head down in class and try to disappear completely. As soon as the bell rings, I practically sprint for the parking lot to get home as quickly as possible.

I finally understand what it means to be gay in Lowry, Texas. It's enough to make you want to kill yourself or head for the hills. Lucky for me, I have my dad and our farm. I spend a lot of time talking to the animals and rediscovering the land, doing manual labor to keep my mind off my troubles. I visit the creek and think about Hiro. In the evenings I search for him online, without much success.

Two weeks after Hiro left, I'm at school picking at a cheeseburger left over from dinner the night before when a kid I don't know approaches me. He looks familiar, but it takes me a second to recognize him as the redheaded kid I saw with Hiro at my football game. Spencer something or other. He's in all the smart classes. I haven't had a class with him since middle school.

"Hey, Berlin," he says and stands kind of far away. Maybe he thinks homosexuality is contagious.

"Spencer, right?"

"Yeah." He looks pleased I remembered his name. He takes a few hesitant steps toward me. I realize then he's afraid of me. I vaguely remember Trent picking on him freshman year, and me not doing anything to stop it.

"Hey, um, I haven't seen Hiroku around school for a couple weeks. Did he transfer or something?"

Hiro didn't tell him where he was going either. That makes me feel a little less sorry for myself.

"He ran away," I say.

Spencer looks surprised, then worried. His face darkens. "Do you know why?"

"I'm not sure." I don't know how close they are, and I'm not going to make the same mistake I did with Hiro's parents. Kids at school know I'm gay, but they don't know about my feelings for Hiro.

"How'd you know I knew Hiro?"

Spencer's eyebrows rise like he's been caught. He glances behind him. "I got this strange text from Hiroku a couple of weeks ago."

"Let me see it," I demand. I didn't mean to sound so stern, but the kid kind of jumps and pulls out his phone. He scrolls through until he finds the text and shows it to me.

Check in on Berlin Webber for me.

Hiro sent it two weeks ago, the same morning he left town. That was probably the last text he sent from his phone, and it was about me. Even then, he was looking out for me. I wish I could do it all over again with Hiro. I'd do so many things different.

"I would have talked to you sooner," Spencer says, "but it's been a little crazy around here with Trent and all."

I shake my head. "Don't worry about it, man." I can hardly blame him.

"Were you and Hiroku… um…." He doesn't finish the question, but I guess at his meaning.

"Yeah. He was my boyfriend." There's no point in hiding it from Spencer. If Hiro trusted him, I should too. Funny how I can say it now that Hiro's gone when I could never say it then.

"I see." He scratches his head, kind of hops from one foot to another. He's a jumpy little guy, kind of looks like that singer all the girls are crazy for, the short one with the red hair.

"So, you two were friends," I say.

"Yeah. I think he told me about you. Over dinner, only he said you were older, out of school. I guess you two were, um, keeping it undercover."

"What did he say?" I ask even though it feels like prying. I'm so desperate to have a little piece of Hiro I don't care about invading his privacy.

Spencer looks me up and down. "He described you, pretty much like this, said you were, um, attractive—"

"Attractive?"

"*Built*, I think is the word he used. And sensitive. Thoughtful. The way he talked about you, it made me kind of jealous."

"You liked him too?" I ask.

"Well, yeah, but it made me jealous that he had someone. It's not easy to find that around here. It's cool you two had each other."

My heart feels heavy as a sandbag inside my chest. "Yeah, it was cool."

Part of me wants to tell Spencer what happened, so that he knows it's not Hiro's fault. It wasn't Hiro who was weak; it was me. The fault is mine.

"Well, here, let me give you my number," he says. "If you ever want to hang out or whatever."

I don't want Spencer to suffer for being kind to me. I can't deal with that on my conscience. "I don't know if that's a good idea. I'm not the most popular guy right now."

"I noticed," he says, "but I'll take my chances."

I don't want him to take any chances on my account, but I do want him to have my number in case Hiro calls him, so I give it to him.

"I'm a good listener," he says, "if you ever want to talk."

I nod. "Thanks and hey, if Hiro calls or texts, could you let me know?"

"For sure." He kind of stares at me. I look away. "You miss him, don't you?"

"Yeah, I do." I rub at my eyes, then my stomach.

I'm falling apart.

HIROKU

THE REST of Petty Crime arrives three weeks after we do. The plan is for the band to spend a week rehearsing, a month or so recording, and then Seth will stay behind and do whatever cleanup is needed on the vocals and instruments. I'm documenting everything to be used in a web series on the band, or maybe to cut up some of the footage for their next video. I have some ideas already for what I want to do with it, a mix between the Red Hot Chili Peppers "Breaking the Girl" and the Smashing Pumpkins "Today," with the desert featured prominently.

On the day everyone arrives, Seth hosts a get-together at our place for the band, significant others, and whatever friends and groupies have come along for the ride. The inside of our trailer is too small, so the party spills into the front, where there's a fire pit and a ring of lawn chairs. Seth sets up a cheap charcoal grill as well.

The smell of the charcoal makes me uneasy, but I try to put it out of my mind.

Mitchell and Dean, the bassist and lead guitarist, are easy enough to reunite with again. A handshake and a *how's it going* suffices. They mostly stayed out of the drama between Seth and me. Mitchell has a wife and young kid, and Dean, who's older, is a recovering alcoholic, tough as nails. The few times he's slipped, he made himself go out and get a tattoo as punishment. I'm not sure how that's a punishment, because his tattoos are pretty rad, but I understand the mind games you play with yourself in order to stay sober. I'm losing mine every day.

My reunion with Sabrina is a little bit rougher.

"The fuck are you doing here, Hiro?" she says by way of greeting. She's the only other person who calls me that.

"Just soaking up the sun," I say. Seth's a few feet away, no doubt within listening range.

"I thought this song had been played out," she says with no trace of amusement.

"It's making a comeback." I want to keep it light. No drama.

"Still powdering our noses, Marie?" For Marie Antoinette. Somehow it turned into a drug reference. We've been friends for years, so we have a lot of coded messages. It's how we communicate when Seth's around.

I shrug in response. I don't want to get into it with her in front of everyone else, Seth included.

"Rehab was that good, huh?" she asks.

Seth comes up then and slings his arm around her shoulders, squeezing a little too tightly. She recoils from him. "You know the thing I like most about drummers, Sabrina?" he purrs. She says nothing. "Yes, that's it. They know exactly when to shut the fuck up."

She glares at him and shoves him off her, walks over to the cooler and pulls out a beer, tilts the bottle my way. "Cheers, Hiro, to the reunion tour."

I need something to do other than wilt under her deep disappointment, so I get a fire going in the pit I made earlier that day out of random rocks that were lying around. I arranged them so it looks like a mosaic of a sunburst. I don't know why I went to the trouble. I could have just piled them up. I guess I have a lot of time on my hands.

Most everyone in the entourage has a guitar, except Sabrina and me. Sometimes she plays the bongos or taps her sticks to keep a beat, but she gets bored quickly. Sabrina has a lot of aggression, and she truly loves beating the hell out of her drum kit.

"So, how was rehab?" she asks me later that evening. The sun has set and the stars are out. I like looking up at the night sky in the desert and seeing the vastness of our universe. I find comfort in being reminded of just how small and insignificant we humans are.

"Fucking sucked," I say.

"And your new school?"

"Same." I'm not going to tell her about Trent or the assault. If she asks me why I came back to Seth, I'll make something up.

"Make any new friends?"

I shrug and pull down on the brim of the hat Berlin gave me. I wear it whenever I can because it reminds me of when we went horseback riding, and the way Berlin greeted me that day with a little dip of his hat. So hot and so sweet at the same time, a perfect gesture. I guess I'm smiling just thinking about him, because Sabrina kind of nudges me. "Tell me about him."

I feel comfortable talking with Sabrina about Berlin. I trust her not to say anything to Seth, and it will do her good to know I was involved with someone else.

"He was a cowboy." That day on his ranch, I wanted to rip off everything else but the hat and just devour him from head to toe. Snapshots of him flit through my mind. His broad chest with his rust-colored hair gleaming in the sunlight, gray-blue eyes that crinkle with kindness and change colors with the sky. His hands, big and callused and surprisingly gentle.

"His friends didn't know," I tell her. "We had to keep it a secret."

"That must have been hard," she says and lays her hand on mine. It's the same thing my father does to my mother when she's upset, which makes me miss them too. Sabrina has always been a good listener. She hears the spaces between the words, the things I don't say.

"It was hard." My eyes start to sting a little. I regret the way I left things with my parents and Berlin. I hope Spencer has reached out to Berlin like I asked. Maybe they'll even get together. Pickings are slim in Lowry. The thought of them having each other kind of makes me feel better about it all.

"Is that why you went back to Seth?" she asks, this time with less judgment.

"Yeah." I sniff a little and drag my arm across my eyes, adjust my hat. I glance across the fire and see Seth staring at me with a crazy look in his eyes.

"Reminiscing over there?" he calls sweetly while continuing to strum his guitar. Sabrina glares at him. Neither of us responds, so he continues. "Hiroku had an interesting year. Why don't you tell us about it?"

"There's nothing to tell," I say shortly. I don't know what he's getting at, but I figure it's nothing good.

"You want to show us that little souvenir you got from your redneck boyfriend?"

I shouldn't be surprised he'd throw that in my face the moment he feels threatened, but I hoped he'd moved past embarrassing me in front of his friends to make himself feel better.

"Hiro, don't tell me you got a tattoo?" Sabrina teases, elbowing my side.

"I don't want to talk about it," I say coldly. Their expressions all flatline, except for Seth. His smile widens.

"Go on, show them," he says like it's funny. Like it wasn't one of the most traumatic experiences of my life.

"No." I wish the word alone would choke him off so he won't utter another goddamned thing.

"They branded him," Seth says, his mouth turning downward. "That's why you came back, Hiroku, isn't it? That's how fucking bad it had to get?"

"Shut the fuck up, Seth," Sabrina growls. She reaches out to me and I evade her, get up and grab my cigarettes on my way out. I hear Seth groan and say something like, "Looks like he's mad at me, again," even though I'm sure he's secretly pleased with himself. Insert knife, turn, then act surprised when the blood starts gushing out.

"Come back, Hiroku, baby," he calls like a condescending asshole. I flip him off and keep walking.

I head out under the starry sky like a lone wanderer, my cheeks wet with tears. That happens to me sometimes—I'll just start crying without really realizing it. I can still get on my bike and get lost in the desert. Pick some random hotel room to hole up in until the withdrawal subsides, but I don't have the money to pay for it. And what place would give a room to a dodgy-looking teenager anyway?

I lie back in the sand and stare up at the stars until the anger drains away, leaving that hard, shriveled knot inside me that passes for a heart. I imagine Berlin's arms around me, the way he made me feel safe without trapping me. I reach under my shirt and trace the tender skin, feeling bitter and confused all at once, thinking about how the scars you can't touch are just as dangerous because of how easy it is to forget they're there.

BERLIN

MY DAD'S worried about me. He thinks I might be depressed, even though he doesn't say the word. Other than school, I don't leave the ranch much. I'm losing weight from all the stress, and I haven't been sleeping so great either. He wants me to go to the doctor, not like the flu doctor, but a therapist.

"There's a lot going on upstairs," Dad says to me over dinner one night. "I'm not the most talkative guy. Might help you to talk to a professional."

"I'm fine, Dad." I don't want to talk to a therapist. I want to talk to Hiro.

But I can't talk to him, so I start following Seth Barrett on Instagram. The first few posts are just Seth in the desert. Then, in the background of one of the pictures, I see Hiro gazing off into the distance. I can't make out his face, but I recognize his posture and the camera slung across his shoulder.

I tell Mrs. H. about it and show her the post, but Seth never gives any clues in his pictures as to where they are. He must know Hiro's parents will come after him.

As the days progress, Hiro is featured more and more. I watch the two of them grow closer in Instagram photos, a different kind of pain. Hiro starts off in the background, then a side profile, then looking at the camera. The first time I see his face, my breath catches and my stomach somersaults like it did when I used to hear his bike coming up the drive or pulling into the parking lot at school. He isn't smiling, though, just staring at the camera with his dark eyes and pouty mouth.

In the most recent one, Seth is kissing Hiro's cheek while Hiro makes a frowny face, a cigarette dangling from his lips. He looks sexy as hell. It guts me, but at the same time, it reassures me to know Hiro is okay. Maybe Seth realized what a treasure he had and he's treating him better.

Still, I recall the way Hiro pulled away from me when I tried to touch him, like he was scared of being hurt again. Sometimes in the photographs, I see Hiro curling into himself or gazing off with a faraway look in his eyes, and it concerns me. I say a prayer for his safety. I hope that even if he isn't calling me, he's staying clean and calling his mother.

Spencer keeps up with me outside of school and invites me to go out with him and some of his other friends. After the conversation about the therapist with my dad, I decide to accept his invitation, if only to prove I'm mentally stable. I meet them at what Spencer calls his "art installation," which turns out to be a bunch of printed photos taped to a cement wall. He and his friends are shooting at it with a paintball gun.

"All the people who've wronged us in the past," Spencer says and takes aim on a blown-up yearbook picture of Trent, Anderson, and me from one of our practices. We're all posing like the guy in the Heisman trophy statue. The Lowry Lions haven't won a game since I quit the team. Their play-off dreams are going down the tubes. It gives me some satisfaction, but it's not nearly enough. They should be punished for what they did to Hiro. I think about it every day, how they got away with it. What's to stop them from doing the same thing to someone else?

Spencer shoots and marks Anderson's shoulder. He shoots again and hits Trent's forehead. "Bull's-eye," Spencer says. "Want to take a shot?" He offers me the gun.

I raise the gun and take aim at the picture. I mark myself square in the chest, then hand the gun back to Spencer.

"Did you mean to hit yourself?"

"That guy is dead and gone."

His eyebrows raise. "How symbolic. Your aim is killer. Take a few more shots." He hands the gun back and tells me who he wants me to hit and where. I tag them all like a mercenary, a machine.

"I'm glad you're playing for our team," Spencer remarks.

"I am now."

I hand the gun to someone else and remember the time I took Hiro shooting, how it felt to hold him in my arms, like that's what my arms were made for. He belonged there and I did too. I feel terribly lonesome, even though I'm surrounded by new friends. I hear my phone ding, the alert I'd set for posting a picture on Instagram. This picture doesn't have Seth in it at all, just Hiro walking away, middle finger raised in the air. It's dark, must be from that same night. On his head I can just make out the hat I gave him.

Seth's words describe the photo. *My sweet Hiroku... hate to see him go, but love to watch him walk away...#loversquarrel*

What were they fighting about? Where was Hiro headed? It's pitch-black wherever he is—no city lights at all. And he's walking off by himself. I think of those cliffs at the quarry and his desire to hurt himself. In my gut I know he's not happy. And there's nothing I can do about it.

I shake my phone. "Just call me."

But my phone stays silent.

HIROKU

AFTER TWO weeks of recording, the stress of having to play nice with his bandmates is wearing on Seth. Most nights he spends drinking in the trailer and complaining about something someone did or said that day. I mostly listen without comment, since Seth has made it clear he doesn't want to hear the other side's perspective.

While they record, I spend most of my time behind the camera, which allows me some distance. When it comes to their familial spats about the guitar solo being too long or the drums being too loud, I stay the hell out of it. Whenever I can get away, I roam around town, meeting the locals, hanging out in the pool halls, the diners, and sometimes the library. I never have much money, only my "allowance," which is the cash Seth leaves for me on the bedside table every few days like I'm some kind of live-in hooker.

Seth doesn't like it when I go to town. He wants me in the studio, even if it's only to stand there and look pretty. We get into arguments about it sometimes. Despite my flirtations, I've never given him a reason not to trust me, but still, it doesn't lessen his desire to control me.

"Sabrina beats those drums like a caveman—no finesse," he says one night after we've just gotten high. I'm lying on the couch staring at the oscillating fan as it pivots back and forth, thinking about how much the two of us have in common, me and that fan. The fan exists to serve me. I exist to serve Seth. We're both trapped in a cage that follows a predestined course, travels only so far as is permitted, then comes right back. In return for this service, the fan gets jolts of electricity and I get painkillers.

Seth is sitting in an old, tattered recliner, working on a collection of empty beer bottles, oblivious to everything save for his own obsessions.

"Maybe I should bring in someone else to do a few of the slower songs so you can actually hear the vocals," he says.

"You do that and it'll break up the band, Billy." Billy Corgan, lead singer of the Smashing Pumpkins, known for being an insane control freak who ended up recording himself playing all the instruments because he didn't think his bandmates were getting it right. They broke up soon after that.

"Maybe you could talk to her, Hiroku," he says with a whine in his voice. "She listens to you."

"Fuck no, Seth. I'd rather have dental work without Novocain."

But he keeps on about it, wearing me down until I finally agree to say something to her if it comes up. The next day, while I'm behind the camera recording them, Seth picks a fight with Sabrina about her heavy hand until they're both mouthing off to each other. Then Seth turns to me and asks me what I think. This isn't how I intended to go about it at all, so I tell him I have no opinion. That pisses him the hell off, so he starts talking shit to me until I finally just pack up my shit and walk out.

Seth doesn't just let me leave, though. He chases after me, into the parking lot of the recording studio, telling me to "get the hell back there" and "don't fucking walk away from me when I'm talking to you."

"Fuck off," I say without stopping. I have my bike with me, thankfully. I'll go down to the local dive and drink a few beers to chill out. The town is small. They know me already, and the band. They serve me even though I'm underage.

Seth catches up to me and grabs my shoulder, spins me around so that I'm facing him, then slaps me square across the face. My cheek stings but I resist the urge to touch it. The look on his face is surprised and then curious, like, *what am I going to do about it?*

"And the beat goes on, huh, Seth?" I turn away and continue to where my bike is parked. I expected to feel… more. More hurt and anger, more betrayal, but something inside me has died ever since I left Lowry. Seth's antics just don't have the same effect they used to. He mostly makes me tired and depressed.

He chases after me, trying on a new character, the contrite boyfriend. I ignore his half-assed apologies, load up my equipment, get on my bike, and make the loop of tinyass towns in the epicenter of nowhere. I think about heading back to Lowry, but then I'll have to face my parents while coming off drugs. I'm too messed up to go back there. I don't want them to see my worst self. I need to quit the drugs first, then Seth.

I stop at a bar in town and get shit-faced, play pool so badly I think the other guys are letting me win, consider going home with one of the bikers who's hitting on me, but in the end decide it probably isn't worth it.

It's late when I get back to the trailer. Walking up to the front door, I'm wobbly on my feet. I should have taken up that biker's offer to bring me home. I open the door to find Seth waiting for me, a meanass look on his face. He's been drinking too.

"Where the fuck have you been?" he fumes, taking up all the space in the trailer. At times like these, the place isn't big enough for the both of us.

"Out," I say. He knows my usual haunts. He could have found me if it was really that important.

"The band left," he says like it's my fault. "Sabrina told me to finish off the drums myself. Are you happy now?"

I'm still pretty drunk. Maybe that's what makes me bold. "You fucking deserve it, Seth. You're an asshole to the band. You're lucky they don't kick your ass out."

He crosses the room in two strides and smacks me again, hard enough to make me see double. I start laughing. It's a nervous reaction.

"You fucked some other guy, didn't you?" he says. Maybe he smells the biker's cologne. I let him show me how to do a trick shot. I wanted to feel another man's arms around me and pretend they were Berlin's.

"No, I didn't." I could have, but I didn't, because I don't want to play games with Seth or give him a reason to be pissed at me.

"Don't fucking lie to me, Hiroku," he says and hits me again. This time it's my lip. I cut the inside of my mouth on my bottom teeth and taste blood.

"Feel better now?" I ask him. The less I react, the more it enrages him. I want to watch him explode. Blow the fucking roof off this crummy trailer.

"You're the same spoiled brat you've always been," he says. His eyes grow larger and more menacing. He bares his teeth, and I think of that fairy tale. *Grandmother, what big teeth you have.* "I bring you out here. I give you every little thing you want, and you still can't wait to get away and slut around town."

I snort. "Yeah, because I'm the one who can't keep my dick in my pants." Another blow, this time to my other cheek to even it out. Maybe I should defend myself, but I don't know how. It'd be like hitting my sister, so instead I wound him with words.

"It was so good, Seth, in the alley behind the pool hall, right next to the dumpster. It was so raw and rough. You ever been with a biker before? God, he was hung like a fucking horse. I had to hold on for dear life." I pump my hips to really drive it home for him. Instead of hitting me, he lunges at me, latches on to my neck with both hands. His fingers clamp around my windpipe and choke off my air. I can't breathe, and he isn't letting up. He shoves me backward so my head knocks against the wall of the trailer. My vision goes black around the edges and I feel like I'm falling. I reach for his wrists to release the pressure. My mouth opens and closes, unable to utter a word or cry out. In his eyes I see his blackest desire. He wants me dead, or at least, he wants the power to kill me.

My mind flashes back to the bigot brigade holding me down, and a rush of superhuman strength surges through me. I tear Seth's wrists away from my neck and collapse into a chair, coughing and sputtering, trying to force air into my lungs. Seth backs away and glances down at his hands like they aren't his own.

"Hiroku," he wails and bursts into tears.

I'm trapped in an oxygen-deprived daze and having trouble speaking. My throat feels like it's been clamped shut with a vise. I have just enough left in me to tell him to piss off. I cross the room to the trailer's bedroom, slam the door behind me, and move the dresser in front of it. He'll have to break a window to get in. I pass out in the bed almost immediately, either from drunkenness or trauma. My last thought before blinking out is that I wish Berlin were here to hold me.

When I wake up the next morning, Seth is gone. Purple and blue marks circle my throat like some ugly pearl choker. I feel like a sad cliché. I still can't talk right and my throat hurts like a bitch.

Jesus, I'm a fucking mess.

I've had enough of Seth's bullshit. I'll sleep in a ditch if I have to. I stuff a backpack with my most critical camera equipment and head outside, but my motorcycle is gone. Seth must have taken it, knowing this would be the last straw. I'd curse him aloud, but my voice is too weak to even say my own name. He's taken my body, my spirit, my voice, and my freedom. Last night he almost took my life.

I walk the two miles into town to Becky's Diner and ask to use their telephone. I dial the number I memorized just in case.

Berlin answers on the second ring.

BERLIN

I DON'T recognize the caller. I almost don't answer it, thinking it might be Trent prank calling me again, but I do, just in case it's Hiro.

"Hello?" I say into the phone.

"Berlin."

The moment I've been praying for the past two months has finally arrived, only Hiro sounds like he's smoked about ten packs of cigarettes. I can barely hear him, his voice is so raspy.

"Hiro." I say his name like a prayer. I'm so happy at the sound of his voice. It's like a shower of pure joy raining down on top of me. "Are you okay?"

Something is wrong, really wrong for him to call me like this, after so much time. It's still early on a Friday morning, which somehow makes it worse.

"I need...." He doesn't finish. Is Seth there with him, preventing him from saying more? There's a lot of noise in the background, like he's in a kitchen. I'm at school, first period, running errands for the office secretary. I duck into an empty classroom in order to hear him better.

"What is it?" I ask. "Anything."

"I need you to come get me," he whispers. He sounds desperate and scared.

"Where are you?"

"You can't...."

"Can't what?" I prompt. It sounds like every word is painful for him.

"You can't tell my mom."

I pause. What if he's hurt and needs to go to the hospital? There are decisions I can't make for him. And his mother loves the hell out of him, no matter what. But I learned my lesson once already, and I don't want to risk losing him again.

"I won't." I'm already jogging down the hallways, on the way to the parking lot where my truck is parked. "Are you safe?"

"For now. I can't talk long and my voice...."

He fades away. I don't want him to spend any more words on me. "Tell me where you are, and I'll be there as soon as I can."

"Allister, Texas. Becky's Diner."

"Allister, Texas. Got it. I missed you...." I hear his wheezy breathing. It sounds like he's having an asthma attack, but I don't think he has asthma. "Are you still there?"

"Yeah, I got to go."

"Stay safe. Call me if you need me."

"I will."

I remember the Petty Crime concert. How he told me if I wanted to go, we had to go right then. How Seth had run after him in the parking lot, screaming like a lunatic. Something bad happened in Allister, Texas. I feel it in my bones.

I check my phone as I climb into my truck. Allister is a six-hour drive.

I'll be there in five.

HIROKU

THE WAITRESS, Denise, is kind to me. I don't have any money, but she gives me hot tea and grits because that's about all I can eat with my throat in the shape it's in. I have a long wait until Berlin gets here. I didn't realize when I called that he was probably at school, and he'll have to cut class to come get me.

I hope whatever hole Seth has crawled into, he'll stay there for the next several hours. I don't want to have to face him.

Denise nods at my neck. "I used to have one of those."

I should have worn a shirt that would hide the bruises a little better. I really don't want Berlin to see my like this, but I need him. I can't do this alone.

"His name was Paul," Denise continues. "Boy, did I think he was the cat's meow. Made me feel like a million bucks, he did. But he got so mean sometimes, especially when he'd been drinking. Liked to take it out on me. Put me in the hospital twice before I finally left him." She shakes her head. "People used to tell me I could do so much better, but I didn't believe them." She looks at me with purpose. "You don't get what you deserve. You get what you think you deserve. Know what I'm saying, sweetheart?"

I nod and sip the tea, trying to keep myself from crying. I don't deserve either of them. Seth because he's a sadistic asshole, Berlin because he's a saint. The two dragons inside me are always battling. One wants darkness and pain; the other wants goodness and light. It's tearing me apart.

Denise pats my hand. "I'm working a double today. I'll wait with you until your friend gets here, okay?"

I nod, scratching at my eyes. "Thank you," I whisper.

I spend the morning reading the newspapers and magazines customers leave behind. Except for school assignments, I haven't read a newspaper in my entire life. It's pretty mundane, but it helps to keep my mind off everything. I didn't get my dose of drugs last night, so by noontime I'm feeling the withdrawal. I pace the parking lot behind the diner, smoking cigarettes, which irritates my throat even more, but I need something to keep myself occupied. My skin is itchy like I have a million mosquito bites. I scratch my arms raw. I try to steady my breathing and think calming thoughts, but it's like a million squawking birds in my head, pecking at my insides.

Around two o'clock, Denise gives me a bowl of tomato soup, which I sip at just to be polite. I feel like I'm going to throw up. I keep glancing at the door when the bell jingles, expecting Berlin at any moment. By three o'clock, I'm worried something has happened to him. Or maybe he wasn't able to get away.

The bell jingles and I glance toward the door again, but it isn't Berlin. It's Seth.

Instead of getting angry and wanting to lash out at him, I get sad and weepy, and even though I hate him and want him to die, I also want him to hold me and apologize and tell me he loves me and that he'll never do that to me again. I also want him to get me high, because my body has turned on me like a hungry dog.

Seth ducks his head when he sees me, clearly ashamed. I swivel back toward the counter. My thoughts can't be trusted. Neither can my words or my actions. *I'm not myself,* I tell myself, but then, when have I ever been? I dig into my seat and hope he'll just walk back out the way he came. He doesn't, though. He sits down next to me at the counter.

"What do you want?" Denise is on him immediately. I haven't told her who did this to me, but she's seen us together before.

"I'll take a coffee, black," he says.

"That's not what I meant," she snarls. She glances over at me. "You want me to get my manager?" I imagine her manager as some superhero with a cape who will use his special abilities to suck out all the pain and agony from my soul and leave me with a bright, shining optimism that makes me think I can tackle anything head-on—addiction, depression, Seth. But no one can do that. Except maybe Berlin.

I shake my head. "It's okay," I whisper. Berlin is two hours late. If he doesn't show up, I at least need my bike. Otherwise, I really am trapped.

"Remember what I said, sweetheart," Denise says to me, then turns to Seth and gives him the evil eye. "I'm watching you." She shuffles away to take someone else's order.

"Hiroku," he says in a voice like silk, with just the right amount of remorse and sadness. He's the only one besides my mother who can make my name sound like a song. But despite his lilting voice, I know there's a knife hidden underneath. I say nothing because speaking is painful and I don't want to give him any more of my pain.

"I can see you're struggling," he says. He must have noticed my hands, which won't stop shaking, the shivers that keep rolling through my body, the sniffling and my red, wild eyes.

"Come home and I'll take care of you," he coos. "You can stay the night, at least. We can talk about it after you feel better."

He wants to get me high in hopes I'll forget all about it. He wants me alone, under his spell, or maybe he wants to kill me. If he can't have me, no one will. The bell jingles and I glance back toward the door, but it's a family of four.

"You expecting someone?" he asks. His clever eyes study me.

"No," I whisper. "Leave some money on the counter."

I stand up and Seth quickly follows suit, dropping a fifty-dollar bill on the counter so there won't be an argument. Denise hustles over to me. "Where do you think you're going?" she asks, hands on her hips. "I thought you had a friend picking you up?"

Seth's head tilts, not missing a beat.

"He's here." I give her a look.

Her eyebrows scrunch together and she nods her head. "You live out there in Joe Vasser's trailer, don'tcha?"

I nod. "Yes, ma'am."

"Well, you take care of yourself, sweetheart." She squeezes my arm and glares at Seth as he ushers me away from her and toward the door.

"Where's my bike?" I ask him when I see the van parked outside.

"We'll pick it up later." He guides me to the passenger side of the van and opens the door. "Let's go home."

I know home isn't with Seth, but I have no place else to go. Seth says he has to stop in town for gas. Then he takes forever getting snacks and whatever else he needs from the convenience store. Meanwhile, my withdrawal is getting worse. I suspect Seth is drawing it out so I'll know just how badly I need him and the drugs. I wouldn't put it past him to make me suffer. Then I wonder if what I'm thinking is real or imagined. Maybe it's only been five minutes and it's the withdrawal that is warping time and making me paranoid and suspicious.

"That took longer than I expected," he says when he's back in the van. I say nothing, just stare out the window. My nose is running, and I can't decide if I'm burning hot or freezing cold. "Almost there," he says, sounding way too excited about it.

Back inside the trailer, Seth takes his time putting away the groceries. I'm only half with it, hunkered down on the couch under a raggedy blanket, but I swear he must be rearranging the cabinets, because he's taking too fucking long. Finally, I can't stand it anymore.

"What the fuck are you waiting for?" I croak.

He glances over at me, a look of mock surprise on his face. "I'm sorry. I didn't realize you were waiting."

"The fuck you didn't," I say viciously. The withdrawal isn't just physical, it's mental and emotional too. I'm my worst self coming off drugs. Maybe that's what Seth wants me to see, the version of myself I hate most. Only then will I believe I deserve him.

"Fuck it," I say and head for the door. He jumps in front of it to block me.

"I got it right here." He pulls a baggie from his pocket. The pills are already crushed into a powder. He could have gotten me high in the diner's bathroom or the front seat of the van. He could have eased my pain, but he chose not to. What an asshole.

"Just have a seat," he coaxes.

"I can't," I whine and circle the tiny trailer like a lion in a cage. He goes over to the counter and starts tapping it out. My circles become smaller until I'm bouncing anxiously on the balls of my feet behind his shoulder. I need it so fucking bad. Just one more hit and I'll be fine. I can quit tomorrow. I just need some right now to get me through.

He cuts up the lines, but instead of letting me go first, he leans over and takes his fill.

I realize then just how selfish he is. It's a moment captured in high-definition, Seth leaned over the counter, taking the first hit while I suffer. Even in this one thing, he can't be generous. Even more than when his fingers were around my throat squeezing the life out of me, in this moment, I truly hate him.

I hear the screech of brakes outside the trailer.

"What was that?" Seth glances around, an alarmed look on his face.

A car door slams. "Hiro?"

It's Berlin. He found me.

Seth shoots me a warning look and puts his finger to his lips. I glance at the lines already laid out before me. Seth moves away from the counter, leaving them wide open to me.

"Hiro?" Berlin calls again, louder this time. The door handle jumps. He's right outside the trailer. I feel his presence and his strength radiating like the sun. He's less than ten feet away, but the drugs are closer and they're calling to me. Just one more hit and then I'll quit forever.

That's the lie I tell myself, but even I don't believe it. I can't have both light and dark, goodness and pain. *You don't get what you deserve, you get what you think you deserve.* The two dragons are circling each other and I have to choose.

"Berlin," I call like it's my last, dying breath.

BERLIN

HIRO CALLS for me from inside the trailer, and I shove my weight against the door. It busts open and I stumble into the dark, dank space. Hiro's leaned against the counter, a blanket wrapped around his shoulders. He looks awful hunched over like that with his nose running and dark raccoon eyes. He looks twitchy too, like he's on something, or maybe coming down from it.

I rush over, and that's when I see the bruises all over his neck. Seth put his hands on him. I'll kill him. That's why he couldn't talk to me on the phone. My blood is boiling, but Hiro is scared and I have to be calm for him.

"Hiro." I pull him to me, wrap him up in my arms, and kiss his hair. I know the right thing would be to take him to the police station so we can put Seth's ass in jail, but I don't want him to run off again. I have to get him the hell out of this shithole and somewhere safe.

"I'm sorry I'm late," I say to him, "but I'm here now. Let's get you home." He sniffles against me, and his body goes limp like he's going to collapse. I grip him tighter.

"You're not taking him anywhere." I glance behind me and see Seth for the first time, holding up an electric guitar like a weapon. The whites of his eyes are huge and his face is twisted up with rage. I could kill him, but my first concern is protecting Hiro. I stand between them.

"You must be Seth," I say.

"You must be the redneck who branded him."

Behind me, Hiro says weakly, "It wasn't him."

"Let's get out of here," I say to Hiro without taking my eyes off Seth. I don't want Hiro using his voice if it's painful and besides, you don't negotiate with terrorists. I glare at Seth, my hands itching to knock him the hell out. If he tries to touch Hiro, I'll destroy him.

"You know it's only going to get worse after this," Seth says, shifting his weight to catch Hiro's eye. I block him. Ten years of football has taught me a thing or two. "Pretty soon you'll be puking. Nosebleeds. Panic attacks. You really want your mother to see you like that?"

Hiro whimpers behind me. Seth knows just what screws to turn to make him cower. I turn slightly so that Hiro knows I'm talking to him. I don't think he's completely with it. "I'm bringing you home with me, Hiro. You can stay in the barn until you feel better. You don't have to see your parents until you're ready."

"It won't be like it was in rehab," Seth continues. "It'll be dirty and disgusting and it'll make you want to die. You really want your beefcake here to see you like that?"

"Ignore him, Hiro. He knows he's losing."

I move sideways toward the door, just a few feet away. Seth jumps into my path and swings the guitar wildly. I snatch it from him and throw it on the ground. I could have clobbered him with it, but I don't want to scare Hiro. I know he's having doubts. If I put Seth in the hospital, Hiro might not leave here with me. Seth turns his crazy eyes on me.

"You know who he ran to when your hillbilly friends branded him? It was me. He loves me, and he always will." He makes another appeal to Hiro. "I made a mistake, Hiroku. I was drunk and high and I didn't know what I was doing, but it'll never happen again, I promise. I love you so much. Please, don't leave me again."

"That's not love," I say to Seth through clenched teeth. "You could have killed him, you sick son of a bitch. Now get the hell out of the way." I reach behind me to make sure Hiro's still with me. He grabs my hand and I squeeze. There's a backpack on the floor I recognize as Hiro's. I sling it over my shoulder, and we scoot sideways out the door.

Outside, I guide Hiro to my truck, with Seth shouting threats the whole way. Hiro is so weak, shivering and hunched over. It scares me to see him like that. I just want to get him out of here. The sooner we can get away, the better.

"All that footage you took of us, Hiroku?" Seth shouts. "Gone. I won't release it to you. You'll never see your bike again. All that camera equipment you left behind, I'll make a bonfire with it."

I boost Hiro into the cab and shut the door behind him. With him secure, I don't worry so much about tangling with Seth. He throws a rock, and it hits me in the thigh. I walk over and stick him good in the gut. He doubles over, gasping, and grips his stomach. I want to hit him again, maybe break his nose, but I know Hiro is watching. I don't want to be the bad guy or stress Hiro out anymore.

It'll take Seth a few minutes to recover anyway, enough time for us to get the hell out of here.

"What about your bike?" I ask as soon as I'm in the truck.

He shakes his head and hides his face in his hands. "Just go, Berlin." My heart breaks for him. The guilt weighs on me too. If I'd protected him from Trent and the others, he would have never run away from home.

We get a couple of miles out of town. He's shivering so bad his teeth are chattering. I pull over and get a couple of flannels from the back of my truck, since the blanket he had in the trailer got lost in the scuffle. I also give him a work rag for his runny nose and some sunglasses because he keeps squinting like the light is painful. My truck doesn't have air-conditioning, so we drive with the windows down. One minute he's sweating. The next he's wrapped up in the flannels.

"Do you need a doctor?" I don't know what's normal in this situation, but he seems to be in a hell of a lot of pain and discomfort.

"No, I'll be fine."

"Try to get some sleep." I pat the bench seat, and he curls up with the flannels and lays his head against my thigh. We don't talk much. He's only partially present, and I know his throat is hurting. In my mind, he's the football and my barn is ten yards downfield. I just have to get him there, and I'll figure out the rest later.

We come up on a gas station, and I ask him if Gatorade and cough syrup might help. He nods pitifully, so I run inside to get him some medicine along with tissues and whatever else I think will help him along.

When I come back outside, he's doubled over in the parking lot, puking and clutching his throat. Judging from the bruises on his neck, I bet it's agonizing. I set the stuff in my truck and rush over to him.

"I'm a fucking mess," he wails, wiping his mouth with the back of his hand. I hug him to me, attracting the attention of everyone in the parking lot and probably those inside the gas station as well. "It's going to get worse than this, Berlin," he moans. "I'm going to say shit I don't mean, just to be nasty. It's not me, though, okay? You have to know that."

"It'll pass," I whisper, patting his head to calm him down. "Be brave now. I know you can do it."

I lead him back to the truck, set him up with a bottle of Gatorade and some cough syrup. He curls into a ball, then shivers and moans until he falls into a fitful, restless sleep.

HIROKU

THE DRUGS aren't going to leave my system without a fight. They have to punish every bit of me on their way out. *You're going to miss me, motherfucker.*

I'm some primitive version of myself, twisting and writhing in my own primordial goo, emptying my guts and bowels with irregularity, the absolute worst and grossest version of myself. God, how I hate Berlin seeing me like this.

"Get out," I say to him in between dry heaves over the toilet. We're in the barn, day two. He stands at the sink, glancing from me to the door, unsure of what to do. "Get the fuck out," I yell as loud as I can, which isn't very loud because my throat is wrecked from all the vomiting and sneezing.

He leaves the barn, and I wash my mouth out and stumble back toward the window to search for him outside. I start to panic he isn't coming back, then see him crossing the yard with a basket in his arms. Once he's upstairs, I see he has all kinds of tea. "For your throat," he says like an apology, which makes me feel even shittier about the way I'm treating him.

I collapse in the bed and squirm in the sheets, trying to get comfortable while Berlin heats up a teakettle. Every nerve in my body is raw and throbbing. The slightest noise sounds like a jet plane. The littlest discomfort is the worst kind of pain. It's like a flu from hell, and all I can think about is getting high, just to end this suffering. One hit is all it will take. I'd give anything to get rid of this sickness.

Berlin makes tea and I drink some of it, feeling resentful and pissy and ungrateful. "You should have left me there," I say. "You shouldn't have brought me back here."

I want him to argue with me, maybe even hit me. It's the drugs, partly, and also because I need to be punished.

"He would have killed you, Hiro. You were right to call me. That guy is bad news."

"I'm bad news," I shout, ripping my throat to shreds.

Berlin shakes his head slowly. His eyes crinkle with kindness. I hate myself even more.

"You're not bad news," he says softly. "You're the best news I've had in a long time."

I tear my eyes away from him. He must be blind. Doesn't he see the ruin of a person that sits before him? What does he even see in me at all? There's nothing here worth saving. "I'm a junkie and a dropout. I'm a fucking loser, Berlin."

He pulls me to him and strokes my back. My tremors subside for the moment. My erratic breath follows his rhythm. I get snot all over his T-shirt and cough into his chest. Pathetic.

"Take it one day at a time," he says. "Just focus right now on getting better, okay?"

I nod miserably and start crying. He rocks me slowly like my mom used to. I don't even have to hold on. He does all the work.

"Everything hurts," I moan. I want to die.

"I know it does," he says soothingly. "You want to try a bath?" I shrug, unable to make even the most basic decisions. He leaves and comes back a few minutes later to tell me the water is ready. He helps me cross the room. My whole body starts quaking. I can't remember the last time I showered. I'm fucking disgusting.

"Do you need help?" he asks. I forget why I'm there and glance around the bathroom, disoriented.

"I don't know," I say testily. He gently helps me remove my shirt and pants. I sit on the toilet while he pulls my jeans the rest of the way. He peels off my stinky socks. Then he helps me climb into the bath. My body's so weak, absolutely wrecked.

His eyes keep darting to the brand, and I don't do anything to hide it. I've given myself over to him completely. My wasted body is in his hands.

"Is the temperature okay?" he asks.

"I don't know," I say again. My internal thermometer is broken, but the water is soothing. I lie back into it and close my eyes. I must have fallen asleep, because Berlin is pulling me up out of the water by my shoulders. He places a pillow behind my head, right there on the back of the bathtub, and I go under.

When I wake up, I'm in bed, wearing one of his T-shirts and boxer shorts. They're big on me. I'm practically swimming in them. It's nighttime and I'm alone. My heart races with panic. He left me by myself. I start freaking out.

"I'm right here," he says quietly. He's lying on his back on the other side of the bed. He rolls over onto his side to face me, opens his arms, and I scoot closer so he can hold me. I breathe in his scent. I must be getting better. I can smell again.

"Don't go," I beg. I can't do this without him.

"I won't."

BERLIN

THE FIRST couple of days are the worst, because Hiro is so sick, and I worry my nursing skills aren't up to snuff. If I ever doubted that drugs are poison, watching Hiro come off them proves it to me. Seeing him suffer like that makes me wish I could take all his pain and discomfort and make it my own.

I picked him up on a Friday. By Tuesday he's acting more like himself, starting to eat again and move around without cringing in pain. The look in his eyes concerns me, though. The lights are out. I don't know if it's coming off drugs or if it's waking up from his stupor to find himself in my barn. I know it wasn't a mistake to bring him here, but maybe he thinks it was.

"What day is it?" he asks. I've made scrambled eggs and toast for him, but he only ever eats half of what I give him, so I usually end up eating the rest. He's lost a lot of weight, especially in the past few days. I'm trying to fatten him up a bit.

"Tuesday."

He counts on his fingers, then glances up at me. "Don't you have school?"

"I'm taking the week off."

"For me?" His head jerks back like he's shocked. He's worth a few missed days of school. He needs me and I want to be here for him. Maybe, too, in my selfishness, I think this could somehow make up for letting him down before.

"It's no big deal," I say. "I'm not too sore about missing school either. It's kind of a bonus."

"Is your dad okay with it?" he asks, a worried look in his eyes.

"He came around." He wasn't on board at first, but I rarely stick my heels in on something. My dad knows it's a fight he's going to lose.

"Has school been bad?" Hiro asks and winces like he knows exactly how bad it's been. I shrug. I don't want to turn this into a pity party. "Are you off the team?"

I nod. "Yeah, I quit."

"I'm sorry." His head slumps forward and his shoulders cave. The last thing I want is for him to feel bad for me. I angle the wooden chair toward him and grab his hands.

"I'm sorry, Hiro. I had the chance to come out to Trent and I didn't. You tried to tell me and I didn't listen. I should have been there to protect you and I wasn't."

He glances away. I can see him going off into the other place he goes whenever the subject at hand becomes too painful.

"I don't want to talk about that," he says quietly and rubs at his chest. I don't think he even knows he's doing it. I swallow. I got a long, hard look at his scar when he fell asleep in the tub the other day. I let that happen.

"I'm glad you're here," I say, tracing his long, slender fingers. "You shouldn't be sorry for my sake. I came out to my dad, school, and my church. I'm not hiding it anymore. You helped me do that."

He smiles, or at least he tries to. I don't think he has it in him just yet.

"I should call my mom," he says. I pull out my phone and hand it to him, grateful that I won't have to stress about it anymore. I've wanted to call her a thousand times, just to tell her he's with me and he's safe, but I didn't want to risk breaking his trust again.

"You mind if I talk to her alone for a few minutes?" he says.

"I'll run up to the store. Want anything?" He shakes his head. I'm worried he's not eating enough, so I ask again, "You sure?"

"Yeah, I'm good."

I drive out to the Pac N Sac and come back with a few bags of groceries. I don't really know what vegetarians eat on a day-to-day basis, other than not meat. I figure beans are a good choice, and peanut butter. Maybe I can get him to make me a list next time. When I get back, Hiro is downstairs in the barn, petting Sheila's nose and talking softly to her. My heart jumps at the sight of him. He glances over at me.

"Sorry to interrupt," I say.

"It's okay. I was waiting for you. Let me help."

I leave the lightest bag for him, and he follows me upstairs. I put the groceries away while he stands in the middle of the room, looking nervous and flighty.

"What's up?" I ask. I pull out two jars of peanut butter. I didn't know if he likes smooth or crunchy, so I got one of each.

"My dad's not happy with me." He scratches at his arms. "I don't think I can go home."

"You don't have to."

He looks at me like I'm being ridiculous. "I can't stay here."

"Of course you can." I never intended for him to leave.

"Your dad—"

"He doesn't mind."

"I can't keep mooching off you, Berlin. You've done more than enough already."

I set down the jar in my hand and join him in the middle of the room. He doesn't always believe what I tell him, but he understands me in other ways. I pull him toward me.

"I don't want you to go. It makes me feel better to know you're here. Safe."

He pulls away and goes over to the window, looks out onto the yard with his hands on his hips. He's too skinny, all angles and jutting bones.

"Talk to me," I say after a spell. I know he's cooking up something. His mind runs a mile a minute.

"I can't stay here without offering you some form of payment," he says at last.

I swallow tightly and remember our first encounter in my truck, the offer he made in exchange for protection. I don't think that's what he means now, but I can't be sure. I also don't want to ask.

"You don't owe me anything," I say cautiously.

"Then I can't stay." He drops his arms and turns like he's going to walk out on me again. I start to panic, wracking my brain for an alternative.

"You can help with the horses." If he needs to feel useful, there's always work to be done around the farm. Our horses never get enough exercise. Some of them are out of shape and out of practice. "I can train you up this week. You can start whenever you're ready."

He glances over his shoulder, knobby underneath the shirt I gave him. He needs some clothes that fit him properly. It'll help him to feel more like himself. Maybe we can stop by his house and pick up some of his clothes.

He nods, but his eyes still look distant and sad.

Evening's coming on, and I realize that other than going out to get more food, I haven't left his side since I picked him up in Allister five days ago. Maybe he needs some time alone. I don't want him to get sick of me or overstay my welcome. "You want me to go?" I ask. "This is your place now."

"No," he says quietly, like it pains him to say it. "Stay."

He shuffles over and I wrap my arms around him. He leans his cheek against my shoulder. "Thank you," he says softly. "For everything."

I hold him closer. "We make a good team." And then, because it's all I can think about, "Just don't run off on me again, okay?"

He nods. "I promise I won't."

HIROKU

COUNTRY LIVING suits me. I like the regularity of chores, and the horses give me plenty to do while Berlin's at school. Over the next couple of weeks, I take all the horses out in turn, exploring more of the property as I gain confidence in my riding. Each one has a different personality and quirks, different preferences for how they're handled and what treats they like best. They were unsure of me at first—after all, no one can compare to Berlin—but I remember what they like and I pay attention to how they're feeling, so they're coming around. They're all special to me, but Sheila is still my favorite. I like her spirit and her spunk.

I get to know Berlin's dad as well. He's a man of few words but a kind heart, like his son. The first week, Mr. Webber eyes me from a distance, kind of like he did the first time we met. By the second week, he's offering suggestions on how to save myself time and energy mucking out the stalls. He gives me a retractable blade for opening hay bales and shows me how to shovel horse manure using the muscles in my legs instead of my back.

"You're young now, but you'll feel it after ten, twenty years. Best to learn good habits from the start," he says.

Like Berlin, when his father talks, it's in longevity. I wonder what it must be like to be born, live, and die on the same plot of land, to know you'll always have a place to belong. I find comfort in it, especially on land as beautiful as this. It must have been so hard for Berlin to come out in this community, knowing that relationships might forever be severed. It's not like he can pick up and move, not without losing a huge piece of his identity.

"Did you always want to be a rancher?" I ask Mr. Webber one afternoon.

"For a spell I wanted to be a ball player. I played for a year in the minor leagues, but I missed the farm too much. My dad was getting on in years and my sister wasn't cut out for ranching—she's a city girl—so it worked out that I came back and took over. Haven't wanted to leave since then. Well, except recently."

"Why's that?" I ask. We've developed an easy rapport. He doesn't offer much in the way of starting conversation, but he doesn't seem to mind answering my questions. He probably gets lonely being out here by himself all day long.

"Berlin's had a hard time of it lately," he says, not looking my way. "I don't think he has any friends left at that school. Didn't want to leave the ranch much. Wasn't sleeping or eating either. I was pretty worried about him."

I turn away, feeling guilty that I left him in his time of need. He's had to suffer alone through the torment of the bigot brigade.

"He's better now," Mr. Webber says, perhaps sensing my troubled thoughts. "He cares a lot for you, Hiro. Kind of reminds me of...." He drifts off. "Well, never mind."

I don't ask who he's thinking of, but I sense it might be Berlin's mother.

"That was a tough lesson for me," he says after a minute. "As a parent, you want to give your kid all the tools they need to survive in this world. But there's some things I can't teach him."

We hear Berlin's truck approaching then. I see him through the windshield, smiling, one arm resting on the open window.

"I think you've done a pretty good job, Mr. Webber."

He adjusts his hat, kind of nods without openly acknowledging the compliment. His modesty reminds me of Berlin. "Remember what I told you about using your legs." He starts to walk away, waving at Berlin as he goes. "Your back will thank you."

BERLIN SPENDS the nights with me out in the barn. Mr. Webber doesn't seem to mind. At least, I don't pick up on it. At first it's very innocent between Berlin and I, fully clothed cuddling, but as the days pass, our fervor for each other grows, and it seems inevitable where we're headed. Berlin doesn't go there, though. Maybe he's waiting for me to make the first move.

One night after we've messed around, I'm laid out beside him with my arms spread, my body still humming with pleasure, when he turns and props himself up on his elbow. I shield my scar out of habit. I catch him looking at it sometimes and I know he feels bad about it, which makes me feel bad. It's like a never-ending cycle of sadness and guilt between us.

"What is it?" I ask. He's staring at me with a thoughtful expression.

"I have some questions." His face darkens in the moonlight. He's blushing.

"Questions?" I prompt.

He ducks his head into the corner of his elbow. "About sex."

I roll over to face him, my posture mimicking his own. "Okay. Shoot."

"Most of what I know comes from what I've read or seen online."

I figured as much, which makes me feel like I have a responsibility to him. It's much easier to learn by doing than by watching or reading about it.

"So, there's different... positions," he says shyly.

"Tops and bottoms," I say. "And some guys do both."

"Right. So, are you...? I mean, I don't want to make you uncomfortable...."

It seems to me that Berlin is the one who's uncomfortable, but I cut him some slack. I want him to feel secure about the prospect of anal sex. The unknown can be scary. "I mainly bottomed with Seth, but I did try topping a few times. I prefer to bottom, I think."

He scratches at the back of his neck, and I admire his muscles. I drift off in a daydream about what it might be like to share that with him. Would it be rough or tender? Wild or controlled? Any which way, I know it'd be good. Berlin is generous and he's a good listener in more ways than one, and even though he's big, he's careful to not use his body to intimidate others, something I really like about him.

"I'm not sure what I am," he says sheepishly and hides his face in the crook of his elbow. I have a hunch on his preference, but I'm not going to state it for him.

I sit up in the bed. I'm usually pretty casual when I talk about sex, but Berlin is kind of a romantic, and he's clearly shy about it. I don't want to sound condescending or unfeeling, so I choose my words carefully. "Do you ever think about having sex with me?"

He nods, avoiding my eyes. I smile a little at his bashfulness. I think about having sex with him the majority of my waking hours and some of my slumbering ones as well.

"So, when you're thinking about it, what's it like? Are you penetrating me or are you being penetrated?"

He looks embarrassed, straining his neck so that the muscles in his shoulders bunch up. "The first one," he says softly.

"Then you're probably a top, not that you have to label yourself that way or stick to one role. You can always try new things."

He sighs with relief. Then his eyes cloud over again. "I have another question."

I bite back a smile and nod. "I'm all ears."

"Were you and Seth... were you guys safe?"

Berlin is a careful guy. The fact that we haven't already had sex shows just how much self-control he has, because in the moment, if he asked me, I wouldn't refuse him. It's something I really admire about him. I'm impulsive and reckless, so I appreciate his caution.

"Yeah, we were safe. He's kind of a slut, so I was strict about that. But I can get tested if it'll make you feel better."

He nods. "I think it would."

He seems to be struggling with something else. I know better than to rush him. Berlin needs time to work up to whatever he's trying to say, so I sit there quietly, until finally his pretty blue eyes meet mine.

"I want you to be my first," he says, and then with less confidence, "if you want that too."

I smile. Inside my chest, my miniscule heart expands. Of course I want him. It's simple chemistry, but Berlin is special and worthy of someone who can love him with the same ardor and commitment. I know from experience how attached you can get to your first. I've only been clean for a few weeks. I worry that when temptation presents itself again, I'll cave, leaving Berlin in my wake of destruction, just like my parents. I don't want to do that to him, and the closer we become, the more I fear I will.

"I do want that, Berlin, but I don't think I'm ready." I don't go into all my doubts and insecurities, just leave it at that.

"I understand," he says. His brow furrows. I don't want him to take it personally or think it's a reflection of my feelings for him.

"It's not you." Our relationship is so much simpler and more honest than what I had with Seth—no mind games or power struggles, no wondering at any given moment where I stand. "I trust you. It's me I don't trust yet."

He glances up at me, his eyes full of compassion and kindness. "I trust you," he says and opens his arms to me. I nestle down beside him, and he nuzzles the back of my neck. He falls asleep almost immediately while I lie awake, wrestling with my own doubts, which have nothing to do with sex or Berlin and everything to do with my addiction.

The more I reflect on all the mistakes I've made, and then made again, the more it becomes clear to me that I have something to prove, which is that I can make it on my own. At present I have Berlin's constant care and affection, and I'm cut off from any source of temptation, which keeps me from sinking back into my old ways. But what happens when I don't have Berlin?

After that night I make a plan. Over the next few weeks, I save up all the money I earn from taking care of the horses, and I ask my mom for a loan to cover the rest. She and I go into Austin one morning and find an apartment. I apply for jobs online with an old laptop Berlin let me borrow. There isn't much out there for a seventeen-year-old high school dropout, and I want to stay away from working at a restaurant or bar, because I know from experience there are a lot of drugs in those environments.

I should have told Berlin straightaway what I was planning, but I didn't want him to try to talk me out of it, because I knew he'd probably succeed. I want to move past living one day at a time and start planning a future for myself, and maybe even for the both of us. I have to prove I'm someone worthy of his affection.

Still, Berlin always knows when I'm hiding something from him. He doesn't pressure me, though, just asks me from time to time what's on my mind. The more I hide it from him, the more it feels like lying. There's no easy way to put it, but I can't keep it from him any longer. It's eating me up inside and probably stressing him out as well.

One night as we're cleaning up after dinner, I just come out with it.

"I'm moving to Austin."

He takes a step back like I've shot him in the chest and sets down the towel he was drying his hands on.

"You're not happy here?" he asks.

"That's not it at all. I love being here with you and your dad, working with the horses, but I need to prove I can be independent."

"You don't need to prove anything to me."

"I need to prove it to myself, then. I have to be able to say no, when the time comes, and as much as I love it here, there's no way I can know if I'm over my addiction or not." If I'm not, I need to self-destruct without Berlin there to witness it. I swear I'll never put him through that hell again.

"But you'll be safe here," Berlin says, and my heart just about breaks.

"You and your dad have been so generous to me. If you hadn't come to get me…." I don't like to think about my sorry shape when Berlin found me, the desperation of my situation with Seth, and the shame I've felt since then.

"We don't have to talk about that," Berlin says, being way too generous, again. I will never be able to repay him for his kindness, and even though I know he wants me to stay, for all his good intentions, I can't be a real partner to him until I know I can stand on my own two feet.

"I want to be someone worthy of someone like you," I tell him.

"You already are, Hiro," he says with more empathy than I deserve.

"Well, I need to show you, through my actions."

He sighs like an ornery bull and says in a heavy voice, "Sounds like you've already made up your mind."

I nod. The look on his face is so sad it makes me have second thoughts. I could still cancel my apartment, even though I'd lose my deposit.

"How long have you been thinking about this?" he asks.

I shrug. "A while."

"Why didn't you tell me before?" He winces like he's in pain. I wonder if it's my secrecy that bothers him more than the fact I'm leaving.

"I didn't want you to talk me out of it."

He nods. "Oh."

I can tell he's hurt, and I resist the urge to say more. I want to give him the time and space he needs to process it.

"Can I visit you?" he asks, his voice thick with emotion.

"Of course. I want you to. I can come back here too."

His knuckles grind into the wood countertop. I've dropped a bomb on him, and he doesn't know how to respond.

"Are you mad at me?" I ask.

He shakes his head and drags one hand through his golden hair. "I'm not mad. I'm just afraid you're going to disappear again. Not knowing where you were or if you were okay, that was hard."

The way his dad described him in my absence, it sounded like he was depressed. I figured it was because of the abuse he was getting at school, but maybe part of it was me leaving as well.

"It won't be like that, Berlin. We can talk or text whenever we want. And after I've had some time to get settled, we can visit each other. It's only a half-hour drive."

He nods, but I don't think he believes me. "Okay," he says. "If that's what you need. I sure am going to miss you, though."

I come over and hug him. He's just so sad. I want to give him everything that night to show him how much I care for him, but I don't want to make it harder for him after I leave. And I don't want our physical closeness to detract from my plan.

Instead, we hold each other like we're each clinging to a life raft.

BERLIN

I DON'T like the fact that Hiro's leaving. Not one bit. I just got him back, and I'm not sure he's strong enough yet to be on his own. But I understand his need to be independent, and I respect him for it.

I think long and hard about what I can do to contribute to his cause. It happens to be what might make me feel better about the whole thing too. So the day before he's set to leave, I bring him down to the stable, make him close his eyes. I made a trade with a neighbor, a piece of machinery for an old Yamaha motorcycle. It isn't as nice as his tricked-out Ninja—I didn't know where to find Seth, and truthfully, I didn't want to tangle with him again—but it's in proper working order, if a little battle-scarred.

"Open your eyes," I say.

I should have taken a picture of his face. I've never seen Hiro show so much emotion before—confusion, surprise, excitement, maybe even some doubt.

"Berlin," he says softly.

"What do you think?"

"I can't accept this. It's too much."

"Would it make you feel better if I told you I didn't have to pay for it?"

He tilts his head and smiles. "A little better."

I squeeze his shoulders. "This way you can get around town, maybe even make it out into the suburbs for a visit."

He throws his arms around me, squeezes tightly. "Thank you," he says and then, almost too quiet to hear, "I don't deserve you." I wonder if he truly believes that.

"Yes, you do."

We spend the rest of the day down by the creek, just throwing pebbles into the water and talking. He's heading out tomorrow morning. I wish I could slow time and live in this day forever. It feels like a gift from God, sharing this with the person I adore most.

"You haven't been going to church," he says. "Unless you've been sneaking out before the sun rises."

I clear my throat. I hope he doesn't think my poor church attendance means I've stopped believing in God. Prayers are all I've had to keep me sane these past few months. Prayers and chores, which for me go together hand in hand. I prayed long and hard on Hiro too. When he called me, those prayers were answered.

"Pastor Craig and I had a difference of opinion," I tell him. Ever since coming out, I haven't felt comfortable in church. There's too much judgment and not enough compassion and understanding. "I feel like some of the things he's preaching aren't being acted upon by the congregation." I'm bitter too that Pastor Craig hasn't done anything to address the violence committed against Hiro by some of his own members. I don't mention that to Hiro, though. I don't want him to think I'm spreading his business around town.

"Do you miss it?" he asks me.

"I miss the sense of community. I miss that about football too—working together as a team, but I'm making new friends at school. Spencer, for one."

Hiro nods and says with a smile, "Are you leaving me for a ginger, Berlin?"

I chuckle, and then, more earnestly, "I'd never leave you."

He ducks his head and smiles, chucks a rock into the water. I want to memorize his face, happy and content, for when I'm feeling lonely in the days and weeks to come.

"How's school been?" he asks. He seems to be bracing himself for the answer.

"Not great."

"Trent," he says. Just saying the name sounds painful for him.

"I didn't realize how bad it was on the other side. I'm sorry for that. I should have been on your side from day one."

"I put you in a difficult position," he says, giving me way too much leeway.

"I put myself there."

He shrugs. "At least you don't have to hide it anymore."

I feel the guilt rising up inside me, a lead balloon that's always there. "I wish I'd done something different. That night or before. I wish it was me they'd come after." I grind my knuckles into the dirt. I know he doesn't want to talk about it, but it feels like, by not talking about it, it's taking up more space than it ought to.

He rubs at his chest like it's sore. It's become a habit of his, one I notice every time.

"Let's not blame ourselves. We were both victims. Trent is the bad guy here, and the culture of homophobia at Lowry High School. It almost destroyed us once. Let's agree to not let that happen again. Deal?"

"Deal."

We ride back on the horses and put them to bed, then spend the rest of the evening upstairs tangled up in each other. The smell and feel and taste of him. There's never enough time, and I feel desperate toward the end, trying not to fall asleep. I'm so worried I'll never see him again. But there's nothing I can do to stop him. His mind is made up.

Hiro leaves the next morning, wearing his signature black, with nothing but his camera equipment in his saddlebags and the clothes on his back. Right before he puts on his helmet, he glances my way and smiles, gives me a thumbs-up. He rides out of my life the same way he rode in. A beautiful storm.

SPENDING ALL that time with Hiro renewed my sense of purpose. Even if I can't get justice for what Trent did to him, I'm not powerless. The Monday after winter break, I ask Mrs. Potts for a meeting with her and the principal.

"Regarding?" she asks.

"Coach Cross," I say somberly. She nods, looking a little fearful. I think she might ask me to come back another time, but she makes a call to the principal, Mr. Jeffries, and he comes in shortly after. The three of us settle in around her desk.

"I'd like to record this," I tell them. I only want to have to say this once. They agree, so I lay my phone on the desk and push Record. Then I tell them everything, beginning with the beatings Trent endured as a kid, the way Coach Cross runs the football team, some of the things he's said to us during practice and games, threats he's made. I tell them about the bullying Trent has doled out over the years. I don't name his victims, but I give them enough detail for them to get a full picture of what's been going on. Then I come to what happened with Hiro, beginning in basketball, the fighting and the cruel pranks, and then how they attacked him.

I get a little teary at that point and have to take a breather. Before Hiro left I told him my intentions, and he let me take a picture of his chest. Mrs. Potts and Principal Jeffries look pretty horrified when I show them. I tell them what Coach Cross said to me about not allowing faggots on the football team. And some of the pranks and vandalism that have happened to me since coming out. I don't need to tell them the shit storm they'll be in if this information gets out. I can tell from their expressions they already know.

"Thank you, Berlin," Mr. Jeffries says when I've finished. "I know it wasn't easy for you to come to us with this. I'm sorry for all that you and Hiroku have endured. I didn't realize…." He trails off. "In any case, we take this matter very seriously. I hope you know that. And please tell your father he's welcome to contact me at anytime."

I pick up my phone and stick it in my pocket. I shake their hands. I don't feel the need to ask them what they're going to do about it. I'll give them time to confer, and if nothing changes, I have this recording. I'll take it to the higher-ups. There's always someone farther up on the food chain.

In the weeks following my statement, there are a lot of changes around Lowry High. Coach Cross is suspended immediately, investigation pending. The rest of the coaches are interviewed about their roles. The tension between me and the football team escalates as well, with them blaming me for the loss of their leader. Strangely, though, Trent doesn't retaliate. It makes me nervous, like maybe he's plotting something big. I'm on my guard all the time, trying to anticipate the next attack.

One afternoon in early February, I'm out in the barn shoveling hay when I spy Trent there in the doorway. I didn't hear his truck come in, which means he must have parked it down the road. I grip the pitchfork, intending to use it as a weapon if needed, but all Trent holds is a near-empty bottle of whiskey. It isn't close to dinnertime, and he's already drunk as a skunk.

"Berlin Webber," he says, kind of slurring my name. He shuffles into the barn, stumbling a bit. I can't believe he drove over here drunk as he is. Luckily the roads that lead to our ranch are wide and empty.

I stab my pitchfork into the ground and wipe the sweat from my brow. A couple of months ago I'd have welcomed the opportunity to beat his ass, but at present I'm not looking for a fight.

He comes in closer. He smells as bad as he looks, which is more than just drunk—ill and a little crazy.

"You the one causing all this trouble?" he asks and digs one finger into my chest. I shove his hand away. Strangely, he doesn't seem as angry as I expected.

"Don't start what you can't finish," I say to him, a throwback to old times when he used to pick fights with me, then end up having to beg for mercy.

"You always were a cocky son of a bitch." He wipes at his mouth and sways a little on his feet. With one good shove, I could send him sprawling. He's sweating more than what seems normal. I can't tell what's going on inside his head, because it isn't rage behind his dark brown eyes, but something else. I square off with him. If he wants to come at me, I'll be ready.

He raises one arm, but instead of punching me, he grips the back of my neck and yanks me in toward him, kissing me full on the mouth. He tastes like the bottom of a bottle. I stumble backward and trip over the pitchfork, landing on my backside in a pile of cold horse shit. My mind is spinning. Trent just had his tongue in my mouth. It's like waking up one day to find the sky underneath you.

"I thought you were a faggot," he says. Now he sounds angry.

"So what?" Does he think me being gay automatically means I'm available?

"So." He kicks at the pitchfork and turns away. I stand up and wipe my hands on my jeans. Hiro was right about him all along. But what's changed for Trent? Why now?

"My dad's going to kill me when he finds out," he says. "Especially now."

I glance over at him. I don't know what to say. I'm not in a position to counsel Trent on how to come out to his father. Honestly, it seems like a bad idea to me too.

"You don't have to tell him."

He grips his head with both hands and tears at his short hair. "You know how hard it is to hide it?"

I sigh, recalling all those times Hiro passed by me at school and I had to ignore him. "Yeah, I do."

He crosses his arms over his chest, sticks his hands in his armpits. He looks like a little kid trying not to fuss. "You never looked at me that way. The way you look at him."

I suppose he means Hiro. He sounds almost… jealous. Was part of his retaliation motivated by envy? That doesn't make it any better. If anything, it's worse that he knew exactly what I was going through. I know forgiveness is a virtue, but I'll never forgive Trent for what he did to Hiro. Never in a million years. At the same time, I know what it's like to struggle alone. I never hated myself for being gay, but I think Trent does, and has for a while.

"Being gay isn't a sin."

"The hell it isn't." He knocks the bottle against his head, and the liquor splashes against the sides. "I can't do this anymore," he moans.

I don't know what he's talking about—being gay or hiding it? "You can't keep hating yourself for something you can't control. Your dad is the sinner here. He's a bully and a meanass man. You don't need his approval or his respect, and no matter how hard you try, you probably won't get it anyway. All you can do is be the best person you can. Being gay, it is what it is."

He rubs his arms and glances over at me with a forlorn look in his eyes. "You probably hate me, don't you?"

I hate him for what he did to Hiro, and the fact that he got away with it, but in this moment, I mainly feel sorry for him. "I feel bad for you, Trent. I know what a struggle it is. It won't always be like this, though. In a couple years, you'll be out on your own. And then, fuck your dad. In the meantime, don't be such a fucking asshole to everyone else, because it's not their fault."

He nods, keeping a stiff upper lip. "You going to tell anyone about this, Webber?"

"I wouldn't do that."

I realize I'm probably the first person he's come out to. It makes me feel guilty. Maybe if we'd both been honest, we could have helped each other along. I get the sense he wants to say more, but he doesn't. He turns to go, and I call out to him, "You want a ride home?" He's still a long way from being sober.

"Getting a ride from a faggot is probably riskier than drunk driving," he says. I shake my head. There are about a hundred nicer ways for him to say it.

"Take care of yourself, Trent."

"Yup." He raises his bottle of whiskey in a good-bye salute.

I go back to mucking the stalls, reflecting on Trent and our friendship over the years, and how sometimes the bravest thing you can do is be honest with yourself about who you are and who you love.

HIROKU

I GET lucky in Austin. I scour the web for wedding videographers until I find one who needs an assistant. I also introduce myself to the editors of the *Beat*, Austin's major music media outfit. I send their photo editor, Emilio Vasquez, a link to my portfolio. A lot of my pictures are of Petty Crime, but I assure him I can cover most any band. He puts me to work right away.

I don't have a good flash anymore—I left mine with Seth in Allister—so I spend my last couple hundred bucks buying one online. It comes in the day before I'm scheduled to shoot, which doesn't give me much time to practice, but I make the most of it.

"These are incredible," Emilio tells me via chat when I send him a link to the photos from my first assignment, a band called Little Sinister playing out in Austin that weekend. I shot them in a graveyard at night. The band was all about it and even contributed their own props, like a shredded umbrella and goth-looking canes and top hats. I added some aftereffects: fog and a filter that made it look like a scene from a silent movie, kind of dirtied it up as well. After that, Emilio gives me a regular gig of photographing the bands that are coming to town. A lot of them like my work and say they'll hire me to do their promo stuff. Within a few weeks of being back in Austin, I'm already making a name for myself.

Between freelancing for the *Beat* and filming and editing wedding footage, I'm earning enough cash to keep me in ramen and peanut butter sandwiches. I talk to my mom almost every day and even get a few words in with my dad. Mai is back in my life and happy for me that I'm doing so well. Berlin and I text throughout the day and FaceTime at night. I know he's anxious to visit, but I still feel like I'm not ready, like I need some kind of proof that I can really do this whole adulting thing on my own.

The next week Emilio makes me an offer.

"Seth Barrett from Petty Crime wants to give us an exclusive interview," he says. I can hear the excitement in Emilio's voice. Petty Crime is the next big thing. They just launched their sophomore album, *China Doll*, the one they recorded in Allister. The song the album is named after is getting played around the country. It's the one I helped Seth write, the one that's supposedly about me.

I argued with Seth about the whole Chinese-Japanese thing, and he told me Japan Doll just doesn't roll off the tongue in the same way. There's a video for it, too, but it's cheesy as hell and feels totally fake. It isn't set in the desert like I wanted, but in some seedy train yard like a bad Bon Jovi video. The guy they found to play me looks Korean. And he isn't nearly as pretty as me, but whatever.

"What an opportunity," I say to Emilio. I already know what comes next.

"Seth requested you specifically. I figured from your portfolio you all must have worked together before. He wants you to do the written piece, too, in addition to the photos. I told him that wasn't your bag, but he was kind of pushy about it. If you get the questions answered, I can pretty it up later. You cool with that?"

Seth must have scoured the web for my name and seen it pop up in a photo credit on the *Beat*. I lie back on my bed and rub at my scar. There's no limit to Seth's insanity and no easy way to escape him. I could refuse Emilio, but if I want to live and work in Austin in this industry, our paths are bound to cross. And maybe this is the test I need to prove I'm over him.

"Hiroku? You still there?"

"Yeah, I'm here." I sit up. "Where does he want to do the interview?"

"At his apartment in Red River. I can text you the address."

"Don't worry about it. I know it already."

We end the call, and I think back to the first time I ever saw Seth, out on the basketball courts with his ripped-up jeans and floppy hair, hard, lean muscles, and sly grin. Even then I knew he was trouble. I was fourteen and just starting to entertain the idea of being with another guy. The first time Seth looked at me with his bedroom eyes and spoke to me in that silken voice, I practically came in my pants right then.

I think about the last time I saw him, through a fog of withdrawal, the crazy look in his eyes and the way he swung that guitar like he was going to bash Berlin's skull in. And me, a hopeless, helpless wretch. It makes me so sad to think about where we started out and where we ended up.

Taking someone as backup feels like cheating. I have to face Seth on my own. I'll treat this like any other job. I pull out my phone and jot down a few interview questions. If I stick to the script, what can possibly go wrong?

I WEAR professional clothes instead of my usual jeans and T-shirt. I have this crazy idea that if Seth sees me as a serious journalist type, he might not try any shenanigans. Wishful thinking.

"Hiroku." He says my name in one long, musical sigh, like he's in the throes of passion. He's shirtless and barefoot when he answers the door with an easy grin on his face, practically oozing smug anticipation. No trace of remorse whatsoever. He must be having one of his manic days.

"Seth," I say as stiffly as I can muster.

He opens the door wide, and I come in just far enough so he can close it behind me. I brought my camera equipment as well. My plan is to snap pictures first, then conduct the interview. That way I can make a speedy exit if I need to.

"How's my bike?" I ask.

"I sold it to help pay for all those drugs. I still have some, though, if you're interested...." He smiles like a fox.

My body twitches and my heart races at the prospect. I remind myself it's not worth it.

"Let's start with pictures." I pull my camera out of its bag.

"Did your beefcake expire?" He eases back into one of his floor cushions like a sultan. I pull back the heavy curtains to let in more light and snap a few pictures of him in his resplendent glory, getting low to the ground to really capture his regal air. That's the fantasy of Seth Barrett and the image he chooses to project, but like most of what he does, it's only an act.

"I still remember the first time I saw you," he says when I don't answer his question about Berlin. He leans in toward me, eyes me hungrily, and licks his lips. "Do you?"

"On the basketball court," I say like I don't give a shit. Seth said he wanted to play even though he wasn't dressed for it. The rest of us, being younger and decidedly less cool than him, said okay. It quickly became apparent that he'd never played before, but he was so charming and funny that nobody cared. From the time he introduced himself to the end of the game, when he asked if he could walk me home, he only had eyes for me. It was such a thrill to have his attention. I felt powerful and cool that this hot, talented, older guy wanted me. Looking back, it was an obsession for the both of us.

"It wasn't playing basketball," he says. He sits back and tugs at his crotch lovingly. I snap a few more pictures; no doubt he'll like those. "It was a couple weeks before. You were walking through the neighborhood, collecting leaves. I was in the garage, tweaking out on my guitar. You were cute as hell, so I followed you to the park. I realized along the way you were only picking up the red ones. Then when you got to the park, you threw them up in the air and snapped pictures of where they'd fallen on the ground. Then you picked them up and did it again." He sighs, a dreamy look on his face. "I can still see the leaves falling all around you like red confetti. You were the prettiest thing I'd ever seen."

I remember that day. At least, I remember those photos. It was during my nature phase. I was trying to emulate a photographer who made complex designs with different colored leaves and sticks. It's strange to think about it from Seth's perspective.

He stands and goes over to the window, winces at the light streaming in. I notice the dark hollows under his eyes and the yellow tinge of his skin. He isn't taking care of himself. I snap a few more pictures. These are more honest portraits.

"You were so young," he whines. "It was practically criminal. That's probably why your mother never liked me." He scratches at the windowpane with his fingernail. My mother didn't like him even when she thought we were just friends. She said she always felt like he was lying when he spoke to her. She wasn't wrong.

"You know what that was like?" he asks me. "To have to be so patient? I had to teach you everything. You remember?"

The first time we had sex I was barely fifteen, and even with all the preparation, it still hurt like hell. Afterward I cried, and he held me and told me over and over how much he loved me and how the next time, I'd like it more. He took it for granted there would be a next time. I guess I did too.

"You remember," he says. He glances over at me with sorrowful eyes. I don't like seeing him in pain, even though I know he's only doing it to manipulate me. He makes me feel like that same vulnerable, trusting kid. His stupid China doll.

I hide behind my camera. I'm here on assignment. *Click. Click. Click.*

"Did you care for me at all, or was I only imagining it?" he asks. It's a trick question. To lie would make me out to be a coldhearted bitch. To answer truthfully would confirm that I'm still not over him. So I say nothing.

"I'm sorry for what happened in the desert." He takes a step toward me. I take a step back, a strange waltz. "Can you ever forgive me?"

I decide I have enough photographs, and the situation is escalating. My body feels like it's pooling at my feet, my mind getting soft and pliable as a piece of wax. I put away my camera and pull out my phone, hit Record.

"A lot of music critics say your sound reminds them of the grunge scene of the early nineties, bands like Candlebox and Alice in Chains. Who are your main influences?"

"Really, Hiroku?" He rolls his eyes. "My influences?"

The question is pretty standard. I stand there silently and wait for a response. When it seems I'm not going to get one, I continue on to the next question. "*China Doll* was recorded in Allister, Texas, just outside the Chihuahuan desert. What was it like working with Van Palamuso on the album?"

"Do you want a bump?" he asks.

"Do you want that included in the interview?"

He throws up his hands. "I just want a straight answer from you, Hiroku. That's all I ever wanted. Did you ever love me, or did I imagine it all?"

Anger floods me head to toe, a liquid fire burning through my veins, that he persists in asking this question when he damn well knows the answer already.

"Fine, Seth. Here it is. I loved you when we were friends, when we were lovers, when we created art together, when we fucked. I loved you when you cheated on me, when you got me hooked on painkillers and took advantage of the most vulnerable side of me. I loved you when you had me suck you off in front of your druggie friends like I was your fucking wind-up toy. I even loved you in the desert when your fingers were around my throat, choking the life out of me. I love you right now. But we both know where that will lead me."

"Where's that?" he asks like he doesn't know already.

"To my fucking grave. You'll kill me or the drugs'll kill me or I'll kill myself. There's no air in the room when you're around, no space in my mind for my own thoughts or will. You make me hate myself. And if you really love me as much as you say you do, why would you want that for me?"

I start crying, or maybe I've been crying. Seth pushes and he pushes and he never relents. He squeezes me so tightly that I have to lash out in all directions. He turns away, unable to face me, and stands there with his shoulders slumped while my own hands shake with rage.

After a moment, he speaks.

"My main influences are The Doors, Muddy Waters, and John Coltrane. For more contemporary acts, I'm a fan of Black Mountain, Kill It Kid, and The Pretty Reckless. I like the contrast of hard sounds with soft melodies. Working with Van Palamuso was one of the best experiences of my life, creatively speaking."

I clear my throat and swipe at my eyes. The next question is one Emilio wants me to ask.

"What inspired you to write the song 'China Doll'?"

"I didn't write it. It was written by a lover of mine, who is actually Japanese."

I sniff and blink away the tears and try again to regain my composure. "What does the song mean to you?"

"Regret."

I wait for him to expand on it, but he doesn't. He turns to face me, and I barrel on so I won't have to confront him. "There have been rumors of your drug use on the road and some late appearances at shows. Is there any truth to these rumors?"

He sighs and stretches his arms over his head. His corded muscles ripple in the light. To watch him is to want him, so I look away. "I struggle with addiction," he says, "but every day is a new chance to make the right decision. It's a never-ending battle."

"You should get help," I say in earnest.

"Are you clean?" he asks. "You look it."

"Yeah, I am."

"You're a better man than me."

I lower my eyes, because I couldn't have done it without Berlin's help. I ask my next question. "You're an openly gay artist in an industry that's known for putting its performers under the microscope. What's been your experience with that?"

"My sexuality is my art. I don't believe in hiding things. My experience, overall, has been very positive. I just wish it was easier for all gay boys and girls in America and worldwide to be who they are and to love who they want."

Seth is an activist in his own way. I've always admired him for that.

"Last question: where do you see yourself in five years?"

"With you," he says hopefully. I stare at my phone, my throat too thick to speak. The silence stretches on. Finally he adds, "Creating music, performing sold-out shows, touring with the band, hooking up with pretty boys, living the dream."

"Is it a dream, Seth?" That isn't a question I penned beforehand.

"Sometimes it's a dream. Sometimes it's a nightmare. Just like me, huh, Hiroku?"

I swallow the lump in my throat and end the recording, put away my phone.

"Do you want to go get lunch?" he asks, even though it's closer to dinnertime. Seth lives according to a musician's clock.

"I can't. I'm on deadline."

"Do you want a blowjob?"

I force myself not to imagine it. "I can't. I'm on deadline."

"Did you practice that line before you came in here?"

"Yes."

He pouts like a kicked puppy. I want to go over and hug him good-bye, but even that is a risk. I turn toward the door.

"Hiroku," he calls. "Whenever you want to come back to me, I'll be waiting."

I nod without turning. "Good-bye, Seth."

"Till next time."

Out on the street, I lean against the brick building and inhale a shaky breath. My limbs feel weak and bendy, but I'm outside his apartment and sober as the bright blue sky. Maybe I haven't completely conquered my addiction, but I took a stand against it.

I mark the occasion by getting my first tattoo.

BERLIN

HIRO CALLS me on a Friday afternoon in late February and invites me for the weekend. I head out within the hour, arriving at his apartment just before dinnertime with an overnight bag. I told my dad I'd be back for school on Monday, and he didn't argue. He's been treating me like an adult ever since we got Hiro back, and I appreciate it.

When Hiro opens the door, I'm pleased at how good he looks— healthy and bright-eyed. His hair is buzzed on both sides and long on the top like a floppy Mohawk. He's gotten back to his fighting weight, and his skin has a healthy glow to it. Most surprising is that he wears a light blue button-down shirt instead of his standard black. He looks kind of nervous when I come inside, or maybe it's just the way I'm feeling.

"What do you think?" he asks with his hands shoved deep into his back pockets.

"You look great."

He shakes his head and smiles bashfully. "Not me, Berlin. My place."

I glance around. His apartment is quirky and artistic like him, with vintage, artsy-looking furniture and original art on the walls. He told me before he was spending a lot of time hitting up thrift stores. It's amazing how he can take the stuff other people don't want and make it beautiful and useful again.

"I love it," I say, unable to take my eyes off him. *I love you* is what I want to say, but I don't want to freak him out in the first five minutes.

"You hungry?" he asks.

"Starving."

Hiro isn't much of a cook, so we go out and grab dinner at an Ethiopian restaurant where you're supposed to pick up your food with this thin pancake-type thing. It's a little weird eating only with my hands, but the food is good. Hiro catches me up with all he's been doing, even though I know most of it already from our texting back and forth. Then he tells me about his interview with Seth, something I didn't know about before. Even though he's sitting and breathing here before me, totally fine, I can't help but get worked up about it.

"You should have told your editor to have someone else do it."
Seth tried to kill him, or had he forgotten? Hiro shouldn't be within five
hundred feet of that son of a bitch. Ever.

"I had to do it," Hiro says as if that's a good enough reason.

"Then you should have had me go with you."

"I needed to face him myself."

"Have you seen him since?" I don't want him to think it's because
I'm jealous, though that might be part of it. Mainly I don't want Seth to
hurt him or tempt him into using drugs and wreck what Hiro's worked
so hard to achieve.

He shakes his head. "No, I haven't."

Then he asks me about school, clearly wanting to change the
subject. I tell him about Trent's visit and Coach Cross being fired, the
football team being suspended, and a new host of coaches coming in for
next year.

"You going to try out for the team?" he asks.

A lot of the guys on the football team are the same, and even
though things with Trent have cooled off, I'm not sure I want to poke the
hornet's nest again. I miss football, but not as much as I thought I would.
"Maybe. Possibly."

Hiro chuckles, and I remember the beginning of the school year,
when I told him I was maybe, possibly, gay.

"You should," he says. "Maybe I'll come to a game, do a couple
of cheers from the sidelines." He winks at me and I imagine it, kind of
getting hot under the collar. Hiro licks his lips and stares at me like he
might be having some bedroom thoughts of his own.

We leave the restaurant shortly after that. Back at his apartment,
the easy conversation we shared over dinner kind of dies away, and we
eye each other with uncertainty. We haven't talked about it, but I know
what I want—I've been reining it in all night long. I'm dammed up and
ready to burst. But I don't want to make him uncomfortable or force him
into something he's not ready for.

"I have to show you something," he says. He unbuttons his shirt
and shrugs it off his shoulders. In the place of his scar, there's a tattoo of
two dragons circling each other, a black one and a white one, kind of like
yin and yang. I come closer to get a better look. The detail is amazing.
The artist did such a good job you can hardly see the scar.

"It's beautiful."

"You like it?" He puffs out his chest in order to see it better.

"I love it." I trace my finger around its shape and get lost in all that smooth, wheat-colored skin. My hands are itchy, my mind a tangle of desire. Hiro glances up at me, parts his lips just a little bit.

It begins with a shuffle in my direction, then a sigh. He drapes one arm over my shoulder and tilts his head as if making an offering of his neck. I go for it, lapping at his sweet-smelling skin, my hand in his hair, the other on the bare skin of his lower back. My hand slides down the smooth slope into his pants, rounding over his ass and cupping him underneath his boxer briefs. A perfect fit.

He tugs at my shirt, so I yank it over my head. He kisses my chest, teeth nibbling at one of my nipples, then the other. I unbutton his pants and reach inside to find him already hard. I kneel in front of him to suck him off, but he stops me.

"Come on."

He pulls me into the bedroom, and we rip off the rest of our clothes along the way like they're on fire. He hooks his elbow around my neck, drawing me down into a bottomless kiss, and we tumble into his bed. He throws one leg over my hip so our cocks knock into each other playfully. I scale my hand down his chest and trace the ridges of his abdomen. I want him so bad. I always have, but now it finally feels right for both of us.

My hand strays farther south, and I stroke his cock a few times, then cup his balls in the palm of my hand. He arches his back and groans.

"I want this," he says with a shudder. "You?"

"Yeah," I whisper, nosing his neck and kissing the underside of his jaw.

"It takes some prep work."

"I've been studying." If you could get a PhD in the study of gay sex, I'd be Dr. Webber by now.

He points to a drawer in the bedside table, and inside it I find condoms and lube. I drop them on the bed and slather my fingers— probably using too much, but I figure that's better than not enough.

Hiro draws up his knees. His thick cock flops against his stomach, and I take a moment to lick it from the base to its tip, sucking on the head like a jawbreaker and then popping it out of my mouth. I sit back and admire the tightness of his cock and balls, the silky black hair glistening in the lamplight. My own cock digs into his thigh as I reach down and massage his ribbed hole with the tip of my index finger, coaxing it open with slow circles.

"Mmmm," he groans, eyes closed, back arching, exposing his neck. With my tongue I trace the line from the base of his throat to his upturned chin. His lips curve into a smile. I slip one finger inside him, sliding it gently up and down, while he clutches my neck and moans into my shoulder. My focus narrows to this one task of getting him ready for me, the warm pulse of his ringed muscle as it clenches around my knuckle. I imagine what that pressure might feel like around my cock, and I shiver with anticipation.

"How's this?" I ask him.

"So good," he utters, drawing his knees higher to give me better access. My cock bobs eagerly and leaves a syrupy trail on his thigh. The grip that held my finger loosens, and before he can tighten up again, I slip a second digit inside him.

"Uhhh," he groans, brow furrowed, mouth open. He jerks at his rigid cock a few times. Watching him in such an unrestrained state of arousal makes me just about lose it. I twist my two fingers inside him, stretching him like a tight rubber band. I don't think three will fit.

"I'm ready," he says in a husky voice.

"You sure?"

He nods, and I carefully withdraw my fingers and wipe them on the sheets, fumble with the condom and more lube like there's a timer attached to a bomb and it's going to go off if I don't get inside him quick enough. Hiro chuckles and lifts his arms over his head, seeming completely at ease, trusting me to take the lead.

I hope I know what I'm doing.

When everything is in place, I kneel with my knees spread wide and knock at his door. Seems like such a tight spot for what I'm offering. I want this more than anything, but I don't want to hurt him.

"You got this," he says, perhaps noticing my hesitation. He places both hands on my hips, urging me on. Something clicks then, and my body takes over. I nudge at his puckered hole with the tip of my sheathed cock, and with the first pulse, I bore into him, pausing with my head just inside as he gasps and tightens up around me. The compression sends a surge of pleasure through me. With a growl, he hugs my ass to him and draws me all the way inside. I shudder down to my toes. I never imagined it could feel this good.

"Stay here a minute," he says.

"Does it hurt?" I start to pull away, and he locks one leg around my lower back, anchoring me to him.

"Stay," he commands, and I make my body still as he takes a few deep breaths. "Okay. Go ahead. Start slow."

I rock my hips gently back and forth, moving only inches, loving the friction and heat of our two bodies locked together. The warmth spreads outward, like a living, throbbing being. I'm sure my cock has never had a true purpose until now.

"That good?" I ask, checking in with him.

"So good," he purrs contentedly.

I lean over him, heart racing, arms braced on either side of him. He meets my eyes, the lazy smirk still on his face, then leans up to kiss me. I drop down on my elbows and deepen the kiss. I'm so far up inside him, on both ends, I don't ever want to surface. His heels dig into my back like spurs, urging me on, and I drive deeper into him.

"Make me come," he says. He reaches for his own cock, and I raise myself up to give him room. Watching him get off with me inside him, steering him, knowing our bodies can do this for each other, I'm overcome by it all. I lean in to kiss his forehead once, and my rhythm quickens—a trot, then a canter. My hips knock into his spread thighs, my balls slap against his ass, skin on skin, flesh pounding against flesh. He wrenches his cock and floods us both with his release, warm and sticky on my chest. I smell his cum mixed with sweat, the tang of our sex, and there's nothing more I can do to hold back.

"I'm about to…." I mutter.

"Go ahead."

I drill in deeper than I thought possible and explode inside him. He grabs my ass with both hands and holds me there until the very last tender pulse.

I'm so dizzy the room is spinning. I must have been holding my breath.

"Hiro," I say softly, stunned and a little disoriented. There's no better feeling in the world than this. There can't be. He hugs me to him and strokes my back. I don't know what else to say.

When we've both caught our breath, I pinch the rim of the condom and pull away from him slowly so it doesn't slip. I wish I didn't have to, though. I'd rather stay inside him, just like that, forever.

"I never thought sex would feel that good," I tell him.

He smiles. "Me neither."

He gets up, a little unsteady on his feet, and I follow him to the bathroom, where we take a shower together. He lets me wash him, including his hair. I want to make it last, my hands on his skin, in his hair, his wet body pressed against mine, kissing the curve of his neck, drawing my hands down his chest and abs, cupping his balls. I think about what we just did, and I can hardly stop myself from blurting out all the thoughts running through my mind. He trusted me enough to make himself vulnerable. That means a lot to me. I don't want to scare him off, though, so I keep my feelings to myself.

"It was good, huh?" I say to him when we're lying in bed again. His head is propped up on my chest, and I play my fingers in his damp hair.

"So good," he says. "I can't wait for your second time." He has a smile on his face. He looks happy.

"I liked it." I can hardly keep the smile off my face.

"I could tell." He looks at me smugly. "I liked it too. Good stuff."

I take a deep breath and watch his head rise and fall on my chest. He gets quiet and thoughtful and I wonder what's on his mind, so I ask.

"There's something I need to tell you." He sits up on the bed, folds his legs crosswise. I must look worried because he reaches over and smooths my forehead with his thumb. "I'm not saying it to get any kind of reaction from you. I just want to be honest."

"Okay," I say with some hesitation. He isn't making me feel any better.

He grabs my hand and stares down at it, his black lashes falling like curtains over his eyes. "I'm developing feelings for you," he says softly.

My smile comes back, and I sigh with relief. "Developing?" I say, mostly to tease him. My own feelings are full-blown. He frowns. He looks so down about it. "Why the face?" I ask.

"I don't deserve you." He shakes his head.

That's horse shit if ever I heard it. It's Seth who brought him down so low. I lift his chin so he'll look at me. "I don't know if you deserve me, Hiro, but you do deserve someone who appreciates you. You've got a big heart and a great sense of humor and you're artsy and smart." I pause, not sure if I should go there, but figure, well why not? "And you're hot and you know it."

He lays his cheek in the valley of my hand and glances away, still troubled. "I'm an addict, Berlin."

He says it like it's some revelation to me, as if I'm not already intimately familiar with the fact. "I'm a rancher, Hiro, and you're a vegetarian, and you're still here with me."

"That's not the same," he says unhappily.

I grab his free hand and squeeze. "Listen, I know you struggle. And I know how serious it is. But we all have obstacles to overcome."

"I'm afraid something will set me off and I'll start using again."

I place his hand over my heart. "Life is long, Hiro. You're stronger now than you've ever been. You have me. You have your mom and dad and your sister. You have your art. You're doing *so good*. You just have to have faith."

"In God?" he asks seriously.

"In yourself."

He chews on his lower lip. I can tell there's a battle going on in his head. Those two dragons on his chest aren't just a pretty picture.

"Do you have faith in me?" he asks, eyes shining.

I squeeze his hand. "Of course I do. I always have."

He looks serious for a moment, then nods. "Me too."

He hunkers down with his head on my chest and I wrap my arms around him. "You know what this means?"

"Tell me," he whispers.

"It means I got you."

I never want to let him go.

HIROKU

I WAKE up the next morning before Berlin. The morning light casts sunbeams on his shoulders and chest, shining on the rusty hairs between his pecs where I like to burrow.

"Berlin Webber," I whisper like an incantation. I'm tempted to get my camera and snap a few pictures, but I don't want to disturb the moment, so I lie there on my side and admire him in the truest light of the day.

God's creation, I think to myself as my eyes travel over the planes of Berlin's body. I couldn't have dreamed up a more stunning work of art. He's beautiful, inside and out, and I think this must be what it's like to feel blessed.

Then I get to thinking about God and wonder if He gave me Berlin to make up for all the shit I had to put up with from Seth. Some people might say God was testing me with my addiction and Seth and Trent to see if I was worthy of the likes of Berlin Webber. But it's convenient to look back and say that now. I could have just as easily overdosed on pills or thrown myself off one of those cliffs.

And when you look at the world itself, there's so much ugliness in it—murder, rape, child abuse, war, slavery, mass shootings. But there's good things too—love and kindness, compassion, pleasure, which makes me think if there is a God, then He must have spun the wheel and walked away from his creation. *Good luck with all that.* And if that's the case, then what's the point in believing at all?

Then I think about the worlds we create ourselves. The world I had with Seth and the one I've begun with Berlin, how vastly different those two worlds are and how we as humans are constantly changing and evolving and bringing new people into our worlds and kicking some of the old ones out. So maybe, in that regard, we're tiny gods ourselves, deeming who's fit to enter our kingdom and who must stay outside the gates.

And as I study Berlin Webber naked as a teenage dream and sleeping soundly in my bed, a sense of gratitude fills me, that I have him in my life.

Whatever brought us together to allow our separate worlds to become one, I know this is a world I want to hold on to for as long as I can. I take a moment to say a prayer of gratitude, not necessarily to any one god, but to the universe in general for not being such a bitch this time and cutting me some goddamned slack for once in my life.

Berlin stirs and opens his eyes to find me staring. He grins and pulls me to him. I breathe him in and rub my cheek against his chest.

"Whatcha thinking about?" he whispers in his rusty morning voice.

"You," I say softly, gazing down at him and drawing my fingertip along his strong jaw and the stubble that lines his chin.

"What about me?"

"How much I love you, and how grateful I am that we found each other."

He smiles bashfully and pulls me to him, kisses my forehead. "I love you too, Hiroku Hayashi."

I shake my head and roll my eyes. God, how he murders my name. Every. Single. Time.

"Just Hiro, Berlin."

He clears his throat and tries again with mischief in his eyes. "I love you too, Just Hiro."

I kiss him and he wraps his big arms around me, bracing me up. I remember what Denise said to me back in that diner in Allister, Texas, how you don't get what you deserve, you get what you think you deserve.

So for now I'll tell myself I'm worthy of Berlin Webber, and maybe one day, through daily devotion and acts of kindness, I'll believe it.

ACKNOWLEDGMENTS

STORIES ARE like children—each one is unique and wonderful in their own way—but this one about a country mouse and a city mouse who overcome so much to be together has a special place in my heart.

Thank you to Angele McQuade, mistress of propaganda, for sharpening my prose and helping Berlin and Hiro grow as characters. Heather Whitaker, mistress of plot, for her never-ending fountain of knowledge and advice on all things of the three-act nature. Trinity 4eva.

Thank you to Dreamspinner Press and the community of DSP authors who are always quick to lend their expertise along with kind words and encouragement. Thanks also to AngstyG for another breathtaking cover—your art inspires me.

To the readers and fans of my work, thank you for traveling on this long, winding road with me. Your support allows me to do what I love best and share it with others.

And finally my darling husband and children, the light of my life, you three help me to be brave.

—Laura

AUTHOR'S NOTE

WHILE I was finishing the first draft of *The Bravest Thing*, my brother-in-law Billy died of a drug overdose. His mother found him in his truck in her driveway in the early morning hours of September 11. He was twenty-nine years old.

Billy had struggled with an addiction to opiates and opioids since high school. Like many addicts, he started with OxyContin, snorting it. Because of this type of rampant abuse, Purdue Pharma, the makers of OxyContin, changed the formula in 2010 so that the pills were more difficult to crush and/or cook. Crushable OxyContin became harder to find and more expensive, and many addicts turned to heroin, which was becoming cheaper and more widely available. Drug dealers then started cutting heroin with fentanyl, which is fifty to a hundred times more potent than heroin and can kill you with an amount the size of a few grains of salt.

As I write this, we are awaiting the toxicology report from the medical examiner, but we believe Billy was snorting heroin cut with fentanyl when he overdosed.

Death by drug overdose, specifically heroin, is a growing epidemic in America. As the *Palm Beach Post* stated in a November 2016 article, "Nationwide, the heroin body count rivals the number of young Americans who died at the height of the Vietnam War." Because of the stigma surrounding drug abuse and addiction, this killing of a generation is happening quietly and without recourse.

At the same time, funding for drug rehabilitation and clean-needle programs is being cut by state legislatures (as is the case in Florida, where Billy died) causing a spike in the spread of HIV. The heroin epidemic is not only a national tragedy, it's a threat to public health.

When he was sober, Billy had a great sense of humor. He used to sneak my daughter candy bars when I wasn't looking and play video games and watch football with my son. We called him Billy Baby because he was the youngest of the family from our generation. He loved surfing, fast cars, and eating apple pie. True to the Florida beach bum that he was, Billy was more often found shirtless than not and had a fun-loving personality that charmed us all. He was a wonderful uncle who one day could have been a great father.

When Billy was using, or more precisely, when he was coming down and out of money to buy drugs, he was a different person. He left threatening voice mails, stole and pawned his mother's belongings for cash, and blamed everyone around him for his addiction.

We. Tried. Everything.

We as a family have learned a few things from watching Billy struggle with addiction:

There is no rock bottom. Over the decade of Billy's drug use, we kept saying *Surely this is the worst it can get. This is what it will take for him to turn it around. This time, he'll understand his life is at stake.* Each time, he went back to using.

You cannot argue, threaten, or love someone out of addiction. While you can help an addict by providing them a safe place to get clean, paying for their rehabilitation, giving them a job, etc., you cannot make a person stay sober. They have to want it themselves. And work at it every day. Every single fucking day.

Addiction is a disease. Prolonged drug use alters brain chemistry and makes it harder for addicts to stay sober. We as a society must get over the stigma of drug abuse if we are going to tackle this epidemic head-on and provide the help and support addicts need to get and stay clean. Ignoring the problem does not make it go away.

Watching someone suffer from addiction is heartbreaking. Billy broke our hearts. If you have a loved one who struggles with addiction, you know what I mean.

If you are an addict, here is my message to you: You are not a bad person. You are not your addiction. Your life is worth saving. You may think you're alone or that you've burned all your bridges, but I can guarantee there are people who love you and want you back. Just like you, they are doing the best they can and dealing with their pain the only way they know how. I hope you see your life has value and you're someone worth saving. Getting and staying sober is the hardest thing you'll ever do, but I believe it's worth it.

And to Billy Baby, wherever you are, we love you and we miss you.

RESOURCES:

Alcoholics Anonymous: aa.org

Alcohol and Drug Abuse Hotline: 1-800-729-6686

Al-Anon for families of alcoholics: al-anon.org

IMAlive, an online crisis network: imalive.org

National Helpline for Substance Abuse: 1-800-262-2463

Suicide Prevention Lifeline: suicidepreventionlifeline.org | 1-800-273-8255

The National Domestic Violence Hotline: thehotline.org | 1-800-799-7233

LAURA LASCARSO lives in north Florida with her darling husband, two children, and a menagerie of animals. Her debut novel, *Counting Backwards* (Simon & Schuster 2012) won the Florida Book Award gold medal for young adult literature. She aims to inspire more questions than answers in her fiction and believes in the power of stories to heal and transform a society.

For social critiques, writer puns, and Parks and Rec gifs, follow her on Twitter @lauralascarso
Website: lauralascarso.com
Facebook: www.facebook.com/lascarso
Twitter: @lauralascarso

LAURA LASCARSO

ANDRE
IN FLIGHT

When up-and-coming Miami painter Martin Fonseca encounters youthful pretty boy Andre Bellamy washing dishes in the kitchen of La Candela, he swears he's known him before, intimately. But Andre only arrived in Miami weeks ago, after running away from small-town Alabama and his abusive father. When Martin discovers Andre trading sexual favors for a place to stay, he offers him a room in his studio apartment. As roommates only.

What starts as a playful friendship turns into something more as Andre begins posing for Martin, whose true passion is painting fantastical portraits. Martin's obsession with Andre grows until they are sharing more than just flirtatious conversation. But when an eccentric art collector buys one of Martin's paintings, Martin's past jealousies resurface and threaten to destroy what he and Andre have so lovingly built.

www.dreamspinnerpress.com

after the
romance
novel

Susan Laine

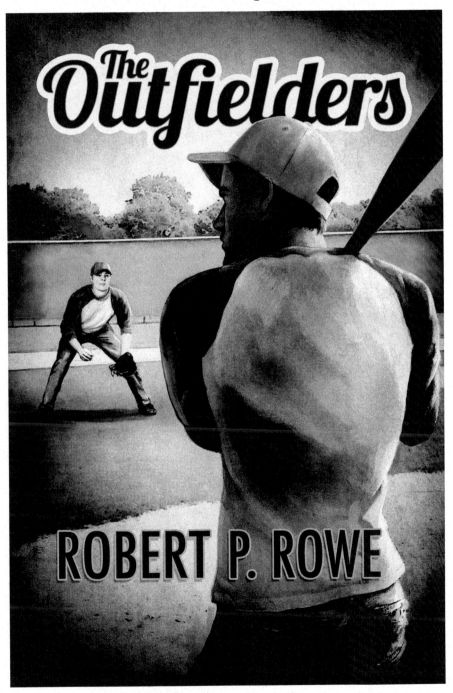

CPSIA information can be obtained
at www.ICGtesting.com
Printed in the USA
LVOW01s1940050517
533420LV00015B/194/P